The Voices of Time

J. G. BALLARD

PHŒNIX

A PHŒNIX PAPERBACK

First published in Great Britain by
Victor Gollancz Ltd under the title
The Four-Dimensional Nightmare, 1963;
revised edition, with the two stories
'Prima Belladonna' and 'Studio 5, The Stars'
replaced by 'The Overloaded Man' and
'Thirteen to Centaurus',
first published by Victor Gollancz Ltd, 1974

First published in paperback by
J. M. Dent & Sons Ltd, 1984

Copyright © J. G. Ballard 1963, 1974

This paperback edition first published in 1992 by
Orion Books Limited, Orion House,
5 Upper St. Martin's Lane, London WC2H 9EA

ISBN 1 85799 000 5

Printed in Great Britain by
The Guernsey Press Co. Ltd, Guernsey, C.I.

British Library Cataloguing in
Publication Data is available.

CONTENTS

ACKNOWLEDGEMENTS

'The Voices of Time', 'Chronopolis', 'The Overloaded Man', and 'The Cage of Sand', copyright 1960 and 1961 by Nova Publications Ltd for *New Worlds Science Fiction*.

'The Sound Sweep', and 'The Watch-Towers', copyright 1960 and 1962 by Nova Publications Ltd for *Science Fantasy*.

'The Garden of Time', copyright 1962 by Mercury Press Inc. for *The Magazine of Fantasy and Science Fiction*.

'Thirteen to Centaurus', copyright 1962 by Ziff-Davis Publishing Company for *Amazing Science Fiction*.

THE VOICES OF TIME

One

LATER Powers often thought of Whitby, and the strange grooves the biologist had cut, apparently at random, all over the floor of the empty swimming pool. An inch deep and twenty feet long, interlocking to form an elaborate ideogram like a Chinese character, they had taken him all summer to complete, and he had obviously thought about little else, working away tirelessly through the long desert afternoons. Powers had watched him from his office window at the far end of the Neurology wing, carefully marking out his pegs and string, carrying away the cement chips in a small canvas bucket. After Whitby's suicide no one had bothered about the grooves, but Powers often borrowed the supervisor's key and let himself into the disused pool, and would look down at the labyrinth of mouldering gulleys, half-filled with water leaking in from the chlorinator, an enigma now past any solution.

Initially, however, Powers was too preoccupied with completing his work at the Clinic and planning his own final withdrawal. After the first frantic weeks of panic he had managed to accept an uneasy compromise that allowed him to view his predicament with the detached fatalism he had previously reserved for his patients. Fortunately he was moving down the physical and mental gradients simultaneously—lethargy and inertia blunted his anxieties, a slackening metabolism made it necessary to concentrate to produce a connected thought-train. In fact, the lengthening intervals of dreamless sleep were almost restful. He found himself beginning to look forward to them, and made no effort to wake earlier than was essential.

At first he had kept an alarm clock by his bed, tried to compress as much activity as he could into the narrowing hours of consciousness, sorting out his library, driving over to Whitby's laboratory every morning to examine the latest batch of X-ray plates, every minute and hour rationed like the last drops of water in a canteen.

Anderson, fortunately, had unwittingly made him realize the pointlessness of this course.

After Powers had resigned from the Clinic he still continued to drive in once a week for his check-up, now little more than a formality. On what turned out to be the last occasion Anderson had perfunctorily taken his blood-count, noting Powers' slacker facial muscles, fading pupil reflexes and unshaven cheeks.

He smiled sympathetically at Powers across the desk, wondering what to say to him. Once he had put on a show of encouragement with the more intelligent patients, even tried to provide some sort of explanation. But Powers was too difficult to reach—neurosurgeon extraordinary, a man always out on the periphery, only at ease working with unfamiliar materials. To himself he thought: *I'm sorry, Robert. What can I say*—"*Even the sun is growing cooler*"—? He watched Powers drum his fingers restlessly on the enamel desk top, his eyes glancing at the spinal level charts hung around the office. Despite his unkempt appearance—he had been wearing the same unironed shirt and dirty white plimsolls a week ago— Powers looked composed and self-possessed, like a Conradian beachcomber more or less reconciled to his own weaknesses.

"What are you doing with yourself, Robert?" he asked. "Are you still going over to Whitby's lab?"

"As much as I can. It takes me half an hour to cross the lake, and I keep on sleeping through the alarm clock. I may leave my place and move in there permanently."

Anderson frowned. "Is there much point? As far as I could make out Whitby's work was pretty speculative—" He broke off, realizing the implied criticism of Powers' own disastrous work at the Clinic, but Powers seemed to ignore this, was examining the pattern of shadows on the ceiling. "Anyway, wouldn't it be better to stay where you are, among your own things, read through Toynbee and Spengler again?"

Powers laughed shortly. "That's the last thing I want to do. I want to *forget* Toynbee and Spengler, not try to remember them. In fact, Paul, I'd like to forget everything. I don't know whether I've got enough time, though. How much can you forget in three months?"

"Everything, I suppose, if you want to. But don't try to race the clock."

Powers nodded quietly, repeating this last remark to himself. Racing the clock was exactly what he had been doing. As he stood up and said good-bye to Anderson he suddenly decided to throw away his alarm clock, escape from his futile obsession with time. To remind himself he unfastened his wrist-watch and scrambled the setting, then slipped it into his pocket. Making his way out to the car park he reflected on the freedom this simple act gave him. He would explore the lateral byways now, the side doors, as it were, in the corridors of time. Three months could be an eternity.

He picked his car out of the line and strolled over to it, shielding his eyes from the heavy sunlight beating down across the parabolic sweep of the lecture theatre roof. He was about to climb in when he saw that someone had traced with a finger across the dust caked over the windshield:

96,688,365,498,721

Looking over his shoulder, he recognized the white Packard parked next to him, peered inside and saw a lean-faced young man with blond sun-bleached hair and a high cerebrotonic forehead watching him behind dark glasses. Sitting beside him at the wheel was a raven-haired girl whom he had often seen around the psychology department. She had intelligent but somehow rather oblique eyes, and Powers remembered that the younger doctors called her "the girl from Mars".

"Hello, Kaldren," Powers said to the young man. "Still following me around?"

Kaldren nodded. "Most of the time, doctor." He sized Powers up shrewdly. "We haven't seen very much of you recently, as a matter of fact. Anderson said you'd resigned, and we noticed your laboratory was closed."

Powers shrugged. "I felt I needed a rest. As you'll understand, there's a good deal that needs re-thinking."

Kaldren frowned half-mockingly. "Sorry to hear that, doctor. But don't let these temporary setbacks depress you." He noticed the girl watching Powers with interest. "Coma's a fan of yours. I gave her your papers from *American Journal of Psychiatry*, and she's read through the whole file."

The girl smiled pleasantly at Powers, for a moment dispelling the hostility between the two men. When Powers nodded to her she leaned across Kaldren and said: "Actually I've just finished Noguchi's autobiography—the great Japanese doctor who discovered the spirochaete. Somehow you remind me of him—there's so much of yourself in all the patients you worked on."

Powers smiled wanly at her, then his eyes turned and locked involuntarily on Kaldren's. They stared at each other sombrely for a moment, and a small tic in Kaldren's right cheek began to flicker irritatingly. He flexed his facial muscles, after a few seconds mastered it with an effort, obviously annoyed that Powers should have witnessed this brief embarrassment.

"How did the clinic go today?" Powers asked. "Have you had any more . . . headaches?"

Kaldren's mouth snapped shut, he looked suddenly irritable. "Whose care am I in, doctor? Yours or Anderson's? Is that the sort of question you should be asking now?"

Powers gestured deprecatingly. "Perhaps not." He cleared his throat; the heat was ebbing the blood from his head and he felt tired and eager to get away from them. He turned towards his car, then realized that Kaldren would probably follow, either try to crowd him into the ditch or block the road and make Powers sit in his dust all the way back to the lake. Kaldren was capable of any madness.

"Well, I've got to go and collect something," he said, adding in a firmer voice: "Get in touch with me, though, if you can't reach Anderson."

He waved and walked off behind the line of cars. From the reflection in the windows he could see Kaldren looking back and watching him closely.

He entered the Neurology wing, paused thankfully in the cool foyer, nodding to the two nurses and the armed guard at the reception desk. For some reason the terminals sleeping in the adjacent dormitory block attracted hordes of would-be sightseers, most of them cranks with some magical anti-narcoma remedy, or merely the idly curious, but a good number of quite normal people, many of whom had travelled thousands of miles, impelled towards the Clinic by some strange instinct, like animals migrating to a preview of their racial graveyards.

He walked along the corridor to the supervisor's office overlooking the recreation deck, borrowed the key and made his way out through the tennis courts and callisthenics rigs to the enclosed swimming-pool at the far end. It had been disused for months, and only Powers' visits kept the lock free. Stepping through, he closed it behind him and walked past the peeling wooden stands to the deep end.

Putting a foot up on the diving-board, he looked down at Whitby's ideogram. Damp leaves and bits of paper obscured it, but the outlines were just distinguishable. It covered almost the entire floor of the pool and at first glance appeared to represent a huge solar disc, with four radiating diamond-shaped arms, a crude Jungian mandala.

Wondering what had prompted Whitby to carve the device before his death, Powers noticed something moving through the debris in the centre of the disc. A black, horny-shelled animal about a foot long was nosing about in the slush, heaving itself on tired legs. Its shell was articulated, and vaguely resembled an armadillo's. Reaching the edge of the disc, it stopped and hesitated, then slowly backed away into the centre again, apparently unwilling or unable to cross the narrow groove.

Powers looked around, then stepped into one of the changing stalls and pulled a small wooden clothes locker off its rusty wall bracket. Carrying it under one arm, he climbed down the chromium ladder into the pool and walked carefully across the slithery floor towards the animal. As he approached it sidled away from him, but he trapped it easily, using the lid to lever it into the box.

The animal was heavy, at least the weight of a brick. Powers tapped its massive olive-black carapace with his knuckle, noting the triangular warty head jutting out below its rim like a turtle's, the thickened pads beneath the first digits of the pentadactyl forelimbs.

He watched the three-lidded eyes blinking at him anxiously from the bottom of the box.

"Expecting some really hot weather?" he murmured. "That lead umbrella you're carrying around should keep you cool."

He closed the lid, climbed out of the pool and made his way back to the supervisor's office, then carried the box out to his car.

"*. . . Kaldren continues to reproach me (Powers wrote in his diary). For some reason he seems unwilling to accept his isolation, is elaborating* *a series of private rituals to replace the missing hours of sleep. Perhaps I should tell him of my own approaching zero, but he'd probably regard this as the final unbearable insult, that I should have in excess what he so desperately yearns for. God knows what might happen. Fortunately the nightmarish visions appear to have receded for the time being . . ."*

Pushing the diary away, Powers leaned forward across the desk and stared out through the window at the white floor of the lake bed stretching towards the hills along the horizon. Three miles away, on the far shore, he could see the circular bowl of the radio-telescope revolving slowly in the clear afternoon air, as Kaldren tirelessly trapped the sky, sluicing in millions of cubic parsecs of sterile ether, like the nomads who trapped the sea along the shores of the Persian Gulf.

Behind him the air-conditioner murmured quietly, cooling the pale blue walls half-hidden in the dim light. Outside the air was bright and oppressive, the heat waves rippling up from the clumps of gold-tinted cacti below the Clinic blurring the sharp terraces of the twenty-storey Neurology block. There, in the silent dormitories behind the sealed shutters, the terminals slept their long dreamless sleep. There were now over 500 of them in the Clinic, the vanguard of a vast somnambulist army massing for its last march. Only five years had elapsed since the first narcoma syndrome had been recognized, but already huge government hospitals in the east were being readied for intakes in the thousands, as more and more cases came to light.

Powers felt suddenly tired, and glanced at his wrist, wondering how long he had to 8 o'clock, his bed-time for the next week or so. Already he missed the dusk, soon would wake to his last dawn.

His watch was in his hip-pocket. He remembered his decision not to use his timepieces, and sat back and stared at the bookshelves beside the desk. There were rows of green-covered AEC publications he had removed from Whitby's library, papers in which the biologist described his work out in the Pacific after the H-tests. Many of them Powers knew almost by heart, read a hundred times in an effort to grasp Whitby's last conclusions. Toynbee would certainly be easier to forget.

His eyes dimmed momentarily, as the tall black wall in the rear of his mind cast its great shadow over his brain. He reached for the diary, thinking of the girl in Kaldren's car—Coma he had called her, another of his insane jokes—and her reference to Noguchi. Actually the comparison should have been made with Whitby, not himself; the monsters in the lab were nothing more than fragmented mirrors of Whitby's mind, like the grotesque radio-shielded frog he had found that morning in the swimming-pool.

Thinking of the girl Coma, and the heartening smile she had given him, he wrote:

Woke 6-33 am. Last session with Anderson. He made it plain he's seen enough of me, and from now on I'm better alone. To sleep 8-00? (these count-downs terrify me.)

He paused, then added:

Good-bye, Eniwetok.

Two

HE saw the girl again the next day at Whitby's laboratory. He had driven over after breakfast with the new specimen, eager to get it into a vivarium before it died. The only previous armoured mutant he had come across had nearly broken his neck. Speeding along the lake road a month or so earlier he had struck it with the off-side front wheel, expecting the small creature to flatten instantly. Instead its hard lead-packed shell had remained rigid, even though the organism within it had been pulped, had flung the car heavily into the ditch. He had gone back for the shell, later weighed it at the laboratory, found it contained over 600 grammes of lead.

Quite a number of plants and animals were building up heavy metals as radiological shields. In the hills behind the beach house a couple of old-time prospectors were renovating the derelict gold-panning equipment abandoned over eighty years ago. They had noticed the bright yellow tints of the cacti, run an analysis and found that the plants were assimilating gold in extractable quantities, although the soil concentrations were unworkable. Oak Ridge was at last paying a dividend!!

Waking that morning just after 6-45—ten minutes later than

the previous day (he had switched on the radio, heard one of the regular morning programmes as he climbed out of bed)—he had eaten a light unwanted breakfast, then spent an hour packing away some of the books in his library, crating them up and taping on address labels to his brother.

He reached Whitby's laboratory half an hour later. This was housed in a 100-foot-wide geodesic dome built beside his chalet on the west shore of the lake about a mile from Kaldren's summer house. The chalet had been closed after Whitby's suicide, and many of the experimental plants and animals had died before Powers had managed to receive permission to use the laboratory.

As he turned into the driveway he saw the girl standing on the apex of the yellow-ribbed dome, her slim figure silhouetted against the sky. She waved to him, then began to step down across the glass polyhedrons and jumped nimbly into the driveway beside the car.

"Hello," she said, giving him a welcoming smile. "I came over to see your zoo. Kaldren said you wouldn't let me in if he came so I made him stay behind."

She waited for Powers to say something while he searched for his keys, then volunteered: "If you like, I can wash your shirt."

Powers grinned at her, peered down ruefully at his dust-stained sleeves. "Not a bad idea. I thought I was beginning to look a little uncared-for." He unlocked the door, took Coma's arm. "I don't know why Kaldren told you that—he's welcome here any time he likes."

"What have you got in there?" Coma asked, pointing at the wooden box he was carrying as they walked between the gear-laden benches.

"A distant cousin of ours I found. Interesting little chap. I'll introduce you in a moment."

Sliding partitions divided the dome into four chambers. Two of them were store-rooms, filled with spare tanks, apparatus, cartons of animal food and test rigs. They crossed the third section, almost filled by a powerful X-ray projector, a giant 250 amp G.E. Maxitron, angled on to a revolving table, concrete shielding blocks lying around ready for use like huge building bricks.

The fourth chamber contained Powers' zoo, the vivaria jammed together along the benches and in the sinks, big coloured cardboard charts and memos pinned on to the draught hoods above them, a tangle of rubber tubing and power leads trailing across the floor. As they walked past the lines of tanks dim forms shifted behind the frosted glass, and at the far end of the aisle there was a sudden scurrying in a large cage by Powers' desk.

Putting the box down on his chair, he picked a packet of peanuts off the desk and went over to the cage. A small black-haired chimpanzee wearing a dented jet pilot's helmet swarmed deftly up the bars to him, chirped happily and then jumped down to a miniature control panel against the rear wall of the cage. Rapidly it flicked a series of buttons and toggles, and a succession of coloured lights lit up like a juke box and jangled out a two-second blast of music.

"Good boy," Powers said encouragingly, patting the chimp's back and shovelling the peanuts into its hands. "You're getting much too clever for that one, aren't you?"

The chimp tossed the peanuts into the back of its throat with the smooth, easy motions of a conjurer, jabbering at Powers in a sing-song voice.

Coma laughed and took some of the nuts from Powers. "He's sweet. I think he's talking to you."

Powers nodded. "Quite right, he is. Actually he's got a two-hundred-word vocabulary, but his voice box scrambles it all up." He opened a small refrigerator by the desk, took out half a packet of sliced bread and passed a couple of pieces to the chimp. It picked an electric toaster off the floor and placed it in the middle of a low wobbling table in the centre of the cage, whipped the pieces into the slots. Powers pressed a tab on the switchboard beside the cage and the toaster began to crackle softly.

"He's one of the brightest we've had here, about as intelligent as a five-year-old child, though much more self-sufficient in a lot of ways." The two pieces of toast jumped out of their slots and the chimp caught them neatly, nonchalantly patting its helmet each time, then ambled off into a small ramshackle kennel and relaxed back with one arm out of a window, sliding the toast into its mouth.

"He built that house himself," Powers went on, switching off the toaster. "Not a bad effort, really." He pointed to a yellow polythene bucket by the front door of the kennel, from which a battered-looking geranium protruded. "Tends that plant, cleans up the cage, pours out an endless stream of wisecracks. Pleasant fellow all round."

Coma was smiling broadly to herself. "Why the space helmet, though?"

Powers hesitated. "Oh, it—er—it's for his own protection. Sometimes he gets rather bad headaches. His predecessors all—" He broke off and turned away. "Let's have a look at some of the other inmates."

He moved down the line of tanks, beckoning Coma with him. "We'll start at the beginning." He lifted the glass lid off one of the tanks, and Coma peered down into a shallow bath of water, where a small round organism with slender tendrils was nestling in a rockery of shells and pebbles.

"Sea anemone. Or was. Simple coelenterate with an open-ended body cavity." He pointed down to a thickened ridge of tissue around the base. "It's sealed up the cavity, converted the channel into a rudimentary notochord, first plant ever to develop a nervous system. Later the tendrils will knot themselves into a ganglion, but already they're sensitive to colour. Look." He borrowed the violet handkerchief in Coma's breast-pocket, spread it across the tank. The tendrils flexed and stiffened, began to weave slowly, as if they were trying to focus.

"The strange thing is that they're completely insensitive to white light. Normally the tendrils register shifting pressure gradients, like the tympanic diaphragms in your ears. Now it's almost as if they can *hear* primary colours, suggests it's re-adapting itself for a non-aquatic existence in a static world of violent colour contrasts."

Coma shook her head, puzzled. "Why, though?"

"Hold on a moment. Let me put you in the picture first." They moved along the bench to a series of drum-shaped cages made of wire mosquito netting. Above the first was a large white cardboard screen bearing a blown-up microphoto of a tall pagoda-like chain, topped by the legend: "Drosophila: 15 röntgens/min."

Powers tapped a small perspex window in the drum. "Fruitfly. Its huge chromosomes make it a useful test vehicle." He bent down, pointed to a grey V-shaped honeycomb suspended from the roof. A few flies emerged from entrances, moving about busily. "Usually it's solitary, a nomadic scavenger. Now it forms itself into well-knit social groups, has begun to secrete a thin sweet lymph something like honey."

"What's this?" Coma asked, touching the screen.

"Diagram of a key gene in the operation." He traced a spray of arrows leading from a link in the chain. The arrows were labelled: "Lymph gland" and subdivided "sphincter muscles, epithelium, templates."

"It's rather like the perforated sheet music of a player-piano," Powers commented, "or a computer punch tape. Knock out one link with an X-ray beam, lose a characteristic, change the score."

Coma was peering through the window of the next cage and pulling an unpleasant face. Over her shoulder Powers saw she was watching an enormous spider-like insect, as big as a hand, its dark hairy legs as thick as fingers. The compound eyes had been built up so that they resembled giant rubies.

"He looks unfriendly," she said. "What's that sort of rope ladder he's spinning?" As she moved a finger to her mouth the spider came to life, retreated into the cage and began spewing out a complex skein of interlinked grey thread which it slung in long loops from the roof of the cage.

"A web," Powers told her. "Except that it consists of nervous tissue. The ladders form an external neural plexus, an inflatable brain as it were, that he can pump up to whatever size the situation calls for. A sensible arrangement, really, far better than our own."

Coma backed away. "Gruesome. I wouldn't like to go into his parlour."

"Oh, he's not as frightening as he looks. Those huge eyes staring at you are blind. Or, rather, their optical sensitivity has shifted down the band, the retinas will only register gamma radiation. Your wrist-watch has luminous hands. When you moved it across the window he started thinking. World War IV should really bring him into his element."

They strolled back to Powers' desk. He put a coffee pan over a bunsen and pushed a chair across to Coma. Then he opened the box, lifted out the armoured frog and put it down on a sheet of blotting-paper.

"Recognize him? Your old childhood friend, the common frog. He's built himself quite a solid little air-raid shelter." He carried the animal across to a sink, turned on the tap and let the water play softly over its shell. Wiping his hands on his shirt, he came back to the desk.

Coma brushed her long hair off her forehead, watched him curiously.

"Well, what's the secret?"

Powers lit a cigarette. "There's no secret. Teratologists have been breeding monsters for years. Have you ever heard of the 'silent pair'?"

She shook her head.

Powers stared moodily at the cigarette for a moment, riding the kick the first one of the day always gave him. "The so-called 'silent pair' is one of modern genetics' oldest problems, the apparently baffling mystery of the two inactive genes which occur in a small percentage of all living organisms, and appear to have no intelligible role in their structure or development. For a long while now biologists have been trying to activate them, but the difficulty is partly in identifying the silent genes in the fertilized germ cells of parents known to contain them, and partly in focusing a narrow enough X-ray beam which will do no damage to the remainder of the chromosome. However, after about ten years' work Dr. Whitby successfully developed a whole-body irradiation technique based on his observation of radiobiological damage at Eniwetok."

Powers paused for a moment. "He had noticed that there appeared to be more biological damage after the tests—that is, a greater transport of energy—than could be accounted for by direct radiation. What was happening was that the protein lattices in the genes were building up energy in the way that any vibrating membrane accumulates energy when it resonates—you remember the analogy of the bridge collapsing under the soldiers marching in step—and it occurred to him that if he could first identify the critical resonance frequency of the lattices in any particular silent gene he could then radiate the entire living organism, and not simply its germ cells, with a low field that would act selectively on the silent gene and cause no damage to the remainder of the chromosomes, whose lattices would resonate critically only at other specific frequencies."

Powers gestured around the laboratory with his cigarette. "You see some of the fruits of this 'resonance transfer' technique around you."

Coma nodded. "They've had their silent genes activated?"

"Yes, all of them. These are only a few of the thousands of specimens who have passed through here, and as you've seen, the results are pretty dramatic."

He reached up and pulled across a section of the sun curtain. They were sitting just under the lip of the dome, and the mounting sunlight had begun to irritate him.

In the comparative darkness Coma noticed a stroboscope winking slowly in one of the tanks at the end of the bench behind her. She stood up and went over to it, examining a tall sunflower with a thickened stem and greatly enlarged receptacle. Packed around the flower, so that only its head protruded, was a chimney of grey-white stones, neatly cemented together and labelled:

Cretaceous Chalk: 60,000,000 years

Beside it on the bench were three other chimneys, these labelled "Devonian Sandstone: 290,000,000 years", "Asphalt: 20 years", "Polyvinylchloride: 6 months".

"Can you see those moist white discs on the sepals," Powers pointed out. "In some way they regulate the plant's metabolism. It literally *sees* time. The older the surrounding environment, the more sluggish its metabolism. With the asphalt chimney it will complete its annual cycle in a week, with the PVC one in a couple of hours."

"Sees time," Coma repeated, wonderingly. She looked up at Powers, chewing her lower lip reflectively. "It's fantastic. Are these the creatures of the future, doctor?"

"I don't know," Powers admitted. "But if they are their world must be a monstrous surrealist one."

Three

HE went back to the desk, pulled two cups from a drawer and poured out the coffee, switching off the bunsen. "Some people have speculated that organisms possessing the silent pair of genes are the forerunners of a massive move up the evolutionary slope, that the silent genes are a sort of code, a divine message that we inferior organisms are carrying for our more highly developed descendants. It may well be true—perhaps we've broken the code too soon."

"Why do you say that?"

"Well, as Whitby's death indicates, the experiments in this laboratory have all come to a rather unhappy conclusion. Without exception the organisms we've irradiated have entered a final phase of totally disorganized growth, producing dozens of specialized sensory organs whose function we can't even guess. The results are catastrophic—the anemone will literally explode, the Drosophila cannibalize themselves, and so on. Whether the future implicit in these plants and animals is ever intended to take place, or whether we're merely extrapolating—I don't know. Sometimes I think, though, that the new sensory organs developed are parodies of their real intentions. The specimens you've seen today are all in an early stage of their secondary growth cycles. Later on they begin to look distinctly bizarre."

Coma nodded. "A zoo isn't complete without its keeper," she commented. "What about Man?"

Powers shrugged. "About one in every 100,000—the usual average—contain the silent pair. You might have them—or I. No one has volunteered yet to undergo whole-body irradiation. Apart from the fact that it would be classified as suicide, if the experiments here are any guide the experience would be savage and violent."

He sipped at the thin coffee, feeling tired and somehow bored. Recapitulating the laboratory's work had exhausted him.

The girl leaned forward. "You look awfully pale," she said solicitously. "Don't you sleep well?"

Powers managed a brief smile. "Too well," he admitted. "It's no longer a problem with me."

"I wish I could say that about Kaldren. I don't think he sleeps anywhere near enough. I hear him pacing around all night." She added: "Still, I suppose it's better than being a terminal. Tell me, doctor, wouldn't it be worth trying this radiation technique on the sleepers at the Clinic? It might wake them up before the end. A few of them must possess the silent genes."

"They all do," Powers told her. "The two phenomena are very closely linked, as a matter of fact." He stopped, fatigue dulling his brain, and wondered whether to ask the girl to leave. Then he climbed off the desk and reached behind it, picked up a tape-recorder.

Switching it on, he zeroed the tape and adjusted the speaker volume.

"Whitby and I often talked this over. Towards the end I took it all down. He was a great biologist, so let's hear it in his own words. It's absolutely the heart of the matter."

He flipped the table on, adding: "I've played it over to myself a thousand times, so I'm afraid the quality is poor."

An older man's voice, sharp and slightly irritable, sounded out above a low buzz of distortion, but Coma could hear it clearly.

WHITBY: . . . for heaven's sake, Robert, look at those FAO statistics. Despite an annual increase of five per cent in acreage sown over the past fifteen years, world wheat crops have continued to decline by a factor of about two per cent. The same story repeats itself *ad nauseam*. Cereals and root crops, dairy yields, ruminant fertility—are all down. Couple these with a mass of parallel symptoms, anything you care to pick from altered migratory routes to longer hibernation periods, and the overall pattern is incontrovertible.

POWERS: Population figures for Europe and North America show no decline, though.

WHITBY: Of course not, as I keep pointing out. It will take a century for such a fractional drop in fertility to have any effect in areas where extensive birth control provides an artificial reservoir. One must look at the countries of the Far East, and particularly at those where infant mortality has remained at a steady level. The population of Sumatra, for example, has declined by over fifteen per cent in the last twenty years. A fabulous decline! Do you realize that only two or three decades ago the Neo-Malthusians were talking about a "world population explosion"? In fact, it's an implosion. Another factor is—

Here the tape had been cut and edited, and Whitby's voice, less querulous this time, picked up again.

. . . just as a matter of interest, tell me something: how long do you sleep each night?

POWERS: I don't know exactly; about eight hours, I suppose.

WHITBY: The proverbial eight hours. Ask anyone and they say automatically "eight hours". As a matter of fact you sleep about ten and a half hours, like the majority of people. I've timed you on a number of occasions. I myself sleep eleven. Yet thirty years ago people did indeed sleep eight hours, and a century before that they slept six or seven. In Vasari's *Lives* one reads of Michelangelo sleeping for only four or five hours, painting all day at the age of eighty and then working through the night over his anatomy table with a candle strapped to his forehead. Now he's regarded as a prodigy, but it was unremarkable then. How do you think the ancients, from Plato to Shakespeare, Aristotle to Aquinas, were able to cram so much work into their lives? Simply because they had an extra six or seven hours every day. Of course, a second disadvantage under which we labour is a lowered basal metabolic rate— another factor no one will explain.

POWERS: I suppose you could take the view that the lengthened sleep interval is a compensation device, a sort of mass neurotic attempt to escape from the terrifying pressures of urban life in the late twentieth century.

WHITBY: You could, but you'd be wrong. It's simply a matter of biochemistry. The ribonucleic acid templates which unravel the protein chains in all living organisms are wearing out, the dies inscribing the protoplasmic signature have become blunted. After all, they've been running now for over a thousand million years. It's time to re-tool. Just as an individual organism's life span is finite, or the life of a yeast colony or a given species, so the life of an entire biological kingdom is of fixed duration. It's always been assumed that the evolutionary slope reaches for ever upwards, but in fact the peak has already been reached, and the pathway now leads downwards to the common biological grave. It's a despairing and at present unacceptable vision of the future, but it's the only one. Five thousand centuries from now our descendants, instead of being multi-brained star-men, will probably be naked prognathous idiots with hair on their foreheads, grunting their way through the remains of this Clinic like Neolithic men caught in a macabre inversion of time. Believe me, I pity them, as I pity myself. My total failure, my absolute lack of any moral or biological right to existence, is implicit in every cell of my body . . .

The tape ended, the spool ran free and stopped. Powers closed the machine, then massaged his face. Coma sat quietly, watching him and listening to the chimp playing with a box of puzzle dice.

"As far as Whitby could tell," Powers said, "the silent genes represent a last desperate effort of the biological kingdom to keep its head above the rising waters. Its total life period is determined by the amount of radiation emitted by the sun, and once this reaches a certain point the sure-death line has been passed and extinction is inevitable. To compensate for this, alarms have been built in which alter the form of the organism and adapt it to living in a hotter radiological climate. Soft-skinned organisms develop hard shells, these contain heavy metals as radiation screens. New organs of perception are developed too. According to Whitby, though, it's all wasted effort in the long run—but sometimes I wonder."

He smiled at Coma and shrugged. "Well, let's talk about something else. How long have you known Kaldren?"

"About three weeks. Feels like ten thousand years."

"How do you find him now? We've been rather out of touch lately."

Coma grinned. "I don't seem to see very much of him either. He makes me sleep all the time. Kaldren has many strange talents, but he lives just for himself. You mean a lot to him, doctor. In fact, you're my one serious rival."

"I thought he couldn't stand the sight of me."

"Oh, that's just a sort of surface symptom. He really thinks of you continually. That's why we spend all our time following you around." She eyed Powers shrewdly. "I think he feels guilty about something."

"Guilty?" Powers exclaimed. "*He* does? I thought I was supposed to be the guilty one."

"Why?" she pressed. She hesitated, then said: "You carried out some experimental surgical technique on him, didn't you?"

"Yes," Powers admitted. "It wasn't altogether a success, like so much of what I seem to be involved with. If Kaldren feels guilty, I suppose it's because he feels he must take some of the responsibility."

He looked down at the girl, her intelligent eyes watching him closely. "For one or two reasons it may be necessary for you to know. You said Kaldren paced around all night and didn't get enough sleep. Actually he doesn't get any sleep at all."

The girl nodded. "You . . ." She made a snapping gesture with her fingers.

". . . narcotomized him," Powers completed. "Surgically speaking, it was a great success, one might well share a Nobel for it. Normally the hypothalamus regulates the period of sleep, raising the threshold of consciousness in order to relax the venous capillaries in the brain and drain them of accumulating toxins. However, by sealing off some of the control loops the subject is unable to receive the sleep cue, and the capillaries drain while he remains conscious. All he feels is a temporary lethargy, but this passes within three or four hours. Physically speaking, Kaldren has had another twenty years added to his life. But the psyche seems to need sleep for its own private reasons, and consequently Kaldren has periodic storms that tear him apart. The whole thing was a tragic blunder."

Coma frowned pensively. "I guessed as much. Your papers in the neuro-surgery journals referred to the patient as K. A touch of pure Kafka that came all too true."

"I may leave here for good, Coma," Powers said. "Make sure that Kaldren goes to his clinics. Some of the deep scar tissue will need to be cleaned away."

"I'll try. Sometimes I feel I'm just another of his insane terminal documents."

"What are those?"

"Haven't you heard? Kaldren's collection of final statements about *homo sapiens*. The complete works of Freud, Beethoven's blind quartets, transcripts of the Nuremberg trials, an automatic novel, and so on." She broke off. "What's that you're drawing?"

"Where?"

She pointed to the desk blotter, and Powers looked down and realized he had been unconsciously sketching an elaborate doodle, Whitby's four-armed sun. "It's nothing," he said. Somehow, though, it had a strangely compelling force.

Coma stood up to leave. "You must come and see us, doctor. Kaldren has so much he wants to show you. He's just got hold of an old copy of the last signals sent back by the Mercury Seven twenty years ago when they reached the moon, and can't think about anything else. You remember the strange messages they recorded before they died, full of poetic ramblings about the white gardens. Now that I think about it they behaved rather like the plants in your zoo here."

She put her hands in her pockets, then pulled something out. "By the way, Kaldren asked me to give you this."

It was an old index card from the observatory library. In the centre had been typed the number:

96,688,365,498,720

"It's going to take a long time to reach zero at this rate," Powers remarked dryly. "I'll have quite a collection when we're finished."

After she had left he chucked the card into the waste bin and sat down at the desk, staring for an hour at the ideogram on the blotter.

Half-way back to his beach house the lake road forked to the left through a narrow saddle that ran between the hills to an abandoned Air Force weapons range on one of the remoter salt lakes. At the nearer end were a number of small bunkers and camera towers, one or two metal shacks and a low-roofed storage hangar. The white hills encircled the whole area, shutting it off from the world outside, and Powers liked to wander on foot down the gunnery aisles that had been marked down the two-mile length of the lake towards the concrete sight-screens at the far end. The abstract patterns made him feel like an ant on a bone-white chess-board, the rectangular screens at one end and the towers and bunkers at the other like opposing pieces.

His session with Coma had made Powers feel suddenly dissatisfied with the way he was spending his last months. *Good-bye, Eniwetok*, he had written, but in fact systematically forgetting everything was exactly the same as remembering it, a cataloguing in reverse, sorting out all the books in the mental library and putting them back in their right places upside down.

Powers climbed one of the camera towers, leaned on the rail and looked out along the aisles towards the sight-screens. Ricocheting shells and rockets had chipped away large pieces of the circular concrete bands that ringed the target bulls, but the outlines of the huge 100-yard-wide discs, alternately painted blue and red, were still visible.

For half an hour he stared quietly at them, formless ideas shifting through his mind. Then, without thinking, he abruptly left the rail and climbed down the companionway. The storage hangar was fifty yards away. He walked quickly across to it, stepped into the cool shadows and peered around the rusting electric trolleys and empty flare drums. At the far end, behind a pile of lumber and bales of wire, were a stack of unopened cement bags, a mound of dirty sand and an old mixer.

Half an hour later he had backed the Buick into the hangar and hooked the cement mixer, charged with sand, cement and water scavenged from the drums lying around outside, on to the rear bumper, then loaded a dozen more bags into the car's trunk and rear seat. Finally he selected a few straight lengths of timber, jammed them through the window and set off across the lake towards the central target bull.

For the next two hours he worked away steadily in the centre of the great blue disc, mixing up the cement by hand, carrying it across to the crude wooden forms he had lashed together from the timber, smoothing it down so that it formed a six-inch high wall around the perimeter of the bull. He worked without pause, stirring the cement with a tyre lever, scooping it out with a hub-cap prised off one of the wheels.

By the time he finished and drove off, leaving his equipment where it stood, he had completed a thirty-foot-long section of wall.

Four

June 7: Conscious, for the first time, of the brevity of each day. As long as I was awake for over twelve hours I still orientated my time around the meridian, morning and afternoon set their old rhythms. Now, with just over eleven hours of consciousness left, they form a continuous interval, like a length of tape-measure. I can see exactly how much is left on the spool and can do little to affect the rate at which it unwinds. Spend the time slowly packing away the library; the crates are too heavy to move and lie where they are filled.

Cell count down to 400,000.

Woke 8-10. To sleep 7-15. (Appear to have lost my watch without realizing it, had to drive into town to buy another.)

June 14: 9½ hours. Time races, flashing past like an expressway. However, the last week of a holiday always goes faster than the first. At the present rate there should be about 4-5 weeks left. This morning I tried to visualize what the last week or so—the final, 3, 2, 1, out— would be like, had a sudden chilling attack of pure fear, unlike anything I've ever felt before. Took me half an hour to steady myself for an intravenous.

Kaldren pursues me like my luminescent shadow, chalked up on the gateway "96,688,365,498,702". Should confuse the mail man.

Woke 9-05. To sleep 6-36.

June 19: 8¾ hours. Anderson rang up this morning. I nearly put the phone down on him, but managed to go through the pretence of making the final arrangements. He congratulated me on my stoicism, even used the word "heroic". Don't feel it. Despair erodes everything—courage, hope, self-discipline, all the better qualities. It's so damned difficult to sustain that impersonal attitude of passive acceptance implicit in the scientific tradition. I try to think of Galileo before the Inquisition, Freud surmounting the endless pain of his jaw cancer surgery.

Met Kaldren down town, had a long discussion about the Mercury Seven. He's convinced that they refused to leave the moon deliberately, after the "reception party" waiting for them had put them in the cosmic picture. They were told by the mysterious emissaries from Orion that the exploration of deep space was pointless, that they were too late as the life of the universe is now virtually over!!! According to K. there are Air Force generals who take this nonsense seriously, but I suspect it's simply an obscure attempt on K.'s part to console me.

Must have the phone disconnected. Some contractor keeps calling me up about payment for 50 bags of cement he claims I collected ten days ago. Says he helped me load them on to a truck himself. I did drive Whitby's pick-up into town but only to get some lead screening. What does he think I'd do with all that cement? Just the sort of irritating thing you don't expect to hang over your final exit. (Moral: don't try too hard to forget Eniwetok.)

Woke 9-40. To sleep 4-15.

June 25: 7½ hours. Kaldren was snooping around the lab again today.

Phoned me there, when I answered a recorded voice he'd rigged up rambled out a long string of numbers, like an insane super-Tim. These practical jokes of his get rather wearing. Fairly soon I'll have to go over and come to terms with him, much as I hate the prospect. Anyway, Miss Mars is a pleasure to look at.

One meal is enough now, topped up with a glucose shot. Sleep is still "black", completely unrefreshing. Last night I took a 16 mm. film of the first three hours, screened it this morning at the lab. The first true horror movie, I looked like a half-animated corpse.

Woke 10-25. To sleep 3-45.

July 3 : 5¾ hours. Little done today. Deepening lethargy, dragged myself over to the lab, nearly left the road twice. Concentrated enough to feed the zoo and get the log up to date. Read through the operating manuals Whitby left for the last time, decided on a delivery rate of 40 röntgens/ min., target distance of 350 cm. Everything is ready now.

Woke 11-05. To sleep 3-15.

Powers stretched, shifted his head slowly across the pillow, focusing on the shadows cast on to the ceiling by the blind. Then he looked down at his feet, saw Kaldren sitting on the end of the bed, watching him quietly.

"Hello, doctor," he said, putting out his cigarette. "Late night? You look tired."

Powers heaved himself on to one elbow, glanced at his watch. It was just after eleven. For a moment his brain blurred, and he swung his legs around and sat on the edge of the bed, elbows on his knees, massaging some life into his face.

He noticed that the room was full of smoke. "What are you doing here?" he asked Kaldren.

"I came over to invite you to lunch." He indicated the bedside phone. "Your line was dead so I drove round. Hope you don't mind me climbing in. Rang the bell for about half an hour. I'm surprised you didn't hear it."

Powers nodded, then stood up and tried to smooth the creases out of his cotton slacks. He had gone to sleep without changing for over a week, and they were damp and stale.

As he started for the bathroom door Kaldren pointed to the camera tripod on the other side of the bed. "What's this? Going into the blue movie business, doctor?"

Powers surveyed him dimly for a moment, glanced at the tripod without replying and then noticed his open diary on the bedside table. Wondering whether Kaldren had read the last entries, he went back and picked it up, then stepped into the bathroom and closed the door behind him.

From the mirror cabinet he took out a syringe and an ampoule, after the shot leaned against the door waiting for the stimulant to pick up.

Kaldren was in the lounge when he returned to him, reading the labels on the crates lying about in the centre of the floor.

"O.K., then," Powers told him, "I'll join you for lunch." He examined Kaldren carefully. He looked more subdued than usual, there was an air almost of deference about him.

"Good," Kaldren said. "By the way, are you leaving?"

"Does it matter?" Powers asked curtly. "I thought you were in Anderson's care?"

Kaldren shrugged. "Please yourself. Come round at about twelve," he suggested, adding pointedly: "That'll give you time to clean up and change. What's that all over your shirt? Looks like lime."

Powers peered down, brushed at the white streaks. After Kaldren had left he threw the clothes away, took a shower and unpacked a clean suit from one of the trunks.

Until his liaison with Coma, Kaldren lived alone in the old abstract summer house on the north shore of the lake. This was a seven-storey folly originally built by an eccentric millionaire mathematician in the form of a spiralling concrete ribbon that wound around itself like an insane serpent, serving walls, floors and ceilings. Only Kaldren had solved the building, a geometric model of $\sqrt{-1}$, and consequently he had been able to take it off the agents' hands at a comparatively low rent. In the evenings Powers had often watched him from the laboratory, striding restlessly from one level to the next, swinging through the labyrinth of inclines and terraces to the roof-top, where his lean angular figure stood out like a gallows against the sky, his lonely eyes sifting out radio lanes for the next day's trapping.

Powers noticed him there when he drove up at noon, poised on a ledge 150 feet above, head raised theatrically to the sky.

"Kaldren!" he shouted up suddenly into the silent air, half-hoping he might be jolted into losing his footing.

Kaldren broke out of his reverie and glanced down into the court. Grinning obliquely, he waved his right arm in a slow semi-circle.

"Come up," he called, then turned back to the sky.

Powers leaned against the car. Once, a few months previously, he had accepted the same invitation, stepped through the entrance and within three minutes lost himself helplessly in a second-floor cul-de-sac. Kaldren had taken half an hour to find him.

Powers waited while Kaldren swung down from his eyrie, vaulting through the wells and stairways, then rode up in the elevator with him to the penthouse suite.

They carried their cocktails through into a wide glass-roofed studio, the huge white ribbon of concrete uncoiling around them like toothpaste squeezed from an enormous tube. On the staged levels running parallel and across them rested pieces of grey abstract furniture, giant photographs on angled screens, carefully labelled exhibits laid out on low tables, all dominated by twenty-foot-high black letters on the rear wall which spelt out the single vast word:

YOU

Kaldren pointed to it. "What you might call the supra-liminal approach." He gestured Powers in conspiratorially, finishing his drink in a gulp. "This is *my* laboratory, doctor," he said with a note of pride. "Much more significant than yours, believe me."

Powers smiled wryly to himself and examined the first exhibit, an old EEG tape traversed by a series of faded inky wriggles. It was labelled: "Einstein, A.; Alpha Waves, 1922."

He followed Kaldren around, sipping slowly at his drink, enjoying the brief feeling of alertness the amphetamine provided. Within two hours it would fade, leave his brain feeling like a block of blotting-paper.

Kaldren chattered away, explaining the significance of the so-called Terminal Documents. "They're end-prints, Powers, final statements, the products of total fragmentation. When I've got enough together I'll build a new world for myself out of them." He picked a thick paper-bound volume off one of the tables, riffled through its pages. "Association tests of the Nuremberg Twelve. I have to include these . . ."

Powers strolled on absently without listening. Over in the corner were what appeared to be three ticker-tape machines, lengths of tape hanging from their mouths. He wondered whether Kaldren was misguided enough to be playing the stock market, which had been declining slowly for twenty years.

"Powers," he heard Kaldren say. "I was telling you about the Mercury Seven." He pointed to a collection of typewritten sheets tacked to a screen. "These are transcripts of their final signals radioed back from the recording monitors."

Powers examined the sheets cursorily, read a line at random.

". . . BLUE . . . PEOPLE . . . RE-CYCLE . . . ORION . . . TELEMETERS . . ."

Powers nodded noncommittally. "Interesting. What are the ticker tapes for over there?"

Kaldren grinned. "I've been waiting for months for you to ask me that. Have a look."

Powers went over and picked up one of the tapes. The machine was labelled: "Auriga 225-G. Interval: 69 hours."

The tape read: 96,688,365,498,695
96,688,365,498,694
96,688,365,498,693
96,688,365,498,692

Powers dropped the tape. "Looks rather familiar. What does the sequence represent?"

Kaldren shrugged. "No one knows."

"What do you mean? It must replicate something."

"Yes, it does. A diminishing mathematical progression. A count-down, if you like."

Powers picked up the tape on the right, tabbed: "Aries 44R951. Interval: 49 days."

Here the sequence ran:

876,567,988,347,779,877,654,434
876,567,988,347,779,877,654,433
876,567,988,347,779,877,654,432

Powers looked round. "How long does it take each signal to come through?"

"Only a few seconds. They're tremendously compressed laterally, of course. A computer at the observatory breaks them down. They were first picked up at Jodrell Bank about twenty years ago. Nobody bothers to listen to them now."

Powers turned to the last tape.

$$6,554$$
$$6,553$$
$$6,552$$
$$6,551$$

"Nearing the end of its run," he commented. He glanced at the label on the hood, which read: "Unidentified radio source, Canes Venatici. Interval: 97 weeks."

He showed the tape to Kaldren. "Soon be over."

Kaldren shook his head. He lifted a heavy directory-sized volume off a table, cradled it in his hands. His face had suddenly become sombre and haunted. "I doubt it," he said. "Those are only the last four digits. The whole number contains over 50 million."

He handed the volume to Powers, who turned to the title page. "Master Sequence of Serial Signal received by Jodrell Bank Radio-Observatory, University of Manchester, England, 0012-59 hours, 21-5-72. Source: NGC 9743, Canes Venatici." He thumbed the thick stack of closely printed pages, millions of numerals, as Kaldren had said, running up and down across a thousand consecutive pages.

Powers shook his head, picked up the tape again and stared at it thoughtfully.

"The computer only breaks down the last four digits," Kaldren explained. "The whole series comes over in each 15-second-long package, but it took IBM more than two years to unscramble one of them."

"Amazing," Powers commented. "But what is it?"

"A count-down, as you can see. NGC 9743, somewhere in Canes Venatici. The big spirals there are breaking up, and they're saying good-bye. God knows who they think we are but they're letting us know all the same, beaming it out on the hydrogen line for everyone in the universe to hear." He paused. "Some people have put other interpretations on them, but there's one piece of evidence that rules out everything else."

"Which is?"

Kaldren pointed to the last tape from Canes Venatici. "Simply that it's been estimated that by the time this series reaches zero the universe will have just ended."

Powers fingered the tape reflectively. "Thoughtful of them to let us know what the real time is," he remarked.

"I agree, it is," Kaldren said quietly. "Applying the inverse square law that signal source is broadcasting at a strength of about three million megawatts raised to the hundredth power. About the size of the entire Local Group. Thoughtful is the word."

Suddenly he gripped Powers' arm, held it tightly and peered into his eyes closely, his throat working with emotion.

"You're not alone, Powers, don't think you are. These are the voices of time, and they're all saying good-bye to you. Think of yourself in a wider context. Every particle in your body, every grain of sand, every galaxy carries the same signature. As you've just said, you know what the time is now, so what does the rest matter? There's no need to go on looking at the clock."

Powers took his hand, squeezed it firmly. "Thanks, Kaldren. I'm glad you understand." He walked over to the window, looked down across the white lake. The tension between himself and Kaldren had dissipated, he felt that all his obligations to him had at last been met. Now he wanted to leave as quickly as possible, forget him as he had forgotten the faces of the countless other patients whose exposed brains had passed between his fingers.

He went back to the ticker machines, tore the tapes from their slots and stuffed them into his pockets. "I'll take these along to remind myself. Say good-bye to Coma for me, will you."

He moved towards the door, when he reached it looked back to see Kaldren standing in the shadow of the three giant letters on the far wall, his eyes staring listlessly at his feet.

As Powers drove away he noticed that Kaldren had gone up on to the roof, watched him in the driving mirror waving slowly until the car disappeared around a bend.

Five

THE outer circle was now almost complete. A narrow segment, an arc about ten feet long, was missing, but otherwise the low perimeter wall ran continuously six inches off the concrete floor around the outer lane of the target bull, enclosing the huge rebus within it. Three concentric circles, the largest a hundred yards in diameter, separated from each other by ten-foot intervals, formed the rim of the device, divided into four segments by the arms of an enormous cross radiating from its centre, where a small round platform had been built a foot above the ground.

Powers worked swiftly, pouring sand and cement into the mixer, tipping in water until a rough paste formed, then carried it across to the wooden forms and tamped the mixture down into the narrow channel.

Within ten minutes he had finished, quickly dismantled the forms before the cement had set and slung the timbers into the back seat of the car. Dusting his hands on his trousers, he went over to the mixer and pushed it fifty yards away into the long shadow of the surrounding hills.

Without pausing to survey the gigantic cipher on which he had laboured patiently for so many afternoons, he climbed into the car and drove off on a wake of bone-white dust, splitting the pools of indigo shadow.

He reached the laboratory at three o'clock, jumped from the car as it lurched back on its brakes. Inside the entrance he first switched on the lights, then hurried round, pulling the sun curtains down and shackling them to the floor slots, effectively turning the dome into a steel tent.

In their tanks behind him the plants and animals stirred quietly, responding to the sudden flood of cold fluorescent light. Only the chimpanzee ignored him. It sat on the floor of its cage, neurotically jamming the puzzle dice into the polythene bucket, exploding in bursts of sudden rage when the pieces refused to fit.

Powers went over to it, noticing the shattered glass fibre reinforcing panels bursting from the dented helmet. Already the chimp's face and forehead were bleeding from self-inflicted blows. Powers picked up the remains of the geranium that had been hurled through the bars, attracted the chimp's attention with it, then tossed a black pellet he had taken from a capsule in the desk drawer. The chimp caught it with a quick flick of the wrist, for a few seconds juggled the pellet with a couple of dice as it concentrated on the puzzle, then pulled it out of the air and swallowed it in a gulp.

Without waiting, Powers slipped off his jacket and stepped towards the X-ray theatre. He pulled back the high sliding doors to reveal the long glassy metallic snout of the Maxitron, then started to stack the lead screening shields against the rear wall. A few minutes later the generator hummed into life.

The anemone stirred. Basking in the warm subliminal sea of radiation rising around it, prompted by countless pelagic memories, it reached tentatively across the tank, groping blindly towards the dim uterine sun. Its tendrils flexed, the thousands of dormant neural cells in their tips regrouping and multiplying, each harnessing the unlocked energies of its nucleus. Chains forged themselves, lattices tiered upwards into multi-faceted lenses, focused slowly on the vivid spectral outlines of the sounds dancing like phosphorescent waves around the darkened chamber of the dome.

Gradually an image formed, revealing an enormous black fountain that poured an endless stream of brilliant light over the circle of benches and tanks. Beside it a figure moved, adjusting the flow through its mouth. As it stepped across the floor its feet threw off vivid bursts of colour, its hands racing along the benches conjured up a dazzling chiaroscuro, balls of blue and violet light that exploded fleetingly in the darkness like miniature star-shells.

Photons murmured. Steadily, as it watched the glimmering screen of sounds around it, the anemone continued to expand. Its ganglia linked, heeding a new source of stimuli from the delicate diaphragms in the crown of its notochord. The silent outlines of the laboratory began to echo softly, waves of muted sound fell from the arc lights and echoed off the benches and furniture below. Etched in sound, their angular forms resonated with sharp persistent overtones. The plastic-ribbed chairs were a buzz of staccato discords, the square-sided desk a continuous double-featured tone.

Ignoring these sounds once they had been perceived, the anemone turned to the ceiling, which reverberated like a shield in the sounds pouring steadily from the fluorescent tubes. Streaming through a narrow skylight, its voice clear and strong, interweaved by numberless overtones, the sun sang . . .

It was a few minutes before dawn when Powers left the laboratory and stepped into his car. Behind him the great dome lay silently in the darkness, the thin shadows of the white moonlit hills falling across its surface. Powers free-wheeled the car down the long curving drive to the lake road below, listening to the tyres cutting across the blue gravel, then let out the clutch and accelerated the engine.

As he drove along, the limestone hills half hidden in the darkness on his left, he gradually became aware that, although no longer looking at the hills, he was still in some oblique way conscious of their forms and outlines in the back of his mind. The sensation was undefined but none the less certain, a strange almost visual impression that emanated most strongly from the deep clefts and ravines dividing one cliff face from the next. For a few minutes Powers let it play upon him, without trying to identify it, a dozen strange images moving across his brain.

The road swung up around a group of chalets built on to the lake shore, taking the car right under the lee of the hills, and Powers suddenly felt the massive weight of the escarpment rising up into the dark sky like a cliff of luminous chalk, and realized the identity of the impression now registering powerfully within his mind. Not only could he see the escarpment, but he was aware of its enormous age, felt distinctly the countless millions of years since it had first reared out of the magma of the earth's crust. The ragged crests three hundred feet above him, the dark gulleys and fissures, the smooth boulders by the roadside at the foot of the cliff, all carried a distinct image of themselves across to him, a thousand voices that together told of the total time that had elapsed in the life of the escarpment, a psychic picture defined and clear as the visual image brought to him by his eyes.

Involuntarily, Powers had slowed the car, and turning his eyes away from the hill face he felt a second wave of time sweep across the first. The image was broader but of shorter perspectives, radiating from the wide disc of the salt lake, breaking over the ancient limestone cliffs like shallow rollers dashing against a towering headland.

Closing his eyes, Powers lay back and steered the car along the interval between the two time fronts, feeling the images deepen and strengthen within his mind. The vast age of the landscape, the inaudible chorus of voices resonating from the lake and from the white hills, seemed to carry him back through time, down endless corridors to the first thresholds of the world.

He turned the car off the road along the track leading towards the target range. On either side of the culvert the cliff faces boomed and echoed with vast impenetrable time fields, like enormous opposed magnets. As he finally emerged between them on to the flat surface of the lake it seemed to Powers that he could feel the separate identity of each sand-grain and salt crystal calling to him from the surrounding ring of hills.

He parked the car beside the mandala and walked slowly towards the outer concrete rim curving away into the shadows. Above him he could hear the stars, a million cosmic voices that crowded the sky from one horizon to the next, a true canopy of time. Like jostling radio beacons, their long aisles interlocking at countless angles, they plunged into the sky from the narrowest recesses of space. He saw the dim red disc of Sirius, heard its ancient voice, untold millions of years old, dwarfed by the huge spiral nebulae in Andromeda, a gigantic carousel of vanished universes, their voices almost as old as the cosmos itself. To Powers the sky seemed an endless babel, the time-song of a thousand galaxies overlaying each other in his mind. As he moved slowly towards the centre of the mandala he craned up at the glittering traverse of the Milky Way, searching the confusion of clamouring nebulae and constellations.

Stepping into the inner circle of the mandala, a few yards from the platform at its centre, he realized that the tumult was beginning to fade, and that a single stronger voice had emerged and was dominating the others. He climbed on to the platform, raised his eyes to the darkened sky, moving through the constellations to the island galaxies beyond them, hearing the thin archaic voices reaching to him across the millennia. In his pockets he felt the paper tapes, and turned to find the distant diadem of Canes Venatici, heard its great voice mounting in his mind.

Like an endless river, so broad that its banks were below the horizons, it flowed steadily towards him, a vast course of time that spread outwards to fill the sky and the universe, enveloping everything within them. Moving slowly, the forward direction of its majestic current almost imperceptible, Powers knew that its source was the source of the cosmos itself. As it passed him, he felt its massive magnetic pull, let himself be drawn into it, borne gently on its powerful back. Quietly it carried him away, and he rotated slowly, facing the direction of the tide. Around him the outlines of the hills and the lake had faded, but the image of the mandala, like a cosmic clock, remained fixed before his eyes, illuminating the broad surface of the stream. Watching it constantly, he felt his body gradually dissolving, its physical dimensions melting into the vast continuum of the current, which bore him out into the centre of the great channel, sweeping him onward, beyond hope but at last at rest, down the broadening reaches of the river of eternity.

As the shadows faded, retreating into the hill slopes, Kaldren stepped out of his car, walked hesitantly towards the concrete rim of the outer circle. Fifty yards away, at the centre, Coma knelt beside Powers' body, her small hands pressed to his dead face. A gust of wind stirred the sand, dislodging a strip of tape that drifted towards Kaldren's feet. He bent down and picked it up, then rolled it carefully in his hands and slipped it into his pocket. The dawn air was cold, and he turned up the collar of his jacket, watching Coma impassively.

"It's six o'clock," he told her after a few minutes. "I'll go and get the police. You stay with him." He paused and then added: "Don't let them break the clock."

Coma turned and looked at him. "Aren't you coming back?"

"I don't know." Nodding to her, Kaldren swung on his heel.

He reached the lake road, five minutes later parked the car in the drive outside Whitby's laboratory.

The dome was in darkness, all its windows shuttered, but the generator still hummed in the X-ray theatre. Kaldren stepped through the entrance and switched on the lights. In the theatre he touched the grilles of the generator, felt the warm cylinder of the beryllium end-window. The circular target table was revolving slowly, its setting at 1 r.p.m., a steel restraining chair shackled to it hastily. Grouped in a semicircle a few feet away were most of the tanks and cages, piled on top of each other haphazardly. In one of them an enormous squid-like plant had almost managed to climb from its vivarium. Its long translucent tendrils clung to the edges of the tank, but its body had burst into a jellified pool of globular mucilage. In another an enormous spider had trapped itself in its own web, hung helplessly in the centre of a huge three-dimensional maze of phosphorescing thread, twitching spasmodically.

All the experimental plants and animals had died. The chimp lay on its back among the remains of the hutch, the helmet forward over its eyes. Kaldren watched it for a moment, then sat down on the desk and picked up the phone.

While he dialled the number he noticed a film reel lying on the blotter. For a moment he stared at the label, then slid the reel into his pocket beside the tape.

After he had spoken to the police he turned off the lights and went out to the car, drove off slowly down the drive.

When he reached the summer house the early sunlight was breaking across the ribbon-like balconies and terraces. He took the lift to the penthouse, made his way through into the museum. One by one he opened the shutters and let the sunlight play over the exhibits. Then he pulled a chair over to a side window, sat back and stared up at the light pouring through into the room.

Two or three hours later he heard Coma outside, calling up to him. After half an hour she went away, but a little later a second voice appeared and shouted up at Kaldren. He left his chair and closed all the shutters overlooking the front courtyard, and eventually he was left undisturbed.

Kaldren returned to his seat and lay back quietly, his eyes gazing across the lines of exhibits. Half-asleep, periodically he leaned up and adjusted the flow of light through the shutter, thinking to himself, as he would do through the coming months of Powers and his strange mandala, and of the seven and their journey to the white gardens of the moon, and the blue people who had come from Orion and spoken in poetry to them of ancient beautiful worlds beneath golden suns in the island galaxies, vanished for ever now in the myriad deaths of the cosmos.

THE SOUND-SWEEP

One

By midnight Madame Gioconda's headache had become intense. All day the derelict walls and ceiling of the sound stage had reverberated with the endless din of traffic accelerating across the mid-town flyover which arched fifty feet above the studio's roof, a frenzied hypermanic babel of jostling horns, shrilling tyres, plunging brakes and engines that hammered down the empty corridors and stairways to the sound stage on the second floor, making the faded air feel leaden and angry.

Exhausting but at least impersonal, these sounds Madame Gioconda could bear. At dusk, however, when the flyover quietened, they were overlaid by the mysterious clapping of her phantoms, the sourceless applause that rustled down on to the stage from the darkness around her. At first a few scattered ripples from the front rows, it soon spread to the entire auditorium, mounting to a tumultuous ovation in which she suddenly detected a note of sarcasm, a single shout of derision that drove a spear of pain through her forehead, followed by an uproar of boos and catcalls that filled the tortured air, driving her away towards her couch where she lay gasping helplessly until Mangon arrived at midnight, hurrying on to the stage with his sonovac.

Understanding her, he first concentrated on sweeping the walls and ceiling clean, draining away the heavy depressing under-layer of traffic noises. Carefully he ran the long snout of the sonovac over the ancient scenic flats (relics of her previous roles at the Metropolitan Opera House) which screened in Madame Gioconda's make-shift home—the great collapsing Byzantine bed (*Othello*) mounted against the microphone turret; the huge framed mirrors with their peeling silver-screen (*Orpheus*) stacked in one corner by the bandstand; the stove (*Trovatore*) set up on the programme director's podium; the gilt-trimmed dressing table and wardrobe (*Figaro*) stuffed with newspaper and magazine cuttings. He swept them methodically, moving the sonovac's nozzle in long strokes, drawing out the dead residues of sound that had accumulated during the day.

By the time he finished the air was clear again, the atmosphere lightened, its overtones of fatigue and irritation dissipated. Gradually Madame Gioconda recovered. Sitting up weakly, she smiled wanly at Mangon. Mangon grinned back encouragingly, slipped the kettle on to the stove for Russian tea, sweetened by the usual phenobarbitone chaser, switched off the sonovac and indicated to her that he was going outside to empty it.

Down in the alley behind the studio he clipped the sonovac on to the intake manifold of the sound truck. The vacuum drained in a few seconds, but he waited a discretionary two or three minutes before returning, keeping up the pretence that Madame Gioconda's phantom audience was real. Of course the cylinder was always empty, containing only the usual daily detritus—the sounds of a door slam, a partition collapsing somewhere or the kettle whistling, a grunt or two, and later, when the headaches began, Madame Gioconda's pitiful moanings. The riotous applause, which would have lifted the roof off the Met, let alone a small radio station, the jeers and hoots of derision were, he knew, quite imaginary, figments of Madame Gioconda's world of fantasy, phantoms from the past of a once great *prima donna* who had been dropped by her public and had retreated into her imagination, each evening conjuring up a blissful dream of being once again applauded by a full house at the Metropolitan, a dream that guilt and resentment turned sour by midnight, inverting it into a nightmare of fiasco and failure.

Why she should torment herself was difficult to understand, but at least the nightmare kept Madame Gioconda just this side of sanity and Mangon, who revered and loved Madame Gioconda, would have been the last person in the world to disillusion her. Each evening, when he finished his calls for the day, he would drive his sound truck all the way over from the West Side to the abandoned radio station under the flyover at the deserted end of F Street, go through the pretence of sweeping Madame Gioconda's apartment on the stage of studio 2, charging no fee, make tea and listen to her reminiscences and plans for revenge, then see her asleep and tiptoe out, a wry but pleased smile on his youthful face.

He had been calling on Madame Gioconda for nearly a year, but what his precise role was in relation to her he had not yet decided. Oddly enough, although he was more or less indispensable now to the effective operation of her fantasy world she showed little personal interest or affection for Mangon, but he assumed that this indifference was merely part of the autocratic personality of a world-famous *prima donna*, particularly one very conscious of the tradition, now alas meaningless, Melba—Callas —Gioconda. To serve at all was the privilege. In time, perhaps, Madame Gioconda might accord him some sign of favour.

Without him, certainly, her prognosis would have been poor. Lately the headaches had become more menacing, as she insisted that the applause was growing stormier, the boos and catcalls more vicious. Whatever the psychic mechanism generating the fantasy system, Mangon realized that ultimately she would need him at the studio all day, holding back the enveloping tides of nightmare and insanity with sham passes of the sonovac. Then, perhaps, when the dream crumbled, he would regret having helped her to delude herself. With luck though she might achieve her ambition of making a comeback. She had told him something of her scheme—a serpentine mixture of blackmail and bribery—and privately Mangon hoped to launch a plot of his own to return her to popularity. By now she had unfortunately reached the point where success alone could save her from disaster.

She was sitting up when he returned, propped back on an enormous gold *lamé* cushion, the single lamp at the foot of the couch throwing a semicircle of light on to the great flats which divided the sound stage from the auditorium. These were all from her last operatic role—*The Medium*—and represented a complete interior of the old spiritualist's seance chamber, the one coherent feature in Madame Gioconda's present existence. Surrounded by fragments from a dozen roles, even Madame Gioconda herself, Mangon reflected, seemed compounded of several separate identities. A tall regal figure, with full shapely shoulders and massive rib-cage, she had a large handsome face topped by a magnificent coiffure of rich blue-black hair—the exact prototype of the classical diva. She must have been almost fifty, yet her soft creamy complexion and small features were those of a child. The eyes, however, belied her. Large and watchful, slashed with mascara, they regarded the world around her balefully, narrowing even as Mangon approached. Her teeth too were bad, stained by tobacco and cheap cocaine. When she was roused, and her full violet lips curled with rage, revealing the blackened hulks of her dentures and the acid flickering tongue, her mouth looked like a very vent of hell. Altogether she was a formidable woman.

As Mangon brought her tea she heaved herself up and made room for him by her feet among the debris of beads, loose diary pages, horoscopes and jewelled address books that littered the couch. Mangon sat down, surreptitiously noting the time (his first calls were at 9.30 the next morning and loss of sleep deadened his acute hearing), and prepared himself to listen to her for half an hour.

Suddenly she flinched, shrank back into the cushion and gestured agitatedly in the direction of the darkened bandstand.

"They're still clapping!" she shrieked. "For God's sake sweep them away, they're driving me insane. Oooohh . . ." she rasped theatrically, "over there, quickly . . . !"

Mangon leapt to his feet. He hurried over to the bandstand and carefully focused his ears on the tiers of seats and plywood music stands. They were all immaculately clean, well below the threshold at which embedded sounds began to radiate detectable echoes. He turned to the corner walls and ceiling. Listening very carefully he could just hear seven muted pads, the dull echoes of his footsteps across the floor. They faded and vanished, followed by a low threshing noise like blurred radio static—in fact Madame Gioconda's present tantrum. Mangon could almost distinguish the individual words, but repetition muffled them.

Madame Gioconda was still writhing about on the couch, evidently not to be easily placated, so Mangon climbed down off the stage and made his way through the auditorium to where he had left his sonovac by the door. The power lead was outside in the truck but he was sure Madame Gioconda would fail to notice.

For five minutes he worked away industriously, pretending to sweep the bandstand again, then put down the sonovac and returned to the couch.

Madame Gioconda emerged from the cushion, sounded the air carefully with two or three slow turns of the head, and smiled at him.

"Thank you, Mangon," she said silkily, her eyes watching him thoughtfully. "You've saved me again from my assassins. They've become so cunning recently, they can even hide from you."

Mangon smiled ruefully to himself at this last remark. So he had been a little too perfunctory earlier on; Madame Gioconda was keeping him up to the mark.

However, she seemed genuinely grateful. "Mangon, my dear," she reflected as she remade her face in the mirror of an enormous compact, painting on magnificent green eyes like a cobra's, "what would I do without you? How can I ever repay you for looking after me?"

The questions, whatever their sinister undertones (had he detected them, Mangon would have been deeply shocked) were purely rhetorical, and all their conversations for that matter entirely one-sided. For Mangon was a mute. From the age of three, when his mother had savagely punched him in the throat to stop him crying, he had been stone dumb, his vocal cords irreparably damaged. In all their endless exchanges of midnight confidences, Mangon had contributed not a single spoken word.

His muteness, naturally, was part of the attraction he felt for Madame Gioconda. Both of them in a sense had lost their voices, he to a cruel mother, she to a fickle and unfaithful public. This bound them together, gave them a shared sense of life's injustice, though Mangon, like all innocents, viewed his misfortune without rancour. Both, too, were social outcasts. Rescued from his degenerate parents when he was four, Mangon had been brought up in a succession of state institutions, a solitary wounded child. His one talent had been his remarkable auditory powers, and at fourteen he was apprenticed to the Metropolitan Sonic Disposal Service. Regarded as little better than garbage collectors, the sound-sweeps were an outcast group of illiterates, mutes (the city authorities preferred these—their discretion could be relied upon) and social cripples who lived in a chain of isolated shacks on the edge of an old explosives plant in the sand dunes to the north of the city which served as the sonic dump.

Mangon had made no friends among the sound-sweeps, and Madame Gioconda was the first person in his life with whom he had been intimately involved. Apart from the pleasure of being able to help her, a considerable factor in Mangon's devotion was that until her decline she had represented (as to all mutes) the most painful possible reminder of his own voiceless condition, and that now he could at last come to terms with years of unconscious resentment.

This soon done, he devoted himself wholeheartedly to serving Madame Gioconda.

Inhaling moodily on a black cigarette clamped into a long jade holder, she was outlining her plans for a comeback. These had been maturing for several months and involved nothing less than persuading Hector LeGrande, chairman-in-chief of Video City, the huge corporation that transmitted a dozen TV and radio channels, into providing her with a complete series of television spectaculars. Built around Madame Gioconda and lavishly dressed and orchestrated, they would spearhead the international revival of classical opera that was her unfading dream.

"La Scala, Covent Garden, the Met—what are they now?" she demanded angrily. "Bowling alleys! Can you believe, Mangon, that in those immortal theatres where I created my Tosca, my Butterfly, my Brünnhilde, they now have—" she spat out a gust of smoke "—beer and skittles!"

Mangon shook his head sympathetically. He pulled a pencil from his breast-pocket and on the wrist-pad stitched to his left sleeve wrote:

Mr. LeGrande?

Madame Gioconda read the note, let it fall to the floor.

"Hector? Those lawyers poison him. He's surrounded by them, I think they steal all my telegrams to him. Of course Hector had a complete breakdown on the spectaculars. Imagine, Mangon, what a scoop for him, a sensation! 'The great Gioconda will appear on television!' Not just some moronic bubblegum girl, but the Gioconda in person."

Exhausted by this vision Madame Gioconda sank back into her cushion, blowing smoke limply through the holder.

Mangon wrote:

Contract?

Madame Gioconda frowned at the note, then pierced it with the glowing end of her cigarette.

"I am having a new contract drawn up. Not for the mere 300,000 I was prepared to take at first, not even 500,000. For each show I shall now demand precisely *one million* dollars. Nothing less! Hector will have to pay for ignoring me. Anyway, think of the publicity value of such a figure. Only a star could think of such vulgar extravagance. If he's short of cash he can sack all those lawyers. Or devalue the dollar, I don't mind."

Madame Gioconda hooted with pleasure at the prospect. Mangon nodded, then scribbled another message.

Be practical.

Madame Gioconda ground out her cigarette. "You think I'm raving, don't you, Mangon? 'Fantastic dreams, million-dollar contracts, poor old fool.' But let me assure you that Hector will be only too eager to sign the contract. And I don't intend to rely solely on his good judgement as an impresario." She smirked archly to herself.

What else?

Madame Gioconda peered round the darkened stage, then lowered her eyes.

"You see, Mangon, Hector and I are very old friends. You know what I mean, of course?" She waited for Mangon, who had swept out a thousand honeymoon hotel suites, to nod and then continued: "How well I remember that first season at Bayreuth, when Hector and I . . ."

Mangon stared unhappily at his feet as Madame Gioconda outlined this latest venture into blackmail. Certainly she and LeGrande had been intimate friends—the cuttings scattered around the stage testified frankly to this. In fact, were it not for the small monthly cheque which LeGrande sent Madame Gioconda she would long previously have disintegrated. To turn on him and threaten ancient scandal (LeGrande was shortly to enter politics) was not only grotesque but extremely dangerous, for LeGrande was ruthless and unsentimental. Years earlier he had used Madame Gioconda as a stepping-stone, reaping all the publicity he could from their affair, then abruptly kicking her away.

Mangon fretted. A solution to her predicament was hard to find. Brought about through no fault of her own, Madame Gioconda's decline was all the harder to bear. Since the introduction a few years earlier of ultrasonic music, the human voice—indeed, audible music of any type—had gone completely out of fashion. Ultrasonic music, employing a vastly greater range of octaves, chords and chromatic scales than are audible by the human ear, provided a direct neural link between the sound stream and the auditory lobes, generating an apparently sourceless sensation of harmony, rhythm, cadence and melody uncontaminated by the noise and vibration of audible music. The re-scoring of the classical repertoire allowed the ultrasonic audience the best of both worlds. The majestic rhythms of Beethoven, the popular melodies of Tchaikovsky, the complex fugal elaborations of Bach, the abstract images of Schoenberg—all these were raised in frequency above the threshold of conscious audibility. Not only did they become inaudible, but the original works were re-scored for the much wider range of the ultrasonic orchestra, became richer in texture, more profound in theme, more sensitive, tender or lyrical as the ultrasonic arranger chose.

The first casualty in this change-over was the human voice. This alone of all instruments could not be re-scored, because its sounds were produced by non-mechanical means which the neurophonic engineer could never hope, or bother, to duplicate.

The earliest ultrasonic recordings had met with resistance, even ridicule. Radio programmes consisting of nothing but silence interrupted at half-hour intervals by commercial breaks seemed absurd. But gradually the public discovered that the silence was golden, that after leaving the radio switched to an ultrasonic channel for an hour or so a pleasant atmosphere of rhythm and melody seemed to generate itself spontaneously around them. When an announcer suddenly stated that an ultrasonic version of Mozart's Jupiter Symphony or Tchaikovsky's Pathétique had just been played the listener identified the real source.

A second advantage of ultrasonic music was that its frequencies were so high they left no resonating residues in solid structures, and consequently there was no need to call in the sound-sweep. After an audible performance of most symphonic music, walls and furniture throbbed for days with disintegrating residues that made the air seem leaden and tumid, an entire room virtually uninhabitable.

An immediate result was the swift collapse of all but a few symphony orchestras and opera companies. Concert halls and opera houses closed overnight. In the age of noise the tranquillizing balms of silence began to be rediscovered.

But the final triumph of ultrasonic music had come with a second development—the short-playing record, spinning at 900 r.p.m., which condensed the 45 minutes of a Beethoven symphony to 20 seconds of playing time, the three hours of a Wagner opera to little more than two minutes. Compact and cheap, SP records sacrificed nothing to brevity. One 30-second SP record delivered as much neurophonic pleasure as a natural length recording, but with deeper penetration, greater total impact.

Ultrasonic SP records swept all others off the market. Sonic LP records became museum pieces—only a crank would choose to listen to an audible full-length version of *Siegfried* or the *Barber of Seville* when he could have both wrapped up inaudibly inside the same five-minute package *and* appreciate their full musical value.

The heyday of Madame Gioconda was over. Unceremoniously left on the shelf, she had managed to survive for a few months vocalizing on radio commercials. Soon these too went ultrasonic. In a despairing act of revenge she bought out the radio station which fired her and made her home on one of the sound stages. Over the years the station became derelict and forgotten, its windows smashed, neon portico collapsing, aerials rusting. The huge eight-lane flyover built across it sealed it conclusively into the past.

Now Madame Gioconda proposed to win her way back at stiletto-point.

Mangon watched her impassively as she ranted on nastily in a cloud of purple cigarette smoke, a large seedy witch. The pheno-barbitone was making her drowsy and her threats and ultimatums were becoming disjointed.

". . . memoirs too, don't forget, Hector. Frank exposure, no holds barred. I mean . . . damn, have to get a ghost. Hotel de Paris at Monte, lots of pictures. Oh yes, I kept the photo-graphs." She grubbed about on the couch, came up with a crumpled soap coupon and a supermarket pay slip. "Wait till those lawyers see them. Hector—" Suddenly she broke off, stared glassily at Mangon and sagged back.

Mangon waited until she was finally asleep, stood up and peered closely at her. She looked forlorn and desperate. He watched her reverently for a moment, then tiptoed to the rheostat mounted on the control panel behind the couch, damped down the lamp at Madame Gioconda's feet and left the stage.

He sealed the auditorium doors behind him, made his way down to the foyer and stepped out, sad but at the same time oddly exhilarated, into the cool midnight air. At last he accepted that he would have to act swiftly if he was to save Madame Gioconda.

Two

DRIVING his sound truck into the city shortly after nine the next morning, Mangon decided to postpone his first call—the weird Neo-Corbusier Episcopalian Oratory sandwiched among the office blocks in the down-town financial sector—and instead turned west on Mainway and across the park towards the white-faced apartment batteries which reared up above the trees and lakes along the north side.

The Oratory was a difficult and laborious job that would take him three hours of concentrated effort. The Dean had recently imported some rare thirteenth-century pediments from the Church of St. Francis at Assisi, beautiful sonic matrices rich with seven centuries of Gregorian chant, overlaid by the timeless tolling of the Angelus. Mounted into the altar they emanated an atmosphere resonant with litany and devotion, a mellow, deeply textured hymn that silently evoked the most sublime images of prayer and meditation.

But at 50,000 dollars each they also represented a terrifying hazard to the clumsy sound-sweep. Only two years earlier the entire north transept of Rheims Cathedral, rose window intact, purchased for a record 1,000,000 dollars and re-erected in the new Cathedral of St. Joseph at San Diego, had been drained of its priceless heritage of tonal inlays by a squad of illiterate sound-sweeps who had misread their instructions and accidentally swept the wrong wall.

Even the most conscientious sound-sweep was limited by his skill, and Mangon, with his auditory super-sensitivity, was greatly in demand for his ability to sweep selectively, draining from the walls of the Oratory all extraneous and discordant noises—coughing, crying, the clatter of coins and mumble of prayer—leaving behind the chorales and liturgical chants which enhanced their devotional overtones. His skill alone would lengthen the life of the Assisi pediments by twenty years; without him they would soon become contaminated by the miscellaneous traffic of the congregation. Consequently he had no fears that the Dean would complain if he failed to appear as usual that morning.

Half-way along the north side of the park he swung off into the forecourt of a huge forty-storey apartment block, a glittering white cliff ribbed by jutting balconies. Most of the apartments were Superlux duplexes occupied by show business people. No one was about, but as Mangon entered the hallway, sonovac in one hand, the marble walls and columns buzzed softly with the echoing chatter of guests leaving parties four or five hours earlier.

In the elevator the residues were clearer—confident male tones, the sharp wheedling of querulous wives, soft negatives of amatory blondes, punctuated by countless repetitions of "dahling". Mangon ignored the echoes, which were almost inaudible, a dim insect hum. He grinned to himself as he rode up to the penthouse apartment; if Madame Gioconda had known his destination she would have strangled him on the spot.

Ray Alto, doyen of the ultrasonic composers and the man more than any other responsible for Madame Gioconda's decline, was one of Mangon's regular calls. Usually Mangon swept his apartment once a week, calling at three in the afternoon. Today, however, he wanted to make sure of finding Alto before he left for Video City, where he was a director of programme music.

The houseboy let him in. He crossed the hall and made his way down the black glass staircase into the sunken lounge. Wide studio windows revealed an elegant panorama of park and mid-town skyscrapers.

A white-slacked young man sitting on one of the long slab sofas—Paul Merrill, Alto's arranger—waved him back.

"Mangon, hold on to your dive breaks. I'm really on reheat this morning." He twirled the ultrasonic trumpet he was playing, a tangle of stops and valves from which half a dozen leads trailed off across the cushions to a cathode tube and tone generator at the other end of the sofa.

Mangon sat down quietly and Merrill clamped the mouth-piece to his lips. Watching the ray tube intently, where he could check the shape of the ultrasonic notes, he launched into a brisk allegretto sequence, then quickened and flicked out a series of brilliant arpeggios, stripping off high P and Q notes that danced across the cathode screen like frantic eels, fantastic glissandos that raced up twenty octaves in as many seconds, each note distinct and symmetrically exact, tripping off the tone generator in turn so that escalators of electronic chords interweaved the original scale, a multi-channel melodic stream that crowded the cathode screen with exquisite, flickering patterns. The whole thing was inaudible, but the air around Mangon felt vibrant and accelerated, charged with gaiety and sparkle, and he applauded generously when Merrill threw off a final dashing riff.

"*Flight of the Bumble Bee*," Merrill told him. He tossed the trumpet aside and switched off the cathode tube. He lay back and savoured the glistening air for a moment. "Well, how are things?"

Just then the door from one of the bedrooms opened and Ray Alto appeared, a tall, thoughtful man of about forty, with thinning blonde hair, wearing pale sunglasses over cool eyes.

"Hello, Mangon," he said, running a hand over Mangon's head. "You're early today. Full programme?" Mangon nodded. "Don't let it get you down." Alto picked a dictaphone off one of the end tables, carried it over to an armchair. "Noise, noise,

noise—the greatest single disease-vector of civilization. The whole world's rotting with it, yet all they can afford is a few people like Mangon fooling around with sonovacs. It's hard to believe that only a few years ago people completely failed to realize that sound left any residues."

"Are we any better?" Merrill asked. "This month's *Transonics* claims that eventually unswept sonic resonances will build up to a critical point where they'll literally start shaking buildings apart. The entire city will come down like Jericho."

"Babel," Alto corrected. "Okay, now, let's shut up. We'll be gone soon, Mangon. Buy him a drink, would you, Paul."

Merrill brought Mangon a coke from the bar, then wandered off. Alto flipped on the dictaphone, began to speak steadily into it. "Memo 7: Betty, when does the copyright on Stravinsky lapse? Memo 8: Betty, file melody for projected nocturne: L, L sharp, BB, Y flat, Q, VT, L, L sharp. Memo 9: Paul, the bottom three octaves of the ultra-tuba are within the audible spectrum of the canine ear—congrats on that SP of the *Anvil Chorus* last night; about three million dogs thought the roof had fallen in on them. Memo 10: Betty—" He broke off, put down the microphone. "Mangon, you look worried."

Mangon, who had been lost in reverie, pulled himself together and shook his head.

"Working too hard?" Alto pressed. He scrutinized Mangon suspiciously. "Are you still sitting up all night with that Gioconda woman?"

Embarrassed, Mangon lowered his eyes. His relationship with Alto was, obliquely, almost as close as that with Madame Gioconda. Although Alto was brusque and often irritable with Mangon, he took a sincere interest in his welfare. Possibly Mangon's muteness reminded him of the misanthropic motives behind his hatred of noise, made him feel indirectly responsible for the act of violence Mangon's mother had committed. Also, one artist to another, he respected Mangon's phenomenal auditory sensitivity.

"She'll exhaust you, Mangon, believe me." Alto knew how much the personal contact meant to Mangon and hesitated to be over-critical. "There's nothing you can do for her. Offering her sympathy merely fans her hopes for a come-back. She hasn't a chance."

Mangon frowned, wrote quickly on his wrist-pad:

She WILL sing again!

Alto read the note pensively. Then, in a harder voice, he said: "She's using you for her own purposes, Mangon. At present you satisfy one whim of hers—the neurotic headaches and fantasy applause. God forbid what the next whim might be."

She is a great artist.

"She *was*," Alto pointed out. "No more, though, sad as it is. I'm afraid that the times change."

Annoyed by this, Mangon gritted his teeth and tore off another sheet.

Entertainment, perhaps. Art, No!

Alto accepted the rebuke silently; he reproved himself as much as Mangon did for selling out to Video City. In his four years there his output of original ultrasonic music consisted of little more than one nearly finished symphony—aptly titled *Opus Zero* —shortly to receive its first performance, a few nocturnes and one quartet. Most of his energies went into programme music, prestige numbers for spectaculars and a mass of straight transcriptions of the classical repertoire. The last he particularly despised, fit work for Paul Merrill, but not for a responsible composer.

He added the sheet to the two in his left hand and asked: "Have you ever heard Madame Gioconda sing?"

Mangon's answer came back scornfully:

No! But you have. Please describe.

Alto laughed shortly, tore up his sheets and walked across to the window.

"All right, Mangon, you've made your point. You're carrying a torch for art, doing your duty to one of the few perfect things the world has ever produced. I hope you're equal to the responsibility. La Gioconda might be quite a handful. Do you know that at one time the doors of Covent Garden, La Scala *and* the Met were closed to her? They said Callas had temperament, but she was a girl guide compared with Gioconda. Tell me, how is she? Eating enough?"

Mangon held up his coke bottle.

"Snow? That's tough. But how does she afford it?" He glanced at his watch. "Dammit, I've got to leave. Clean this place out thoroughly, will you. It gives me a headache just listening to myself think."

He started to pick up the dictaphone but Mangon was scribbling rapidly on his pad.

Give Madame Gioconda a job.

Alto read the note, then gave it back to Mangon, puzzled. "Where? In this apartment?" Mangon shook his head. "Do you mean at V.C.? *Singing?*" When Mangon began to nod vigorously he looked up at the ceiling with a despairing groan. "For heaven's sake, Mangon, the last vocalist sang at Video City over ten years ago. No audience would stand for it. If I even suggested such an idea they'd tear my contract into a thousand pieces." He shuddered, only half-playfully. "I don't know about you, Mangon, but I've got my ulcer to support."

He made his way to the staircase, but Mangon intercepted him, pencil flashing across the wrist-pad.

Please. Madame Gioconda will start blackmail soon. She is desperate. Must sing again. Could arrange make-believe programme in research studios. Closed circuit.

Alto folded the note carefully, left the dictaphone on the staircase and walked slowly back to the window.

"This blackmail. Are you absolutely sure? Who, though, do you know?" Mangon nodded, but looked away. "Okay, I won't press you. LeGrande, probably, eh?" Mangon turned round in surprise, then gave an elaborate parody of a shrug.

"Hector LeGrande. Obvious guess. But there are no secrets there, it's all on open file. I suppose she's just threatening to make enough of an exhibition of herself to block his governorship." Alto pursed his lips. He loathed LeGrande, not merely for having bribed him into a way of life he could never renounce, but also because, once having exploited his weakness, LeGrande never hesitated to remind Alto of it, treating him and his music with contempt. If Madame Gioconda's blackmail had the slightest hope of success he would have been only too happy, but he knew LeGrande would destroy her, probably take Mangon too.

Suddenly he felt a paradoxical sense of loyalty for Madame Gioconda. He looked at Mangon, waiting patiently, big spaniel eyes wide with hope.

"The idea of a closed circuit programme is insane. Even if we went to all the trouble of staging it she wouldn't be satisfied. She

doesn't want to sing, she wants to be a *star*. It's the trappings of
stardom she misses—the cheering galleries, the piles of bouquets,
the green room parties. I could arrange a half-hour session on
closed circuit with some trainee technicians—a few straight
selections from *Tosca* and *Butterfly*, say, with even a sonic piano
accompaniment, I'd be glad to play it myself—but I can't provide
the gossip columns and theatre reviews. What would happen
when she found out?"

She wants to SING.

Alto reached out and patted Mangon on the shoulder. "Good
for you. All right, then, I'll think about it. God knows how we'd
arrange it. We'd have to tell her that she'll be making a surprise
guest appearance on one of the big shows—that'll explain the
absence of any programme announcement and we'll be able to
keep her in an isolated studio. Stress the importance of surprise,
to prevent her from contacting the newspapers . . . Where are
you going?"

Mangon reached the staircase, picked up the dictaphone and
returned to Alto with it. He grinned happily, his jaw working
wildly as he struggled to speak. Strangled sounds quavered in his
throat.

Touched, Alto turned away from him and sat down. "Okay,
Mangon," he snapped brusquely, "you can get on with your
job. Remember, I haven't promised anything." He flicked on
the dictaphone, then began: "Memo 11: Ray . . ."

Three

IT was just after four o'clock when Mangon braked the sound
truck in the alley behind the derelict station. Overhead the traffic
hammered along the flyover, dinning down on to the cobbled
walls. He had been trying to finish his rounds early enough to
bring Madame Gioconda the big news before her headaches
began. He had swept out the Oratory in an hour, whirled through
a couple of movie theatres, the Museum of Abstract Art, and a
dozen private calls in half his usual time, driven by his almost
overwhelming joy at having won a promise of help from Ray Alto.

He ran through the foyer, already fumbling at his wrist-pad.

For the first time in many years he really regretted his muteness, his inability to tell Madame Gioconda orally of his triumph that morning.

Studio 2 was in darkness, the rows of seats and litter of old programmes and ice-cream cartons reflected dimly in the single light masked by the tall flats. His feet slipped in some shattered plaster fallen from the ceiling and he was out of breath when he clambered up on to the stage and swung round the nearest flat.

Madame Gioconda had gone!

The stage was deserted, the couch a rumpled mess, a clutter of cold saucepans on the stove. The wardrobe door was open, dresses wrenched outwards off their hangers.

For a moment Mangon panicked, unable to visualize why she should have left, immediately assuming that she had discovered his plot with Alto.

Then he realized that never before had he visited the studio until midnight at the earliest, and that Madame Gioconda had merely gone out to the supermarket. He smiled at his own stupidity and sat down on the couch to wait for her, sighing with relief.

As vivid as if they had been daubed in letters ten feet deep, the words leapt out from the walls, nearly deafening him with their force.

"*You grotesque old witch, you must be insane! You ever threaten me again and I'll have you destroyed! LISTEN, you pathetic—*"

Mangon spun round helplessly, trying to screen his ears. The words must have been hurled out in a paroxysm of abuse, they were only an hour old, vicious sonic scars slashed across the immaculately swept walls.

His first thought was to rush out for the sonovac and sweep the walls clear before Madame Gioconda returned. Then it dawned on him that she had already heard the original of the echoes—in the background he could just detect the muffled rhythms and intonations of her voice.

All too exactly, he could identify the man's voice.

He had heard it many times before, raging in the same ruthless tirades, when, deputizing for one of the sound-sweeps, he had swept out the main board-room at Video City.

Hector LeGrande! So Madame Gioconda had been more desperate than he thought.

The bottom drawer of the dressing-table lay on the floor, its contents upended. Propped against the mirror was an old silver portrait frame, dull and verdigrised, some cotton wool and a tin of cleansing fluid next to it. The photograph was one of LeGrande, taken twenty years earlier. She must have known LeGrande was coming and had searched out the old portrait, probably regretting the threat of blackmail.

But the sentiment had not been shared.

Mangon walked round the stage, his heart knotting with rage, filling his ears with LeGrande's taunts. He picked up the portrait, pressed it between his palms, and suddenly smashed it across the edge of the dressing-table.

"*Mangon!*"

The cry riveted him to the air. He dropped what was left of the frame, saw Madame Gioconda step quietly from behind one of the flats.

"Mangon, please," she protested gently. "You frighten me." She sidled past him towards the bed, dismantling an enormous purple hat. "And do clean up all that glass, or I shall cut my feet."

She spoke drowsily and moved in a relaxed, sluggish way that Mangon first assumed indicated acute shock. Then she drew from her handbag six white vials and lined them up carefully on the bedside table. These were her favourite confectionery—so LeGrande had sweetened the pill with another cheque. Mangon began to scoop the glass together with his feet, at the same time trying to collect his wits. The sounds of LeGrande's abuse dinned the air, and he broke away and ran off to fetch the sonovac.

Madame Gioconda was sitting on the edge of the bed when he returned, dreamily dusting a small bottle of bourbon which had followed the cocaine vials out of the handbag. She hummed to herself melodically and stroked one of the feathers in her hat.

"Mangon," she called when he had almost finished. "Come here."

Mangon put down the sonovac and went across to her.

She looked up at him, her eyes suddenly very steady. "Mangon, why did you break Hector's picture?" She held up a piece of the frame. "Tell me."

Mangon hesitated, then scribbled on his pad:

I am sorry. I adore you very much. He said such foul things to you.

Madame Gioconda glanced at the note, then gazed back thoughtfully at Mangon. "Were you hiding here when Hector came?"

Mangon shook his head categorically. He started to write on his pad but Madame Gioconda restrained him.

"That's all right, dear. I thought not." She looked around the stage for a moment, listening carefully. "Mangon, when you came in could you hear what Mr. LeGrande said?"

Mangon nodded. His eyes flickered to the obscene phrases on the walls and he began to frown. He still felt LeGrande's presence and his attempt to humiliate Madame Gioconda.

Madame Gioconda pointed around them. "And you can actually hear what he said even now? How remarkable. Mangon, you have a wondrous talent."

I am sorry you have to suffer so much.

Madame Gioconda smiled at this. "We all have our crosses to bear. I have a feeling you may be able to lighten mine considerably." She patted the bed beside her. "Do sit down, you must be tired." When he was settled she went on, "I'm very interested, Mangon. Do you mean you can distinguish entire phrases and sentences in the sounds you sweep? You can hear complete conversations hours after they have taken place?"

Something about Madame Gioconda's curiosity made Mangon hesitate. His talent, so far as he knew, was unique, and he was not so naïve as to fail to appreciate its potentialities. It had developed in his late adolescence and so far he had resisted any temptation to abuse it. He had never revealed the talent to anyone, knowing that if he did his days as a sound-sweeper would be over.

Madame Gioconda was watching him, an expectant smile on her lips. Her thoughts, of course, were solely of revenge. Mangon listened again to the walls, focused on the abuse screaming out into the air.

Not complete conversations. Long fragments, up to twenty syllables. Depending on resonances and matrix. Tell no one. I will help you have revenge on LeGrande.

Madame Gioconda squeezed Mangon's hand. She was about to reach for the bourbon bottle when Mangon suddenly remembered the point of his visit. He leapt off the bed and started frantically scribbling on his wrist-pad.

He tore off the first sheet and pressed it into her startled hands, then filled three more, describing his encounter with the musical director at V.C., the latter's interest in Madame Gioconda and the conditional promise to arrange her guest appearance. In view of LeGrande's hostility he stressed the need for absolute secrecy.

He waited happily while Madame Gioconda read quickly through the notes, tracing out Mangon's child-like script with a long scarlet finger-nail. When she finished he nodded his head rapidly and gestured triumphantly in the air.

Bemused, Madame Gioconda gazed uncomprehendingly at the notes. Then she reached out and pulled Mangon to her, taking his big faun-like head in her jewelled hands and pressing it to her lap.

"My dear child, how much I need you. You must never leave me now."

As she stroked Mangon's hair her eyes roved questingly around the walls.

The miracle happened shortly before eleven o'clock the next morning.

After breakfast, sprawled across Madame Gioconda's bed with her scrapbooks, an old gramophone salvaged by Mangon from one of the studios playing operatic selections, they had decided to drive out to the stockades—the sound-sweeps left for the city at nine and they would be able to examine the sonic dumps unmolested. Having spent so much time with Madame Gioconda and immersed himself so deeply in her world, Mangon was eager now to introduce Madame Gioconda to his. The stockades, bleak though they might be, were all he had to show her.

For Mangon, Madame Gioconda had now become the entire universe, a source of certainty and wonder as potent as the sun. Behind him his past life fell away like the discarded chrysalis of a brilliant butterfly, the grey years of his childhood at the orphanage dissolving into the magical kaleidoscope that revolved around him. As she talked and murmured affectionately to him, the drab flats and props in the studio seemed as brightly coloured and meaningful as the landscape of a mescalin fantasy, the air tingling with a thousand vivid echoes of her voice.

They set off down F Street at ten, soon left behind the dingy warehouses and abandoned tenements that had enclosed Madame Gioconda for so long. Squeezed together in the driving-cab of the sound truck they looked an incongruous pair—the gangling Mangon, in zip-fronted yellow plastic jacket and yellow peaked cap, at the wheel, dwarfed by the vast flamboyant Madame Gioconda, wearing a parrot-green cartwheel hat and veil, her huge creamy breast glittering with pearls, gold stars and jewelled crescents, a small selection of the orders that had showered upon her in her heyday.

She had breakfasted well, on one of the vials and a tooth-glass of bourbon. As they left the city she gazed out amiably at the fields stretching away from the highway, and trilled out a light recitative from *Figaro*.

Mangon listened to her happily, glad to see her in such good form. Determined to spend every possible minute with Madame Gioconda, he had decided to abandon his calls for the day, if not for the next week and month. With her he at last felt completely secure. The pressure of her hand and the warm swell of her shoulder made him feel confident and invigorated, all the more proud that he was able to help her back to fame.

He tapped on the windshield as they swung off the highway on to the narrow dirt track that led towards the stockades. Here and there among the dunes they could see the low ruined outbuildings of the old explosives plant, the white galvanized iron roof of one of the sound-sweep's cabins. Desolate and unfrequented, the dunes ran on for miles. They passed the remains of a gateway that had collapsed to one side of the road; originally a continuous fence ringed the stockade, but no one had any reason for wanting to penetrate it. A place of strange echoes and festering silences, overhung by a gloomy miasma of a million compacted sounds, it remained remote and haunted, the grave-yard of countless private babels.

The first of the sonic dumps appeared two or three hundred yards away on their right. This was reserved for aircraft sounds swept from the city's streets and municipal buildings, and was a tightly packed collection of sound-absorbent baffles covering several acres. The baffles were slightly larger than those in the other stockades; twenty feet high and fifteen wide, each supported by heavy wooden props, they faced each other in a random labyrinth of alleyways, like a store lot of advertisement hoardings.

Only the top two or three feet were visible above the dunes, but the charged air hit Mangon like a hammer, a pounding niagara of airliners blaring down the glideway, the piercing whistle of jets jockeying at take-off, the ceaseless mind-sapping roar that hangs like a vast umbrella over any metropolitan complex.

All around, odd sounds shaken loose from the stockades were beginning to reach them. Over the entire area, fed from the dumps below, hung an unbroken phonic high, invisible but nonetheless as tangible and menacing as an enormous black thundercloud. Occasionally, when super-saturation was reached after one of the summer holiday periods, the sonic pressure fields would split and discharge, venting back into the stockades a nightmarish cataract of noise, raining on to the sound-sweeps not only the howling of cats and dogs, but the multi-lunged tumult of cars, express trains, fairgrounds and aircraft, the cacophonic *musique concrète* of civilization.

To Mangon the sounds reaching them, though scaled higher in the register, were still distinct, but Madame Gioconda could hear nothing and felt only an overpowering sense of depression and irritation. The air seemed to grate and rasp. Mangon noticed her beginning to frown and hold her hand to her forehead. He wound up his window and indicated to her to do the same. He switched on the sonovac mounted under the dashboard and let it drain the discordancies out of the sealed cabin.

Madame Gioconda relaxed in the sudden blissful silence. A little further on, when they passed another stockade set closer to the road, she turned to Mangon and began to say something to him.

Suddenly she jerked violently in alarm, her hat toppling. Her voice had frozen! Her mouth and lips moved frantically, but no sounds emerged. For a moment she was paralysed. Clutching her throat desperately, she filled her lungs and screamed.

A faint squeak piped out of her cavernous throat, and Mangon swung round in alarm to see her gibbering apoplectically, pointing helplessly to her throat.

He stared at her bewildered, then doubled over the wheel in a convulsion of silent laughter, slapping his thigh and thumping the dashboard. He pointed to the sonovac, then reached down and turned up the volume.

". . . aaauuuoooh," Madame Gioconda heard herself groan.

She grasped her hat and secured it. "Mangon, what a dirty trick, you should have warned me."

Mangon grinned. The discordant sounds coming from the stockades began to fill the cabin again, and he turned down the volume. Gleefully, he scribbled on his wrist-pad:

Now you know what it is like!

Madame Gioconda opened her mouth to reply, then stopped in time, hiccupped and took his arm affectionately.

Four

MANGON slowed down as they approached a side road. Two hundred yards away on their left a small pink-washed cabin stood on a dune overlooking one of the stockades. They drove up to it, turned into a circular concrete apron below the cabin and backed up against one of the unloading bays, a battery of red-painted hydrants equipped with manifold gauges and release pipes running off into the stockade. This was only twenty feet away at its nearest point, a forest of door-shaped baffles facing each other in winding corridors, like a set from a surrealist film.

As she climbed down from the truck Madame Gioconda expected the same massive wave of depression and overload that she had felt from the stockade of aircraft noises, but instead the air seemed brittle and frenetic, darting with sudden flashes of tension and exhilaration.

As they walked up to the cabin Mangon explained:

Party noises—company for me.

The twenty or thirty baffles nearest the cabin he reserved for those screening him from the miscellaneous chatter that filled the rest of the stockade. When he woke in the mornings he would listen to the laughter and small talk, enjoy the gossip and wise-cracks as much as if he had been at the parties himself.

The cabin was a single room with a large window overlooking the stockade, well insulated from the hubbub below. Madame Gioconda showed only a cursory interest in Mangon's meagre belongings, and after a few general remarks came to the point and went over to the window. She opened it slightly, listened experimentally to the stream of atmospheric shifts that crowded past her.

She pointed to the cabin on the far side of the stockade. "Mangnon, whose is that?"

Gallagher's. My partner. He sweeps City Hall, University, V.C., big mansions on 5th and A. Working now.

Madame Gioconda nodded and surveyed the stockade with interest. "How fascinating. It's like a zoo. All that talk, talk, talk. And *you* can hear it all." She snapped back her bracelets with swift decisive flicks of the wrist.

Mangon sat down on the bed. The cabin seemed small and dingy, and he was saddened by Madame Gioconda's disinterest. Having brought her all the way out to the dumps he wondered how he was going to keep her amused. Fortunately the stockade intrigued her. When she suggested a stroll through it he was only too glad to oblige.

Down at the unloading bay he demonstrated how he emptied the tanker, clipping the exhaust leads to the hydrant, regulating the pressure through the manifold and then pumping the sound away into the stockade.

Most of the stockade was in a continuous state of uproar, sounding something like a crowd in a football stadium, and as he led her out among the baffles he picked their way carefully through the quieter aisles. Around them voices chattered and whined fretfully, fragments of conversation drifted aimlessly over the air. Somewhere a woman pleaded in thin nervous tones, a man grumbled to himself, another swore angrily, a baby bellowed. Behind it all was the steady background murmur of countless TV programmes, the easy patter of announcers, the endless monotones of race-track commentators, the shrieking audiences of quiz shows, all pitched an octave up the scale so that they sounded an eerie parody of themselves.

A shot rang out in the next aisle, followed by screams and shouting. Although she heard nothing, the pressure pulse made Madame Gioconda stop.

"Mangon, wait. Don't be in so much of a hurry. Tell me what they're saying."

Mangon selected a baffle and listened carefully. The sounds appeared to come from an apartment over a launderette. A battery of washing machines chuntered to themselves, a cash register slammed interminably, there was a dim almost sub-threshold echo of 60-cycle hum from an SP record-player.

He shook his head, waved Madame Gioconda on.

"Mangon, what did they *say*?" she pestered him. He stopped again, sharpened his ears and waited. This time he was more lucky, an over-emotional female voice was gasping ". . . but if he finds you here he'll kill you, he'll kill us both, what shall we do . . ." He started to scribble down this outpouring, Madame Gioconda craning breathlessly over his shoulder, then recognized its source and screwed up the note.

"Mangon, for heaven's sake, what was it? Don't throw it away! Tell me!" She tried to climb under the wooden super-structure of the baffle to recover the note, but Mangon restrained her and quickly scribbled another message.

Adam and Eve. Sorry.

"What, the film? Oh, how ridiculous! Well, come on, try again."

Eager to make amends, Mangon picked the next baffle, one of a group serving the staff married quarters of the University. Always a difficult job to keep clean, he struck paydirt almost at once.

". . . my God, there's Bartok all over the place, that damned Steiner woman, I'll swear she's sleeping with her . . ."

Mangon took it all down, passing the sheets to Madame Gioconda as soon as he covered them. Squinting hard at his crabbed handwriting, she gobbled them eagerly, disappointed when, after half a dozen, he lost the thread and stopped.

"Go on, Mangon, what's the matter?" She let the notes fall to the ground. "Difficult, isn't it. We'll have to teach you short-hand."

They reached the baffles Mangon had just filled from the previous day's rounds. Listening carefully he heard Paul Merrill's voice: ". . . month's *Transonics* claims that . . . the entire city will come down like Jericho."

He wondered if he could persuade Madame Gioconda to wait for fifteen minutes, when he would be able to repeat a few carefully edited fragments from Alto's promise to arrange her guest appearance, but she seemed eager to move deeper into the stockade.

"You said your friend Gallagher sweeps out Video City, Mangon. Where would that be?"

Hector LeGrande. Of course, Mangon realized, why had he been so obtuse. This was the chance to pay the man back.

He pointed to an area a few aisles away. They climbed between the baffles, Mangon helping Madame Gioconda over the beams and props, steering her full skirt and wide hat brim away from splinters and rusted metalwork.

The task of finding LeGrande was simple. Even before the baffles were in sight Mangon could hear the hard, unyielding bite of the tycoon's voice, dominating every other sound from the Video City area. Gallagher in fact swept only the senior dozen or so executive suites at V.C., chiefly to relieve their occupants of the distasteful echoes of LeGrande's voice.

Mangon steered their way among these, searching for LeGrande's master suite, where anything of a really confidential nature took place.

There were about twenty baffles, throwing off an unending chorus of "Yes, H.L.," "Thanks, H.L.," "Brilliant, H.L." Two or three seemed strangely quiet, and he drew Madame Gioconda over to them.

This was LeGrande with his personal secretary and PA. He took out his pencil and focused carefully.

". . . of Third National Bank, transfer two million to private holding and threaten claim for stock depreciation . . . redraft escape clauses, including non-liability purchase benefits . . ."

Madame Gioconda tapped his arm but he gestured her away. Most of the baffle appeared to be taken up by dubious financial dealings, but nothing that would really hurt LeGrande if revealed.

Then he heard—

". . . Bermuda Hilton. Private Island, with anchorage, have the beach cleaned up, last time the water was full of fish . . . I don't care, poison them, hang some nets out . . . Imogene will fly in from Idlewild as Mrs. Edna Burgess, warn Customs to stay away . . ."

". . . call Cartiers, something for the Contessa, 17 carats say, ceiling of ten thousand. No, make it eight thousand . . ."

". . . hat-check girl at the Tropicabana. Usual dossier . . ."

Mangon scribbled furiously, but LeGrande was speaking at rapid dictation speed and he could get down only a few fragments. Madame Gioconda barely deciphered his handwriting, and became more and more frustrated as her appetite was whetted. Finally she flung away the notes in a fury of exasperation.

"This is absurd, you're missing everything!" she cried. She pounded on one of the baffles, then broke down and began to sob angrily. "Oh God, God, *God*, how ridiculous! Help me, I'm going insane . . ."

Mangon hurried across to her, put his arms round her shoulders to support her. She pushed him away irritably, railing at herself to discharge her impatience. "It's useless, Mangon, it's stupid of me, I was a fool—"

"*STOP!*"

The cry split the air like the blade of a guillotine.

They both straightened, stared at each other blankly. Mangon put his fingers slowly to his lips, then reached out tremulously and put his hands in Madame Gioconda's. Somewhere within him a tremendous tension had begun to dissolve.

"Stop," he said again in a rough but quiet voice. "Don't cry. I'll help you."

Madame Gioconda gaped at him with amazement. Then she let out a tremendous whoop of triumph.

"Mangon, you can talk! You've got your voice back! It's absolutely astounding! Say something, quickly, for heaven's sake!"

Mangon felt his mouth again, ran his fingers rapidly over his throat. He began to tremble with excitement, his face brightened, he jumped up and down like a child.

"I can talk," he repeated wonderingly. His voice was gruff, then seesawed into a treble. "I can talk," he said louder, controlling its pitch. "I can talk, I can talk, *I can talk*!" He flung his head back, let out an ear-shattering shout. "I CAN TALK! HEAR ME!" He ripped the wrist-pad off his sleeve, hurled it away over the baffles.

Madame Gioconda backed away, laughing agreeably. "We can hear you, Mangon. Dear me, how sweet." She watched Mangon thoughtfully as he cavorted happily in the narrow interval between the aisles. "Now don't tire yourself out or you'll lose it again."

Mangon danced over to her, seized her shoulders and squeezed them tightly. He suddenly realized that he knew no diminutive or Christian name for her.

"Madame Gioconda," he said earnestly, stumbling over the syllables, the words that were so simple yet so enormously complex to pronounce. "You gave me back my voice. Anything you want—" He broke off, stuttering happily, laughing through his tears. Suddenly he buried his head in her shoulder, exhausted by his discovery, and cried gratefully, "It's a *wonderful* voice."

Madame Gioconda steadied him maternally. "Yes, Mangon," she said, her eyes on the discarded notes lying in the dust. "You've got a wonderful voice, all right." *Sotto voce*, she added: "But your hearing is even more wonderful."

Paul Merrill switched off the SP player, sat down on the arm of the sofa and watched Mangon quizzically.

"Strange. You know, my guess is that it was psychosomatic."

Mangon grinned. "Psychosemantic," he repeated, garbling the word half-deliberately. "Clever. You can do amazing things with words. They help to crystallize the truth."

Merrill groaned playfully. "God, you sit there, you drink your coke, you philosophize. Don't you realize you're supposed to stand quietly in a corner, positively dumb with gratitude? Now you're even ramming your puns down my throat. Never mind, tell me again how it happened."

"Once a pun a time—" Mangon ducked the magazine Merrill flung at him, let out a loud "Olé!"

For the last two weeks he had been *en fête*.

Every day he and Madame Gioconda followed the same routine; after breakfast at the studio they drove out to the stockade, spent two or three hours compiling their confidential file on LeGrande, lunched at the cabin and then drove back to the city, Mangon going off on his rounds while Madame Gioconda slept until he returned shortly before midnight. For Mangon their existence was idyllic; not only was he rediscovering himself in terms of the complex spectra and patterns of speech—a completely new category of existence—but at the same time his relationship with Madame Gioconda revealed areas of sympathy, affection and understanding that he had never previously seen. If he sometimes felt that he was too preoccupied with his side of their relationship and the extraordinary benefits it had brought him, at least Madame Gioconda had been equally well served. Her headaches and mysterious phantoms had gone, she had cleaned up the studio and begun to salvage a little dignity and self-confidence, which made her single-minded sense of ambition seem less obsessive. Psychologically, she needed Mangon less now than he needed her, and he was sensible to restrain his high spirits and give her plenty of attention. During the first week Mangon's incessant chatter had been rather wearing, and once, on their way to the stockade, she had switched on the sonovac in the driving-cab and left Mangon mouthing silently at the air like a stranded fish. He had taken the hint.

"What about the sound-sweeping?" Merrill asked. "Will you give it up?"

Mangon shrugged. "It's my talent, but living at the stockade, let in at back doors, cleaning up the verbal garbage—it's a degraded job. I want to help Madame Gioconda. She will need a secretary when she starts to go on tour."

Merrill shook his head warily. "You're awfully sure there's going to be a sonic revival, Mangon. Every sign is against it."

"They have not heard Madame Gioconda sing. Believe me, I know the power and wonder of the human voice. Ultrasonic music is great for atmosphere, but it has no content. It can't express ideas, only emotions."

"What happened to that closed circuit programme you and Ray were going to put on for her?"

"It—fell through," Mangon lied. The circuits Madame Gioconda would perform on would be open to the world. He had told them nothing of the visits to the stockade, of his power to read the baffles, of the accumulating file on LeGrande. Soon Madame Gioconda would strike.

Above them in the hallway a door slammed, someone stormed through into the apartment in a tempest, kicking a chair against a wall. It was Alto. He raced down the staircase into the lounge, jaw tense, fingers flexing angrily.

"Paul, don't interrupt me until I've finished," he snapped racing past without looking at them. "You'll be out of a job but I warn you, if you don't back me up one hundred per cent I'll shoot you. That goes for you too, Mangon, I need you in on this." He whirled over to the window, bolted out the traffic noises below, then swung back and watched them steadily, feet planted firmly in the carpet. For the first time in the three years Mangon had known him he looked aggressive and confident.

"Headline," he announced. "The Gioconda is to sing again! Incredible and terrifying though the prospect may seem, exactly two weeks from now the live, uncensored voice of the Gioconda will go out coast to coast on all three V.C. radio channels. Surprised, Mangon? It's no secret, they're printing the bills right now. Eight-thirty to nine-thirty, right up on the peak, even if they have to give the time away."

Merrill sat forward. "Bully for her. If LeGrande wants to drive the whole ship into the ground, why worry?"

Alto punched the sofa viciously. "Because you and I are going to be on board! Didn't you hear me? Eight-thirty, a fortnight today! *We* have a programme on then. Well, guess who our guest star is?"

Merrill struggled to make sense of this. "Wait a minute, Ray. You mean she's actually going to appear—she's going to *sing*—in the middle of *Opus Zero*?" Alto nodded grimly. Merrill threw up his hands and slumped back. "It's crazy, she can't. Who says she will?"

"Who do you think? The great LeGrande." Alto turned to Mangon. "She must have raked up some real dirt to frighten him into this. I can hardly believe it."

"But why on *Opus Zero*?" Merrill pressed. "Let's switch the première to the week after."

"Paul, you're missing the point. Let me fill you in. Sometime yesterday Madame Gioconda paid a private call on LeGrande. Something she told him persuaded him that it would be absolutely wonderful for her to have a whole hour to herself on one of the feature music programmes, singing a few old-fashioned songs from the old-fashioned shows, with a full-scale ultrasonic backing. Eager to give her a completely free hand he even asked her which of the regular programmes she'd like. Well, as the last show she appeared on ten years ago was cancelled to make way for Ray Alto's *Total Symphony* you can guess which one she picked."

Merrill nodded. "It all fits together. We're broadcasting from the concert studio. A single ultrasonic symphony, no station breaks, not even a commentary. Your first world première in three years. There'll be a big invited audience. White tie, something like the old days. Revenge is sweet." He shook his head sadly. "Hell, all that work."

Alto snapped: "Don't worry, it won't be wasted. Why should we pay the bill for LeGrande? This symphony is the one piece of serious music I've written since I joined V.C. and it isn't going to be ruined." He went over to Mangon, sat down next to him. "This afternoon I went down to the rehearsal studios. They'd found an ancient sonic grand somewhere and one of the old-timers was accompanying her. Mangon, it's ten years since she sang last. If she'd practised for two or three hours a day she might have preserved her voice, but you sweep her radio station, you know she hasn't sung a note. She's an old woman now. What time alone hasn't done to her, cocaine and self-pity have." He paused, watching Mangon searchingly. "I hate to say it, Mangon, but it sounded like a cat being strangled."

You lie, Mangon thought icily. *You are simply so ignorant, your taste in music is so debased, that you are unable to recognize real genius when you see it.* He looked at Alto with contempt, sorry for the man, with his absurd silent symphonies. He felt like shouting: *I know what silence is! The voice of the Gioconda is a stream of gold, molten and pure, she will find it again as I found mine.* However, something about Alto's manner warned him to wait.

He said: "I understand." Then: "What do you want me to do?"

Alto patted him on the shoulder. "Good boy. Believe me, you'll be helping her in the long run. What I propose will save all of us from looking foolish. We've got to stand up to LeGrande, even if it means a one-way ticket out of V.C. Okay, Paul?" Merrill nodded firmly and he went on: "Orchestra will continue as scheduled. According to the programme Madame Gioconda will be singing to an accompaniment by *Opus Zero*, but that means nothing and there'll be no connection at any point. In fact she won't turn up until the night itself. She'll stand well down-stage on a special platform, and the only microphone will be an aerial about twenty feet diagonally above her. It will be live—*but her voice will never reach it*. Because you, Mangon, will be in the cue-box directly in front of her, with the most powerful sonovac we can lay our hands on. As soon as she opens her mouth you'll let her have it. She'll be at least ten feet away from you so she'll hear herself and won't suspect what is happening."

"What about the audience?" Merrill asked.

"They'll be listening to my symphony, enjoying a neurophonic experience of sufficient beauty and power, I hope, to distract them from the sight of a blowzy *prima donna* gesturing to herself in a cocaine fog. They'll probably think she's conducting. Remember, they may be expecting her to sing but how many people still know what the word really means? Most of them will assume it's ultrasonic."

"And LeGrande?"

"He'll be in Bermuda. Business conference."

Five

MADAME GIOCONDA was sitting before her dressing-table mirror, painting on a face like a Hallowe'en mask. Beside her the gramophone played scratchy sonic selections from *Traviata*. The stage was still a disorganized jumble, but there was now an air of purpose about it.

Making his way through the flats, Mangon walked up to her quietly and kissed her bare shoulder. She stood up with a flourish, an enormous monument of a woman in a magnificent black silk dress sparkling with thousands of sequins.

"Thank you, Mangon," she sang out when he complimented her. She swirled off to a hat-box on the bed, pulled out a huge peacock feather and stabbed it into her hair.

Mangon had come round at six, several hours before usual; over the past two days he had felt increasingly uneasy. He was convinced that Alto was in error, and yet logic was firmly on his side. Could Madame Gioconda's voice have preserved itself? Her spoken voice, unless she was being particularly sweet, was harsh and uneven, recently even more so. He assumed that with only a week to her performance nervousness was making her irritable.

Again she was going out, as she had done almost every night. With whom, she never explained; probably to the theatre restaurants, to renew contacts with agents and managers. He would have liked to go with her, but he felt out of place on this plane of Madame Gioconda's existence.

"Mangon, I won't be back until very late," she warned him.

"You look rather tired and pasty. You'd better go home and get some sleep."

Mangon noticed he was still wearing his yellow peaked cap. Unconsciously he must already have known he would not be spending the night there.

"Do you want to go to the stockade tomorrow?" he asked.

"Hmmmh . . . I don't think so. It gives me rather a headache. Let's leave it for a day or two."

She turned on him with a tremendous smile, her eyes glittering with sudden affection.

"Good-bye, Mangon, it's been wonderful to see you." She bent down and pressed her cheek maternally to his, engulfing him in a heady wave of powder and perfume. In an instant all his doubts and worries evaporated, he looked forward to seeing her the next day, certain that they would spend the future together.

For half an hour after she had gone he wandered around the deserted sound stage, going through his memories. Then he made his way out to the alley and drove back to the stockade.

As the day of Madame Gioconda's performance drew closer Mangon's anxieties mounted. Twice he had been down to the concert studio at Video City, had rehearsed with Alto his entry beneath the stage to the cue-box, a small compartment off the corridor used by the electronics engineers. They had checked the power points, borrowed a sonovac from the services section—a heavy duty model used for shielding VIPs and commentators at airports—and mounted its nozzle in the cue-hood.

Alto stood on the platform erected for Madame Gioconda, shouted at the top of his voice at Merrill sitting in the third row of the stalls.

"Hear anything?" he called afterwards.

Merrill shook his head. "Nothing, no vibration at all."

Down below Mangon flicked the release toggle, vented a long-drawn-out "Fiivvveeee! . . . Foouuurrr! . . . Thrreeeee! . . . Twooooo! . . . Onnneeee . . . !"

"Good enough," Alto decided. Chicago-style, they hid the sonovac in a triple-bass case, stored it in Alto's office.

"Do you want to hear her sing, Mangon?" Alto asked. "She should be rehearsing now."

Mangon hesitated, then declined.

"It's tragic that she's unable to realize the truth herself," Alto commented. "Her mind must be fixed fifteen or twenty years in the past, when she sang her greatest roles at La Scala. That's the voice she hears, the voice she'll probably always hear."

Mangon pondered this. Once he tried to ask Madame Gioconda how her practice sessions were going, but she was moving into a different zone and answered with some grandiose remark. He was seeing less and less of her, whenever he visited the station she was either about to go out or else tired and eager to be rid of him. Their trips to the stockade had ceased. All this he accepted as inevitable; after the performance, he assured himself, after her triumph, she would come back to him.

He noticed, however, that he was beginning to stutter.

On the final afternoon, a few hours before the performance that evening, Mangon drove down to F Street for what was to be the last time. He had not seen Madame Gioconda the previous day and he wanted to be with her and give her any encouragement she needed.

As he turned into the alley he was surprised to see two large removal vans parked outside the station entrance. Four or five men were carrying out pieces of furniture and the great scenic flats from the sound stage.

Mangon ran over to them. One of the vans was full; he recognized all Madame Gioconda's possessions—the rococo wardrobe and dressing-table, the couch, the huge Desdemona bed, up-ended and wrapped in corrugated paper—as he looked at it he felt that a section of himself had been torn from him and rammed away callously. In the bright daylight the peeling threadbare flats had lost all illusion of reality; with them Mangon's whole relationship with Madame Gioconda seemed to have been dismantled.

The last of the workmen came out with a gold cushion under his arm, tossed it into the second van. The foreman sealed the doors and waved on the driver.

"W . . . wh . . . where are you going?" Mangon asked him urgently.

The foreman looked him up and down. "You're the sweeper, are you?" He jerked a thumb towards the station. "The old girl said there was a message for you in there. Couldn't see one myself."

Mangon left him and ran into the foyer and up the stairway towards Studio 2. The removers had torn down the blinds and a grey light was flooding into the dusty auditorium. Without the flats the stage looked exposed and derelict.

He raced down the aisle, wondering why Madame Gioconda had decided to leave without telling him.

The stage had been stripped. The music stands had been kicked over, the stove lay on its side with two or three old pans around it, underfoot there was a miscellaneous litter of paper, ash and empty vials.

Mangon searched around for the message, probably pinned to one of the partitions.

Then he heard it screaming at him from the walls, violent and concise.

"GO AWAY YOU UGLY CHILD! NEVER TRY TO SEE ME AGAIN!"

He shrank back, involuntarily tried to shout as the walls seemed to fall in on him, but his throat had frozen.

As he entered the corridor below the stage shortly before eight-twenty, Mangon could hear the sounds of the audience arriving and making their way to their seats. The studio was almost full, a hubbub of well-heeled chatter. Lights flashed on and off in the corridor, and oblique atmospheric shifts cut through the air as the players on the stage tuned their instruments.

Mangon slid past the technicians manning the neurophonic rigs which supplied the orchestra, trying to make the enormous triple-bass case as inconspicuous as possible. They were all busy checking the relays and circuits, and he reached the cue-box and slipped through the door unnoticed.

The box was almost in darkness, a few rays of coloured light filtering through the pink and white petals of the chrysanthemums stacked over the hood. He bolted the door, then opened the case, lifted out the sonovac and clipped the snout into the canister. Leaning forward, with his hands he pushed a small aperture among the flowers.

Directly in front of him he could see a velvet-lined platform, equipped with a white metal rail to the centre of which a large floral ribbon had been tied. Beyond was the orchestra, disposed in a semicircle, each of the twenty members sitting at a small box-like desk on which rested his instrument, tone generator and cathode tube. They were all present, and the light reflected from the ray screens threw a vivid phosphorescent glow on to the silver wall behind them.

Mangon propped the nozzle of the sonovac into the aperture, bent down, plugged in the lead and switched on.

Just before eight-twenty-five someone stepped across the platform and paused in front of the cue-hood. Mangon crouched back, watching the patent leather shoes and black trousers move near the nozzle.

"Mangon!" he heard Alto snap. He craned forward, saw Alto eyeing him. Mangon waved to him and Alto nodded slowly, at the same time smiling to someone in the audience, then turned on his heel and took his place in the orchestra.

At eight-thirty a sequence of red and green lights signalled the start of the programme. The audience quietened, waiting while an announcer in an off-stage booth introduced the programme.

A compère appeared on stage, standing behind the cue-hood, and addressed the audience. Mangon sat quietly on the small wooden seat fastened to the wall, staring blankly at the canister of the sonovac. There was a round of applause, and a steady green light shone downwards through the flowers. The air in the cue-box began to sweeten, a cool motionless breeze eddied vertically around him as a rhythmic ultrasonic pressure wave pulsed past. It relaxed the confined dimensions of the box, with a strange mesmeric echo that held his attention. Somewhere in his mind he realized that the symphony had started, but he was too distracted to pull himself together and listen to it consciously.

Suddenly, through the gap between the flowers and the sonovac nozzle, he saw a large white mass shifting about on the platform. He slipped off the seat and peered up.

Madame Gioconda had taken her place on the platform. Seen from below she seemed enormous, a towering cataract of glistening white satin that swept down to her feet. Her arms were folded loosely in front of her, fingers flashing with blue and white stones. He could only just glimpse her face, the terrifying witch-like mask turned in profile as she waited for some off-stage signal.

Mangon mobilized himself, slid his hand down to the trigger

of the sonovac. He waited, feeling the steady subliminal music of Alto's symphony swell massively within him, its tempo accelerating. Presumably Madame Gioconda's arranger was waiting for a climax at which to introduce her first aria.

Abruptly Madame Gioconda looked forward at the audience and took a short step to the rail. Her hands parted and opened palms upward, her head moved back, her bare shoulders swelled.

The wave front pulsing through the cue-box stopped, then soared off in a continuous unbroken crescendo. At the same time Madame Gioconda thrust her head out, her throat muscles contracted powerfully.

As the sound burst from her throat Mangon's finger locked rigidly against the trigger guard. An instant later, before he could think, a shattering blast of sound ripped through his ears, followed by a slightly higher note that appeared to strike a hidden ridge half-way along its path, wavered slightly, then recovered and sped on, like an express train crossing lines.

Mangon listened to her numbly, hands gripping the barrel of the sonovac. The voice exploded in his brain, flooding every nexus of cells with its violence. It was grotesque, an insane parody of a classical soprano. Harmony, purity, cadence had gone. Rough and cracked, it jerked sharply from one high note to a lower, its breath intervals uncontrolled, sudden precipices of gasping silence which plunged through the volcanic torrent, dividing it into a loosely connected sequence of *bravura* passages.

He barely recognized what she was singing : the Toreador song from *Carmen*. Why she had picked this he could not imagine. Unable to reach its higher notes she fell back on the swinging rhythm of the refrain, hammering out the rolling phrases with tosses of her head. After a dozen bars her pace slackened, she slipped into an extempore humming, then broke out of this into a final climactic assault.

Appalled, Mangon watched as two or three members of the orchestra stood up and disappeared into the wings. The others had stopped playing, were switching off their instruments and conferring with each other. The audience was obviously restive ; Mangon could hear individual voices in the intervals when Madame Gioconda refilled her lungs.

Behind him someone hammered on the door. Startled, Mangon nearly tripped across the sonovac. Then he bent down and wrenched the plug out of its socket. Snapping open the two catches beneath the chassis of the sonovac, he pulled off the canister to reveal the valves, amplifier and generator. He slipped his fingers carefully through the leads and coils, seized them as firmly as he could and ripped them out with a single motion. Tearing his nails, he stripped the printed circuit off the bottom of the chassis and crushed it between his hands.

Satisfied, he dropped the sonovac to the floor, listened for a moment to the caterwauling above, which was now being drowned by the mounting vocal opposition of the audience, then unlatched the door.

Paul Merrill, his bow tie askew, burst in. He gaped blankly at Mangon, at the blood dripping from his fingers and the smashed sonovac on the floor.

He seized Mangon by the shoulders, shook him roughly. "Mangon, are you crazy? What are you trying to do?"

Mangon attempted to say something, but his voice had died. He pulled himself away from Merrill, pushed past into the corridor.

Merrill shouted after him. "Mangon, help me fix this! Where are you going?" He got down on his knees, started trying to piece the sonovac together.

From the wings Mangon briefly watched the scene on the stage.

Madame Gioconda was still singing, her voice completely inaudible in the uproar from the auditorium. Half the audience were on their feet, shouting towards the stage and apparently remonstrating with the studio officials. All but a few members of the orchestra had left their instruments, these sitting on their desks and watching Madame Gioconda in amazement.

The programme director, Alto and one of the compères stood in front of her, banging on the rail and trying to attract her attention. But Madame Gioconda failed to notice them. Head back, eyes on the brilliant ceiling lights, hands gesturing majestically, she soared along the private causeways of sound that poured unrelentingly from her throat, a great white angel of discord on her homeward flight.

Mangon watched her sadly, then slipped away through the stage-hands pressing around him. As he left the theatre by the stage door a small crowd was gathering by the main entrance.

He flicked away the blood from his fingers, then bound his handkerchief round them.

He walked down the side street to where the sound truck was parked, climbed into the cab and sat still for a few minutes, looking out at the bright evening lights in the bars and shop-fronts.

Opening the dashboard locker, he hunted through it and pulled out an old wrist-pad, clipped it into his sleeve.

In his ears the sounds of Madame Gioconda singing echoed like an insane banshee.

He switched on the sonovac under the dashboard, turned it full on, then started the engine and drove off into the night.

THE OVERLOADED MAN

FAULKNER was slowly going insane.

After breakfast he waited impatiently in the lounge while his wife tidied up in the kitchen. She would be gone within two or three minutes, but for some reason he always found the short wait each morning almost unbearable. As he drew the Venetian blinds and readied the reclining chair on the veranda he listened to Julia moving about efficiently. In the same strict sequence she stacked the cups and plates in the dish-washer, slid the pot roast for that evening's dinner into the auto-cooker and selected the alarm, lowered the air-conditioner refrigerator and immersion heater settings, switched open the oil storage manifolds for the delivery tanker that afternoon, and retracted her section of the garage door.

Faulkner followed the sequence with admiration, counting off each successive step as the dials clicked and snapped.

You ought to be in B-52's, he thought, or in the control house of a petrochemicals plant. In fact Julia worked in the personnel section at the Clinic, and no doubt spent all day in the same whirl of efficiency, stabbing buttons marked "Jones",

"Smith", and "Brown", shunting paraplegics to the left, para-
noids to the right.

She stepped into the lounge and came over to him, the standard
executive product in brisk black suit and white blouse.

"Aren't you going to the school today?" she asked.

Faulkner shook his head, played with some papers on the
desk. "No, I'm still on creative reflection. Just for this week.
Professor Harman thought I'd been taking too many classes
and getting stale."

She nodded, looking at him doubtfully. For three weeks
now he had been lying around at home, dozing on the veranda,
and she was beginning to get suspicious. Sooner or later, Faulkner
realized, she would find out, but by then he hoped to be out of
reach. He longed to tell her the truth, that two months ago he
had resigned from his job as a lecturer at the Business School
and had no intention of ever going back. She'd get a damn big
surprise when she discovered they had almost expended his last
pay cheque, might even have to put up with only one car. Let
her work, he thought, she earns more than I did anyway.

With an effort Faulkner smiled at her. *Get out!* his mind
screamed, but she still hovered around him indecisively.

"What about your lunch? There's no—"

"Don't worry about me," Faulkner cut in quickly, watching
the clock. "I gave up eating six months ago. You have lunch
at the Clinic."

Even talking to her had become an effort. He wished they
could communicate by means of notes; had even bought two
scribble pads for this purpose. However, he had never quite
been able to suggest that she use hers, although he did leave
messages around for her, on the pretext that his mind was so
intellectually engaged that talking would break up his thought
trains.

Oddly enough, the idea of leaving her never seriously occurred
to him. Such an escape would prove nothing. Besides, he had
an alternative plan.

"You'll be all right?" she asked, still watching him warily.

"Absolutely," Faulkner told her, maintaining the smile. It
felt like a full day's work.

Her kiss was quick and functional, like the automatic peck
of some huge bottle-topping machine. The smile was still on his

face as she reached the door. When she had gone he let it fade slowly, then found himself breathing again and gradually relaxed, letting the tension drain down through his arms and legs. For a few minutes he wandered blankly around the empty house, then made his way into the lounge again, ready to begin his serious work.

His programme usually followed the same course. First, from the centre drawer of his desk he took a small alarm clock, fitted with a battery and wrist strap. Sitting down on the veranda, he fastened the strap to his wrist, wound and set the clock and placed it on the table next to him, binding his arm to the chair so that there was no danger of dragging the clock onto the floor.

Ready now, he lay back and surveyed the scene in front of him.

Menninger Village, or the "Bin" as it was known locally, had been built about ten years earlier as a self-contained housing unit for the graduate staff of the Clinic and their families. In all there were some sixty houses in the development, each designed to fit into a particular architectonic niche, preserving its own identity from within and at the same time merging into the organic unity of the whole development. The object of the architects, faced with the task of compressing a great number of small houses into a four-acre site, had been, firstly, to avoid producing a collection of identical hutches, as in most housing estates, and secondly, to provide a showpiece for a major psychiatric foundation which would serve as a model for the corporate living units of the future.

However, as everyone there had found out, living in the Bin was hell on earth. The architects had employed the so-called psycho-modular system—a basic L-design—and this meant that everything under- or overlapped everything else. The whole development was a sprawl of interlocking frosted glass, white rectangles and curves, at first glance exciting and abstract (*Life* magazine had done several glossy photographic treatments of the new "living trends" suggested by the Village) but to the people within formless and visually exhausting. Most of the Clinic's senior staff had soon taken off, and the Village was now rented to anyone who could be persuaded to live there.

Faulkner gazed out across the veranda, separating from the clutter of white geometric shapes the eight other houses he could see without moving his head. On his left, immediately adjacent, were the Penzils, with the McPhersons on the right; the other six houses were directly ahead, on the far side of a muddle of interlocking garden areas, abstract rat-runs divided by waist-high white panelling, glass angle-pieces and slatted screens.

In the Penzil's garden was a collection of huge alphabet blocks, each three high, which their two children played with. Often they left messages out on the grass for Faulkner to read, sometimes obscene, at others merely gnomic and obscure. This morning's came into the latter category. The blocks spelled out:

STOP AND GO

Speculating on the total significance of this statement, Faulkner let his mind relax, his eyes staring blankly at the houses. Gradually their already obscured outlines began to merge and fade, and the long balconies and ramps partly hidden by the intervening trees became disembodied forms, like gigantic geometric units.

Breathing slowly, Faulkner steadily closed his mind, then without any effort erased his awareness of the identity of the houses opposite.

He was now looking at a cubist landscape, a collection of random white forms below a blue backdrop, across which several powdery green blurs moved slowly backwards and forwards. Idly, he wondered what these geometric forms really represented—he knew that only a few seconds earlier they had constituted an immediately familiar part of his everyday existence—but however he rearranged them spatially in his mind, or sought their associations, they still remained a random assembly of geometric forms.

He had discovered this talent only about three weeks ago. Balefully eyeing the silent television set in the lounge one Sunday morning, he had suddenly realized that he had so completely accepted and assimilated the physical form of the plastic cabinet that he could no longer remember its function. It had required a considerable mental effort to recover himself and re-identify it. Out of interest he had tried out the new talent on other objects, found that it was particularly successful with over-associated ones such as washing machines, cars and other consumer goods. Stripped of their accretions of sales slogans and status imperatives, their real claim to reality was so tenuous that it needed little mental effort to obliterate them altogether.

The effect was similar to that of mescaline and other hallucinogens, under whose influence the dents in a cushion became as vivid as the craters of the moon, the folds in a curtain the ripples in the waves of eternity.

During the following weeks Faulkner had experimented carefully, training his ability to operate the cut-out switches. The process was slow, but gradually he found himself able to eliminate larger and larger groups of objects, the mass-produced furniture in the lounge, the overenamelled gadgets in the kitchen, his car in the garage—de-identified, it sat in the half-light like an enormous vegetable marrow, flaccid and gleaming; trying to identify it had driven him almost out of his mind. "What on earth could it *possibly* be?" he had asked himself helplessly, splitting his sides with laughter—and as the facility developed he had dimly perceived that here was an escape route from the intolerable world in which he found himself at the Village.

He had described the facility to Ross Hendricks, who lived a few houses away, also a lecturer at the Business School and Faulkner's only close friend.

"I may actually be stepping out of time," Faulkner speculated. "Without a time sense consciousness is difficult to visualize. That is, eliminating the vector of time from the de-identified object frees it from all its everyday cognitive associations. Alternatively, I may have stumbled on a means of repressing the photo-associative centres that normally identify visual objects, in the same way that you can so listen to someone speaking your own language that none of the sounds has any meaning. Everyone's tried this at some time."

Hendricks had nodded. "But don't make a career out of it, though." He eyed Faulkner carefully. "You can't simply turn a blind eye to the world. The subject-object relationship is not as polar as Descartes' 'Cogito ergo sum' suggests. By any degree to which you devalue the external world so you devalue yourself.

It seems to me that your real problem is to reverse the process."

But Hendricks, however sympathetic, was beyond helping Faulkner. Besides, it was pleasant to see the world afresh again, to wallow in an endless panorama of brilliantly coloured images. What did it matter if there was form but no content?

A sharp click woke him abruptly. He sat up with a jolt, fumbling with the alarm clock, which had been set to wake him at 11 o'clock. Looking at it, he saw that it was only 10.55. The alarm had not rung, nor had he received a shock from the battery. Yet the click had been distinct. However, there were so many servos and robots around the house that it could have been anything.

A dark shape moved across the frosted glass panel which formed the side wall of the lounge. Through it, into the narrow drive separating his house from the Penzils', he saw a car draw to a halt and park, a young woman in a blue smock climb out and walk across the gravel. This was Penzil's sister-in-law, a girl of about twenty who had been staying with them for a couple of months. As she disappeared into the house Faulkner quickly unstrapped his wrist and stood up. Opening the veranda doors, he sauntered down into the garden, glancing back over his shoulder.

The girl, Louise (he had never spoken to her), went to sculpture classes in the morning, and on her return regularly took a leisurely shower before going out onto the roof to sunbathe.

Faulkner hung around the bottom of the garden, flipping stones into the pond and pretending to straighten some of the pergola slats, then noticed that the McPhersons' 15-year-old son Harvey was approaching along the other garden.

"Why aren't you at school?" he asked Harvey, a gangling youth with an intelligent ferretlike face under a mop of brown hair.

"I should be," Harvey told him easily. "But I convinced Mother I was overtense, and Morrison"—his father—"said I was ratiocinating too much." He shrugged. "Patients here are overpermissive."

"For once you're right," Faulkner agreed, watching the shower stall over his shoulder. A pink form moved about, adjusting taps, and there was the sound of water jetting.

"Tell me, Mr. Faulkner," Harvey asked. "Do you realize

that since the death of Einstein in 1955 there hasn't been a single living genius? From Michelangelo, through Shakespeare, Newton, Beethoven, Goethe, Darwin, Freud and Einstein there's always been a living genius. Now for the first time in 500 years we're on our own."

Faulkner nodded, his eyes engaged. "I know," he said. "I feel damned lonely about it too."

When the shower was over he grunted to Harvey, wandered back to the veranda, and took up his position again in the chair, the battery lead strapped to his wrist.

Steadily, object by object, he began to switch off the world around him. The houses opposite went first. The white masses of the roofs and balconies he resolved quickly into flat rectangles, the lines of windows into small squares of colour like the grids in a Mondrian abstract. The sky was a blank field of blue. In the distance an aircraft moved across it, engines hammering. Carefully Faulkner repressed the identity of the image, then watched the slim silver dart move slowly away like a vanishing fragment from a cartoon dream.

As he waited for the engines to fade he was conscious of the sourceless click he had heard earlier that morning. It sounded only a few feet away, near the French window on his right, but he was too immersed in the unfolding kaleidoscope to rouse himself.

When the plane had gone he turned his attention to the garden, quickly blotted out the white fencing, the fake pergola, the elliptical disc of the ornamental pool. The pathway reached out to encircle the pool, and when he blanked out his memories of the countless times he had wandered up and down its length it reared up into the air like a terracotta arm holding an enormous silver jewel.

Satisfied that he had obliterated the Village and the garden, Faulkner then began to demolish the house. Here the objects around him were more familiar, highly personalized extensions of himself. He began with the veranda furniture, transforming the tubular chairs and glass-topped table into a trio of involuted green coils, then swung his head slightly and selected the TV set inside the lounge on his right. It clung limply to its identity. Easily he unfocussed his mind and reduced the brown plastic box, with its fake wooden veining, to an amorphous blur.

One by one he cleared the bookcase and desk of all associations, the standard lamps and picture frames. Like lumber in some psychological warehouse, they were suspended behind him *in vacuo*, the white armchairs and sofas like blunted rectangular clouds.

Anchored to reality only by the alarm mechanism clamped to his wrist, Faulkner craned his head from left to right, systematically obliterating all traces of meaning from the world around him, reducing everything to its formal visual values.

Gradually these too began to lose their meaning, the abstract masses of colour dissolving, drawing Faulkner after them into a world of pure psychic sensation, where blocks of ideation hung like magnetic fields in a cloud chamber. . . .

With a shattering blast, the alarm rang out, the battery driving sharp spurs of pain into Faulkner's forearm. Scalp tingling, he pulled himself back into reality and clawed away the wrist strap, massaging his arm rapidly, then slapped off the alarm.

For a few minutes he sat kneading his wrist, re-identifying all the objects around him, the houses opposite, the gardens, his home, aware that a glass wall had been inserted between them and his own psyche. However carefully he focussed his mind on the world outside, a screen still separated them, its opacity thickening imperceptibly.

On other levels as well, bulkheads were shifting into place.

His wife reached home at 6.00, tired out after a busy intake day, annoyed to find Faulkner ambling about in a semistupor, the veranda littered with dirty glasses.

"Well, clean it up!" she snapped when Faulkner vacated his chair for her and prepared to take off upstairs. "Don't leave the place like this. What's the matter with you? Come on, *connect!*"

Cramming a handful of glasses together, Faulkner mumbled to himself and started for the kitchen, found Julia blocking the way out when he tried to leave. Something was on her mind. She sipped quickly at her martini, then began to throw out probes about the school. He assumed she had rung there on some pretext and had found her suspicions reinforced when she referred in passing to himself.

"Liaison is terrible," Faulkner told her. "Take two days

off and no one remembers you work there." By a massive effort of concentration he had managed to avoid looking his wife in the face since she arrived. In fact, they had not exchanged a direct glance for over a week. Hopefully he wondered if this might be getting her down.

Supper was slow agony. The smells of the auto-cooked pot roast had permeated the house all afternoon. Unable to eat more than a few mouthfuls, he had nothing on which to focus his attention. Luckily Julia had a brisk appetite and he could stare at the top of her head as she ate, let his eyes wander around the room when she looked up.

After supper, thankfully, there was television. Dusk blanked out the other houses in the Village, and they sat in the darkness around the set, Julia grumbling at the programmes.

"Why do we watch *every* night?" she asked. "It's a total time waster."

Faulkner gestured airily. "It's an interesting social document." Slumped down into the wing chair, hands apparently behind his neck, he could press his fingers into his ears, at will blot out the sounds of the programme. "Don't pay any attention to what they're saying," he told his wife. "It makes more sense." He watched the characters mouthing silently like demented fish. The close-ups in melodramas were particularly hilarious; the more intense the situation the broader was the farce.

Something kicked his knee sharply. He looked up to see his wife bending over him, eyebrows knotted together, mouth working furiously. Fingers still pressed to his ears, Faulkner examined her face with detachment, for a moment speculated whether to complete the process and switch her off as he had switched off the rest of the world earlier that day. When he did he wouldn't bother to set the alarm . . .

"Harry!" he heard his wife bellow.

He sat up with a start, the row from the set backing up his wife's voice.

"What's the matter? I was asleep."

"You were in a trance, you mean. For God's sake answer when I talk to you. I was saying that I saw Harriet Tizzard this afternoon." Faulkner groaned and his wife swerved on him.

"I know you can't stand the Tizzards but I've decided we ought to see more of them . . ."

As his wife rattled on, Faulkner eased himself down behind the wings. When she was settled back in her chair he moved his hands up behind his neck. After a few discretionary grunts, he slid his fingers into his ears and blotted out her voice, then lay quietly watching the silent screen.

By 10 o'clock the next morning he was out on the veranda again, alarm strapped to his wrist. For the next hour he lay back enjoying the disembodied forms suspended around him, his mind free of its anxieties. When the alarm woke him at 11.00 he felt refreshed and relaxed. For a few moments he was able to survey the nearby houses with the visual curiosity their architects had intended. Gradually, however, everything began to secrete its poison again, its overlay of nagging associations, and within ten minutes he was looking fretfully at his wrist watch.

When Louise Penzil's car pulled into the drive he disconnected the alarm and sauntered out into the garden, head down to shut out as many of the surrounding houses as possible. As he was idling around the pergola, replacing the slats torn loose by the roses, Harvey McPherson suddenly popped his head over the fence.

"Harvey, are you still around? Don't you ever go to school?"

"Well, I'm on this relaxation course of Mother's," Harvey explained. "I find the competitive context of the classroom is—"

"I'm trying to relax too," Faulkner cut in. "Let's leave it at that. Why don't you beat it?"

Unruffled, Harvey pressed on. "Mr. Faulkner, I've got a sort of problem in metaphysics that's been bothering me. Maybe you could help. The only absolute in space-time is supposed to be the speed of light. But as a matter of fact any estimate of the speed of light involves the component of time, which is subjectively variable—so, bam, what's left?"

"Girls," Faulkner said. He glanced over his shoulder at the Penzil house and then turned back moodily to Harvey.

Harvey frowned, trying to straighten his hair. "What are you talking about?"

"Girls," Faulkner repeated. "You know, the weaker sex, the distaff side."

"Oh, for Pete's sake." Shaking his head, Harvey walked back to his house, muttering to himself.

That'll shut you up, Faulkner thought. He started to scan the Penzils' house through the slats of the pergola, then suddenly spotted Harry Penzil standing in the centre of his veranda window, frowning out at him.

Quickly Faulkner turned his back and pretended to trim the roses. By the time he managed to work his way indoors he was sweating heavily. Harry Penzil was the sort of man liable to straddle fences and come out leading with a right swing.

Mixing himself a drink in the kitchen, Faulkner brought it out onto the veranda and sat down waiting for his embarrassment to subside before setting the alarm mechanism.

He was listening carefully for any sounds from the Penzils' when he heard a familiar soft metallic click from the house on his right.

Faulkner sat forward, examining the veranda wall. This was a slab of heavy frosted glass, completely opaque, carrying white roof timbers, clipped onto which were slabs of corrugated polythene sheeting. Just beyond the veranda, screening the proximal portions of the adjacent gardens, was a ten-foot-high metal lattice extending about twenty feet down the garden fence and strung with japonica.

Inspecting the lattice carefully, Faulkner suddenly noticed the outline of a square black object on a slender tripod propped up behind the first vertical support just three feet from the open veranda window, the disc of a small glass eye staring at him unblinkingly through one of the horizontal slots.

A camera! Faulkner leapt out of his chair, gaping incredulously at the instrument. For days it had been clicking away at him. God alone knew what glimpses into his private life Harvey had recorded for his own amusement.

Anger boiling, Faulkner strode across to the lattice, prised one of the metal members off the support beam and seized the camera. As he dragged it through the space the tripod fell away with a clatter and he heard someone on the McPhersons' veranda start up out of a chair.

Faulkner wrestled the camera through, snapping off the

remote control cord attached to the shutter lever. Opening the camera, he ripped out the film, then put it down on the floor and stamped its face in with the heel of his shoe. Then, ramming the pieces together, he stepped forward and hurled them over the fence towards the far end of the McPhersons' garden.

As he returned to finish his drink the phone rang in the hall.

"Yes, what is it?" he snapped into the receiver.

"Is that you, Harry? Julia here."

"Who?" Faulkner said, not thinking. "Oh, yes. Well, how are things?"

"Not too good, by the sound of it." His wife's voice had become harder. "I've just had a long talk with Professor Harman. He told me that you resigned from the school two months ago. Harry, what are you playing at? I can hardly believe it."

"I can hardly believe it either," Faulkner retorted jocularly. "It's the best news I've had for years. Thanks for confirming it."

"Harry!" His wife was shouting now. "Pull yourself together! If you think I'm going to support you you're very much mistaken. Professor Harman said—"

"That idiot Harman!" Faulkner interrupted. "Don't you realize he was trying to drive me insane?" As his wife's voice rose to an hysterical squawk he held the receiver away from him, then quietly replaced it in the cradle. After a pause he took it off again and laid it down on the stack of directories.

Outside, the spring morning hung over the Village like a curtain of silence. Here and there a tree stirred in the warm air, or a window opened and caught the sunlight, but otherwise the quiet and stillness were unbroken.

Lying on the veranda, the alarm mechanism discarded on the floor below his chair, Faulkner sank deeper and deeper into his private reverie, into the demolished world of form and colour which hung motionlessly around him. The houses opposite had vanished, their places taken by long white rectangular bands. The garden was a green ramp at the end of which poised the silver ellipse of the pond. The veranda was a transparent cube, in the centre of which he felt himself suspended like an image floating on a sea of ideation. He had obliterated not only the world around him, but his own body, and his limbs and trunk seemed an extension of his mind, disembodied forms whose physical dimensions pressed upon it like a dream's awareness of its own identity.

Some hours later, as he rotated slowly through his reverie, he was aware of a sudden intrusion into his field of vision. Focussing his eyes, with surprise he saw the dark-suited figure of his wife standing in front of him, shouting angrily and gesturing with her handbag.

For a few minutes Faulkner examined the discrete entity she familiarly presented, the proportions of her legs and arms, the planes of her face. Then, without moving, he began to dismantle her mentally, obliterating her literally limb by limb. First he forgot her hands, forever snapping and twisting like frenzied birds, then her arms and shoulders, erasing all his memories of their energy and motion. Finally, as it pressed closer to him, mouth working wildly, he forgot her face, so that it presented nothing more than a blunted wedge of pink-grey dough, deformed by various ridges and grooves, split by apertures that opened and closed like the vents of some curious bellows.

Turning back to the silent dreamscape, he was aware of her jostling insistently behind him. Her presence seemed ugly and formless, a bundle of obtrusive angles.

Then at last they came into brief physical contact. Gesturing her away, he felt her fasten like a dog upon his arm. He tried to shake her off but she clung to him, jerking about in an outpouring of anger.

Her rhythms were sharp and ungainly. To begin with he tried to ignore them; then he began to restrain and smooth her, moulding her angular form into a softer and rounder one.

As he worked away, kneading her like a sculptor shaping clay, he noticed a series of crackling noises, over which a persistent scream was just barely audible. When he finished he let her fall to the floor, a softly squeaking lump of spongy rubber.

Faulkner returned to his reverie, re-assimilating the unaltered landscape. His brush with his wife had reminded him of the one encumbrance that still remained—his own body. Although he had forgotten its identity it none the less felt heavy and warm, vaguely uncomfortable, like a badly made bed to a

restless sleeper. What he sought was pure ideation, the undisturbed sensation of psychic being untransmuted by any physical
medium. Only thus could he escape the nausea of the external
world.

Somewhere in his mind an idea suggested itself. Rising from
his chair, he walked out across the veranda, unaware of the
physical movements involved, but propelling himself towards
the far end of the garden.

Hidden by the rose pergola, he stood for five minutes at the
edge of the pond, then stepped into the water. Trousers billowing
around his knees, he waded out slowly. When he reached the
centre he sat down, pushing the weeds apart, and lay back in
the shallow water.

Slowly he felt the puttylike mass of his body dissolving, its
temperature growing cooler and less oppressive. Looking out
through the surface of the water six inches above his face, he
watched the blue disc of the sky, cloudless and undisturbed,
expanding to fill his consciousness. At last he had found the
perfect background, the only possible field of ideation, an
absolute continuum of existence uncontaminated by material
excrescences.

Steadily watching it, he waited for the world to dissolve and
set him free.

THIRTEEN TO CENTAURUS

ABEL knew.

Three months earlier, just after his sixteenth birthday, he had
guessed, but had been too unsure of himself, too overwhelmed by
the logic of his discovery, to mention it to his parents. At times,
lying back half asleep in his bunk while his mother crooned one
of the old lays to herself, he would deliberately repress the knowledge, but always it came back, nagging at him insistently,

forcing him to jettison most of what he had long regarded as the real world.

None of the other children at the Station could help. They were immersed in their games in Playroom, or chewing pencils over their tests and homework.

"Abel, what's the matter?" Zenna Peters called after him as he wandered off to the empty store-room on D-Deck. "You're looking sad again."

Abel hesitated, watching Zenna's warm, puzzled smile, then slipped his hands into his pockets and made off, springing down the metal stairway to make sure she didn't follow him. Once she sneaked into the store-room uninvited and he had pulled the light-bulb out of the socket, shattered about three weeks of conditioning. Dr. Francis had been furious.

As he hurried along the D-Deck corridor he listened carefully for the doctor, who had recently been keeping an eye on Abel, watching him shrewdly from behind the plastic models in Playroom. Perhaps Abel's mother had told him about the nightmare, when he would wake from a vice of sweating terror, an image of a dull burning disc fixed before his eyes.

If only Dr. Francis could cure him of that dream.

Every six yards down the corridor he stepped through a bulk-head, and idly touched the heavy control boxes on either side of the doorway. Deliberately unfocussing his mind, Abel identified some of the letters above the switches

M–T—R   SC—N

but they scrambled into a blur as soon as he tried to read the entire phrase. Conditioning was too strong. After he trapped her in the store-room Zenna had been able to read a few of the notices, but Dr. Francis whisked her away before she could re-peat them. Hours later, when she came back, she remembered nothing.

As usual when he entered the store-room, he waited a few seconds before switching on the light, seeing in front of him the small disc of burning light that in his dreams expanded until it filled his brain like a thousand arc lights. It seemed endlessly distant, yet somehow mysteriously potent and magnetic, arousing dormant areas of his mind close to those which responded to his mother's presence.

As the disc began to expand he pressed the switch tab.

To his surprise, the room remained in darkness. He fumbled for the switch, a short cry slipping involuntarily through his lips.

Abruptly, the light went on.

"Hello, Abel," Dr. Francis said easily, right hand pressing the bulb into its socket. "Quite a shock, that one." He leaned against a metal crate. "I thought we'd have a talk together about your essay." He took an exercise book out of his white plastic suit as Abel sat down stiffly. Despite his dry smile and warm eyes there was something about Dr. Francis that always put Abel on his guard.

Perhaps Dr. Francis knew too?

"The Closed Community," Dr. Francis read out. "A strange subject for an essay, Abel."

Abel shrugged. "It was a free choice. Aren't we really expected to choose something unusual?"

Dr. Francis grinned. "A good answer. But seriously, Abel, why pick a subject like that?"

Abel fingered the seals on his suit. These served no useful purpose, but by blowing through them it was possible to inflate the suit. "Well, it's a sort of study of life at the Station, how we all get on with each other. What else is there to write about? I don't see that it's so strange."

"Perhaps not. No reason why you shouldn't write about the Station. All four of the others did too. But you called yours 'The Closed Community.' The Station isn't closed, Abel, is it?"

"It's closed in the sense that we can't go outside." Abel explained slowly. "That's all I meant."

"Outside," Dr. Francis repeated. "It's an interesting concept You must have given the whole subject a lot of thought. When did you first start thinking along these lines?"

"After the dream," Abel said. Dr. Francis had deliberately sidestepped his use of the word "outside" and he searched for some means of getting to the point. In his pocket he felt the small plumbline he carried around. "Dr. Francis, perhaps you can explain something to me. Why is the Station revolving?"

"Is it?" Dr. Francis looked up with interest. "How do you know?"

Abel reached up and fastened the plumbline to the ceiling stanchion. "The interval between the ball and the wall is about an eighth of an inch greater at the bottom than at the top. Centrifugal forces are driving it outwards. I calculated that the Station is revolving at about two feet per second."

Dr. Francis nodded thoughtfully. "That's just about right," he said matter-of-factly. He stood up. "Let's take a trip to my office. It looks as if it's time you and I had a serious talk."

The Station was on four levels. The lower two contained the crew's quarters, two circular decks of cabins which housed the 14 people on board the Station. The senior clan was the Peters, led by Captain Theodore, a big stern man of taciturn disposition who rarely strayed from Control. Abel had never been allowed there, but the Captain's son, Matthew, often described the hushed dome-like cabin filled with luminous dials and flickering lights, the strange humming music.

All the male members of the Peters clan worked in Control —grandfather Peters, a white-haired old man with humorous eyes, had been Captain before Abel was born—and with the Captain's wife and Zenna they constituted the elite of the Station.

However, the Grangers, the clan to which Abel belonged, was in many respects more important, as he had begun to realize. The day-to-day running of the Station, the detailed programming of emergency drills, duty rosters and commissary menus, was the responsibility of Abel's father, Matthias, and without his firm but flexible hand the Bakers, who cleaned the cabins and ran the commissary, would never have known what to do. And it was only the deliberate intermingling in Recreation which his father devised that brought the Peters and Bakers together, or each family would have stayed indefinitely in its own cabins.

Lastly, there was Dr. Francis. He didn't belong to any of the three clans. Sometimes Abel asked himself where Dr. Francis had come from, but his mind always fogged at a question like that, as the conditioning blocks fell like bulkheads across his thought trains (logic was a dangerous tool at the Station). Dr. Francis' energy and vitality, his relaxed good humour—in a way,

he was the only person in the Station who ever made any jokes—
were out of character with everyone else. Much as he sometimes
disliked Dr. Francis for snooping around and being a know-all,
Abel realized how dreary life in the Station would seem without
him.

Dr. Francis closed the door of his cabin and gestured Abel
into a seat. All the furniture in the Station was bolted to the
floor, but Abel noticed that Dr. Francis had unscrewed his chair
so that he could tilt it backwards. The huge vacuum-proof
cylinder of the doctor's sleeping tank jutted from the wall, its
massive metal body able to withstand any accident the Station
might suffer. Abel hated the thought of sleeping in the cylinder
—luckily the entire crew quarters were accident-secure—and
wondered why Dr. Francis chose to live alone up on A-Deck.

"Tell me, Abel," Dr. Francis began, "has it ever occurred to you
to ask why the Station is here?"

Abel shrugged. "Well, it's designed to keep us alive, it's
our home."

"Yes, that's true, but obviously it has some other object than
just our own survival. Who do you think built the Station in the
first place?"

"Our fathers, I suppose, or grandfathers. Or *their* grandfathers."

"Fair enough. And where were they before they built it?"

Abel struggled with the *reductio ad absurdum*. "I don't know,
they must have been floating around in mid-air!"

Dr. Francis joined in the laughter. "Wonderful thought. Actually it's not that far from the truth. But we can't accept that as it
stands."

The doctor's self-contained office gave Abel an idea. "Perhaps
they came from another Station? An even bigger one?"

Dr. Francis nodded encouragingly. "Brilliant, Abel. A first-
class piece of deduction. All right, then, let's assume that. Somewhere away from us, a huge Station exists, perhaps a hundred
times bigger than this one, maybe even a thousand. Why not?"

"It's possible," Abel admitted, accepting the idea with surprising ease.

"Right. Now you remember your course in advanced mechanics—the imaginary planetary system, with the orbiting bodies

held together by mutual gravitational attraction? Let's assume further that such a system actually exists. O.K.?"

"Here?" Abel said quickly. "In your cabin?" Then he added "In your sleeping cylinder?"

Dr. Francis sat back. "Abel, you do come up with some amazing things. An interesting association of ideas. No, it would be too big for that. Try to imagine a planetary system orbiting around a central body of absolutely enormous size, each of the planets a million times larger than the Station." When Abel nodded, he went on. "And suppose that the big Station, the one a thousand times larger than this, were attached to one of the planets, and that the people in it decided to go to another planet. So they build a smaller Station, about the size of this one, and send it off through the air. Make sense?"

"In a way." Strangely, the completely abstract concepts were less remote than he would have expected. Deep in his mind dim memories stirred, interlocking with what he had already guessed about the Station. He gazed steadily at Dr. Francis. "You're saying that's what the Station is doing? That the planetary system exists?"

Dr. Francis nodded. "You'd more or less guessed before I told you. Unconsciously, you've known all about it for several years. A few minutes from now I'm going to remove some of the conditioning blocks, and when you wake up in a couple of hours you'll understand everything. You'll know then that in fact the Station is a space ship, flying from our home planet, Earth, where our grandfathers were born, to another planet millions of miles away, in a distant orbiting system. Our grandfathers always lived on Earth, and we are the first people ever to undertake such a journey. You can be proud that you're here. Your grandfather, who volunteered to come, was a great man, and we've got to do everything to make sure that the Station keeps running."

Abel nodded quickly. "When do we get there—the planet we're flying to?"

Dr. Francis looked down at his hands, his face growing sombre. "We'll never get there, Abel. The journey takes too long. This is a multi-generation space vehicle, only our children will land and they'll be old by the time they do. But don't worry, you'll go on thinking of the Station as your only home, and that's deliberate, so that you and your children will be happy here."

He went over to the TV monitor screen by which he kept in touch with Captain Peters, his fingers playing across the control tabs. Suddenly the screen lit up, a blaze of fierce points of light flared into the cabin, throwing a brilliant phosphorescent glitter across the walls, dappling Abel's hands and suit. He gaped at the huge balls of fire, apparently frozen in the middle of a giant explosion, hanging in vast patterns.

"This is the celestial sphere," Dr. Francis explained. "The starfield into which the Station is moving." He touched a bright speck of light in the lower half of the screen. "Alpha Centauri, the star around which revolves the planet the Station will one day land upon." He turned to Abel. "You remember all these terms I'm using, don't you, Abel? None of them seems strange."

Abel nodded, the wells of his unconscious memory flooding into his mind as Dr. Francis spoke. The TV screen blanked and then revealed a new picture. They appeared to be looking down at an enormous top-like structure, the flanks of a metal pylon sloping towards its centre. In the background the starfield rotated slowly in a clockwise direction. "This is the Station," Dr. Francis explained, "seen from a camera mounted in the nose boom. All visual checks have to be made indirectly, as the stellar radiation would blind us. Just below the ship you can see a single star, the Sun, from which we set out 50 years ago. It's now almost too distant to be visible, but a deep inherited memory of it is the burning disc you see in your dreams. We've done what we can to erase it, but unconsciously all of us see it too."

He switched off the set and the brilliant pattern of light swayed and fell back. "The social engineering built into the ship is far more intricate than the mechanical, Abel. It's three generations since the Station set off, and birth, marriage and birth again have followed exactly as they were designed to. As your father's heir great demands are going to be made on your patience and understanding. Any disunity here would bring disaster. The conditioning programmes are not equipped to give you more than a general outline of the course to follow. Most of it will be left to you."

"Will you always be here?"

Dr. Francis stood up. "No, Abel, I won't. No one here lives

forever. Your father will die, and Captain Peters and myself."
He moved to the door. "We'll go now to Conditioning. In three
hours' time, when you wake up, you'll find yourself a new man."

Letting himself back into his cabin, Francis leaned wearily
against the bulkhead, feeling the heavy rivets with his fingers,
here and there flaking away as the metal slowly rusted. When he
switched on the TV set he looked tired and dispirited, and gazed
absently at the last scene he had shown Abel, the boom camera's
view of the ship. He was just about to select another frame when
he noticed a dark shadow swing across the surface of the hull.

He leaned forward to examine it, frowning in annoyance as
the shadow moved away and faded among the stars. He pressed
another tab, and the screen divided into a large chessboard, five
frames wide by five deep. The top line showed Control, the main
pilot and navigation deck lit by the dim glow of the instrument
panels, Captain Peters sitting impassively before the compass
screen.

Next, he watched Matthias Granger begin his afternoon inspection of the ship. Most of the passengers seemed reasonably
happy, but their faces lacked any lustre. All spent at least 2–3
hours each day bathing in the UV light flooding through the
recreation lounge, but the pallor continued, perhaps an unconscious realization that they had been born and were living in what
would also be their own tomb. Without the continuous conditioning sessions, and the hypnotic reassurance of the sub-sonic
voices, they would long ago have become will-less automatons.

Switching off the set, he prepared to climb into the sleeping
cylinder. The airlock was three feet in diameter, waist-high off
the floor. The time seal rested at zero, and he moved it forward
12 hours, then set it so that the seal could only be broken from
within. He swung the lock out and crawled in over the moulded
foam mattress, snapping the door shut behind him.

Lying back in the thin yellow light, he slipped his fingers
though the ventilator grille in the rear wall, pressed the unit into
its socket and turned it sharply. Somewhere an electric motor
throbbed briefly, the end wall of the cylinder swung back slowly
like a vault door and bright daylight poured in.

Quickly, Francis climbed out onto a small metal platform that jutted from the upper slope of a huge white asbestos-covered dome. Fifty feet above was the roof of a large hangar. A maze of pipes and cables traversed the surface of the dome, interlacing like the vessels of a giant bloodshot eye, and a narrow stairway led down to the floor below. The entire dome, some 150 feet wide, was revolving slowly. A line of five trucks was drawn up by the stores depot on the far side of the hangar, and a man in a brown uniform waved to him from one of the glass-walled offices.

At the bottom of the ladder he jumped down on to the hangar floor, ignoring the curious stares from the soldiers unloading the stores. Half-way across he craned up at the revolving bulk of the dome. A black perforated sail, 50 feet square, like a fragment of a planetarium, was suspended from the roof over the apex of the dome, a TV camera directly below it, a large metal sphere mounted about five feet from the lens. One of the guy-ropes had snapped and the sail tilted slightly to reveal the catwalk along the centre of the roof.

He pointed this out to a maintenance sergeant warming his hands in one of the ventilator outlets from the dome. "You'll have to string that back. Some fool was wandering along the catwalk and throwing his shadow straight on to the model. I could see it clearly on the TV screen. Luckily no one spotted it."

"O.K., Doctor, I'll get it fixed." He chuckled sourly. "That would have been a laugh, though. Really give them something to worry about."

The man's tone annoyed Francis. "They've got plenty to worry about as it is."

"I don't know about that, Doctor. Some people here think they have it all ways. Quiet and warm in there, nothing to do except sit back and listen to those hypno-drills." He looked out bleakly at the abandoned airfield stretching away to the cold tundra beyond the perimeter, and turned up his collar. "We're the boys back here on Mother Earth who do the work, out in this Godforsaken dump. If you need any more spacecadets, Doctor, remember me."

Francis managed a smile and stepped into the control office, made his way through the clerks sitting at trestle tables in front of the progress charts. Each carried the name of one of the dome passengers and a tabulated breakdown of progress through the psychometric tests and conditioning programmes. Other charts listed the day's rosters, copies of those posted that morning by Matthias Granger.

Inside Colonel Chalmers' office Francis relaxed back gratefully in the warmth, describing the salient features of his day's observation. "I wish you could go in there and move around them, Paul," he concluded. "It's not the same spying through the TV cameras. You've got to talk to them, measure yourself against people like Granger and Peters."

"You're right, they're fine men, like all the others. It's a pity they're wasted there."

"They're not wasted," Francis insisted. "Every piece of data will be immensely valuable when the first space ships set out." He ignored Chalmers' muttered "If they do" and went on: "Zenna and Abel worry me a little. It may be necessary to bring forward the date of their marriage. I know it will raise eyebrows, but the girl is as fully mature at 15 as she will be four years from now, and she'll be a settling influence on Abel, stop him from thinking too much."

Chalmers shook his head doubtfully. "Sounds a good idea, but a girl of 15 and a boy of 16—? You'd raise a storm, Roger. Technically they're wards of court, every decency league would be up in arms."

Francis gestured irritably. "Need they know? We've really got a problem with Abel, the boy's too clever. He'd more or less worked out for himself that the Station was a space ship, he merely lacked the vocabulary to describe it. Now that we're starting to lift the conditioning blocks he'll want to know everything. It will be a big job to prevent him from smelling a rat, particularly with the slack way this place is being run. Did you see the shadow on the TV screen? We're damn lucky Peters didn't have a heart attack."

Chalmers nodded. "I'm getting that tightened up. A few mistakes are bound to happen, Roger. It's damn cold for the control crew working around the dome. Try to remember that the people outside are just as important as those inside."

"Of course. The real trouble is that the budget is ludicrously out of date. It's only been revised once in 50 years. Perhaps General Short can generate some official interest, get a new deal for us. He sounds like a pretty brisk new broom." Chalmers pursed his lips doubtfully, but Francis continued "I don't know whether the tapes are wearing out, but the negative conditioning doesn't hold as well as it used to. We'll probably have to tighten up the programmes. I've made a start by pushing Abel's graduation forward."

"Yes, I watched you on the screen here. The control boys became quite worked up next door. One or two of them are as keen as you, Roger, they'd been programming ahead for three months. It meant a lot of time wasted for them. I think you ought to check with me before you make a decision like that. The dome isn't your private laboratory."

Francis accepted the reproof. Lamely, he said "It was one of those spot decisions, I'm sorry. There was nothing else to do."

Chalmers gently pressed home his point. "I'm not so sure. I thought you rather overdid the long-term aspects of the journey. Why go out of your way to tell him he would never reach planetfall? It only heightens his sense of isolation, makes it that much more difficult if we decide to shorten the journey."

Francis looked up. "There's no chance of that, is there?"

Chalmers paused thoughtfully. "Roger, I really advise you not to get too involved with the project. Keep saying to yourself they're-not-going-to-Alpha-Centauri. They're here on Earth, and if the government decided it they'd be let out tomorrow. I know the courts would have to sanction it but that's a formality. It's 50 years since this project was started and a good number of influential people feel that it's gone on for too long. Ever since the Mars and Moon colonies failed, space programmes have been cut right back. They think the money here is being poured away for the amusement of a few sadistic psychologists."

"You know that isn't true," Francis retorted. "I may have been over-hasty, but on the whole this project has been scrupulously conducted. Without exaggeration, if you did send a dozen people on a multi-generation ship to Alpha Centauri you couldn't do better than duplicate everything that's taken place here, down to the last cough and sneeze. If the information we've obtained had been available the Mars and Moon colonies never would have failed!"

"True. But irrelevant. Don't you understand, when everyone was eager to get into space they were prepared to accept the idea of a small group being sealed into a tank for 100 years, particularly when the original team volunteered. Now, when interest has evaporated, people are beginning to feel that there's something obscene about this human zoo; what began as a grand adventure of the spirit of Columbus, has become a grisly joke. In one sense we've learned too much.—the social stratification of the three families is the sort of unwelcome datum that doesn't do the project much good. Another is the complete ease with which we've manipulated them, made them believe anything we've wanted." Chalmers leaned forward across the desk. "Confidentially, Roger, General Short has been put in command for one reason only—to close this place down. It may take years, but it's going to be done, I warn you. The important job now is to get those people out of there, not keep them in."

Francis stared bleakly at Chalmers. "Do you really believe that?"

"Frankly, Roger, yes. This project should never have been launched. You can't manipulate people the way we're doing— the endless hypno-drills, the forced pairing of children—look at yourself, five minutes ago you were seriously thinking of marrying two teen-age children just to stop them using their minds. The whole thing degrades human dignity, all the taboos, the increasing degree of introspection—sometimes Peters and Granger don't speak to anyone for two or three weeks—the way life in the dome has become tenable only by accepting the insane situation as the normal one. I think the reaction against the project is healthy."

Francis stared out at the dome. A gang of men were loading the so-called "compressed food" (actually frozen foods with the brand names removed) into the commissary hatchway. Next morning, when Baker and his wife dialled the pre-arranged menu, the supplies would be promptly delivered, apparently from the space-hold. To some people, Francis knew, the project might well seem a complete fraud.

Quietly he said: "The people who volunteered accepted the sacrifice, and all it involved. How's Short going to get them out? Just open the door and whistle?"

Chalmers smiled, a little wearily. "He's not a fool, Roger. He's as sincerely concerned about their welfare as you are. Half the crew, particularly the older ones, would go mad within five minutes. But don't be disappointed, the project has more than proved its worth."

"It won't do that until they 'land'. If the project ends it will be we who have failed, not them. We can't rationalize by saying it's cruel or unpleasant. We owe it to the 14 people in the dome to keep it going."

Chalmers watched him shrewdly. "14? You mean 13, don't you, Doctor? Or are you inside the dome too?"

This ship had stopped rotating. Sitting at his desk in Command, planning the next day's fire drill, Abel noticed the sudden absence of movement. All morning, as he walked around the ship—he no longer used the term Station—he had been aware of an inward drag that pulled him towards the wall, as if one leg were shorter than the other.

When he mentioned this to his father the older man merely said: "Captain Peters is in charge of Control. Always let him worry where the navigation of the ship is concerned."

This sort of advice now meant nothing to Abel. In the previous two months his mind had attacked everything around him voraciously, probing and analysing, examining every facet of life in the Station. An enormous, once suppressed vocabulary of abstract terms and relationships lay latent below the surface of his mind, and nothing would stop him applying it.

Over their meal trays in the commissary he grilled Matthew Peters about the ship's flight path, the great parabola which would carry it to Alpha Centauri.

"What about the currents built into the ship?" he asked. "The rotation was designed to eliminate the magnetic poles set up when the ship was originally constructed. How are you compensating for that?"

Matthew looked puzzled. "I'm not sure, exactly. Probably the instruments are automatically compensated." When Abel smiled sceptically he shrugged. "Anyway, Father knows all about it. There's no doubt we're right on course.

"We hope," Abel murmured *sotto voce*. The more Abel asked Matthew about the navigational devices he and his father operated in Control the more obvious it became that they were merely carrying out low-level instrument checks, and that their role was limited to replacing burnt-out pilot lights. Most of the instruments operated automatically, and they might as well have been staring at cabinets full of mattress flock.

What a joke if they were!

Smiling to himself, Abel realized that he had probably stated no more than the truth. It would be unlikely for the navigation to be entrusted to the crew when the slightest human error could throw the space ship irretrievably out of control, send it hurtling into a passing star. The designers of the ship would have sealed the automatic pilots well out of reach, given the crew light supervisory duties that created an illusion of control.

That was the real clue to life aboard the ship. None of their roles could be taken at face value. The day-to-day, minute-to-minute programming carried out by himself and his father was merely a set of variations on a pattern already laid down; the permutations possible were endless, but the fact that he could send Matthew Peters to the commissary at 12 o'clock rather than 12.30 didn't give him any real power over Matthew's life. The master programmes printed by the computers selected the day's menus, safety drills and recreation periods, and a list of names to choose from, but the slight leeway allowed, the extra two or three names supplied, were there in case of illness, not to give Abel any true freedom of choice.

One day, Abel promised himself, he would programme himself out of the conditioning sessions. Shrewdly he guessed that the conditioning still blocked out a great deal of interesting material, that half his mind remained submerged. Something about the ship suggested that there might be more to it than—

"Hello, Abel, you look far away." Dr. Francis sat down next to him. "What's worrying you?"

"I was just calculating something," Abel explained quickly. "Tell me, assuming that each member of the crew consumes about three pounds of non-circulated food each day, roughly half a ton per year, the total cargo must be about 800 tons, and that's not allowing for any supplies after planet-fall. There should be at least 1,500 tons aboard. Quite a weight."

"Not in absolute terms, Abel. The Station is only a small fraction of the ship. The main reactors, fuel tanks and space holds together weigh over 30,000 tons. They provide the gravitational pull that holds you to the floor."

Abel shook his head slowly. "Hardly, Doctor. The attraction must come from the stellar gravitational fields, or the weight of the ship would have to be about 6×10^{20} tons."

Dr. Francis watched Abel reflectively, aware that the young man had led him into a simple trap. The figure he had quoted was near enough the Earth's mass. "These are complex problems, Abel. I wouldn't worry too much about stellar mechanics. Captain Peters has that responsibility."

"I'm not trying to usurp it," Abel assured him. "Merely to extend my own knowledge. Don't you think it might be worth departing from the rules a little? For example, it would be interesting to test the effects of continued isolation. We could select a small group, subject them to artificial stimuli, even seal them off from the rest of the crew and condition them to believe they were back on Earth. It could be a really valuable experiment, Doctor."

As he waited in the conference room for General Short to finish his opening harangue, Francis repeated the last sentence to himself, wondering idly what Abel, with his limitless enthusiasm, would have made of the circle of defeated faces around the table.

". . . regret as much as you do, gentlemen, the need to discontinue the project. However, now that a decision has been made by the Space Department, it is our duty to implement it. Of course, the task won't be an easy one. What we need is a phased withdrawal, a gradual readjustment of the world around the crew that will bring them down to Earth as gently as a parachute." The General was a brisk, sharp-faced man in his fifties, with burly shoulders but sensitive eyes. He turned to Dr. Kersh, who was responsible for the dietary and bietric controls aboard the dome. "From what you tell me, Doctor, we might not have as much time as we'd like. This boy Abel sounds something of a problem."

Kersh smiled. "I was looking in at the commissary, overheard him tell Dr. Francis that he wanted to run an experiment on a small group of the crew. An isolation drill, would you believe it. He's estimated that the two-man tractor crews may be isolated for up to two years when the first foraging trips are made."

Captain Sanger, the engineering officer, added: "He's also trying to duck his conditioning sessions. He's wearing a couple of foam pads under his earphones, missing about 90 per cent of the subsonics. We spotted it when the EEG tape we record showed no alpha waves. At first we thought it was a break in the cable, but when we checked visually on the screen we saw that he had his eyes open. He wasn't listening."

Francis drummed on the table. "It wouldn't have mattered. The sub-sonic was a maths instruction sequence—the four-figure antilog system."

"A good thing he did miss them," Kersh said with a laugh. "Sooner or later he'll work out that the dome is travelling in an elliptical orbit 93 million miles from a dwarf star of the G_0 spectral class."

"What are you doing about this attempt to evade conditioning, Dr. Francis?" Short asked. When Francis shrugged vaguely he added: "I think we ought to regard the matter fairly seriously. From now on we'll be relying on the programming."

Flatly, Francis said: "Abel will resume the conditioning. There's no need to do anything. Without the regular daily contact he'll soon feel lost. The sub-sonic voice is composed of his mother's vocal tones; when he no longer hears it he'll lose his orientations, feel completely deserted."

Short nodded slowly. "Well, let's hope so." He addressed Dr. Kersh. "At a rough estimate, Doctor, how long will it take to bring them back? Bearing in mind they'll have to be given complete freedom and that every TV and newspaper network in the world will interview each one a hundred times."

Kersh chose his words carefully. "Obviously a matter of years, General. All the conditioning drills will have to be gradually rescored; as a stop-gap measure we may need to introduce a meteor collision . . . guessing, I'd say three to five years. Possibly longer."

"Fair enough. What would you estimate, Dr. Francis?"

Francis fiddled with his blotter, trying to view the question seriously. "I've no idea. *Bring them back*. What do you really mean, General? Bring what back?" Irritated, he snapped: "A hundred years."

Laughter crossed the table, and Short smiled at him, not unamiably. "That's fifty years more than the original project, Doctor. You can't have been doing a very good job here."

Francis shook his head. "You're wrong, General. The original project was to get them to Alpha Centauri. Nothing was said about bringing them *back*." When the laughter fell away Francis cursed himself for his foolishness; antagonizing the General wouldn't help the people in the dome.

But Short seemed unruffled. "All right, then, it's obviously going to take some time." Pointedly, with a glance at Francis, he added: "It's the men and women in the ship we're thinking of, not ourselves; if we need a hundred years we'll take them, not one less. You may be interested to hear that the Space Department chiefs feel about fifteen years will be necessary. At least." There was a quickening of interest around the table. Francis watched Short with surprise. In fifteen years a lot could happen, there might be another spaceward swing of public opinion.

"The Department recommends that the project continue as before, with whatever budgetary parings we can make—stopping the dome is just a start—and that we condition the crew to believe that a round trip is in progress, that their mission is merely one of reconnaissance, and that they are bringing vital information back to Earth. When they step out of the spaceship they'll be treated as heroes and accept the strangeness of the world around them." Short looked across the table, waiting for someone to reply. Kersh stared doubtfully at his hands, and Sanger and Chalmers played mechanically with their blotters.

Just before Short continued Francis pulled himself together, realizing that he was faced with his last opportunity to save the project. However much they disagreed with Short, none of the others would try to argue with him.

"I'm afraid that won't do, General," he said, "though I appreciate the Department's foresight and your own sympathetic approach. The scheme you've outlined sounds plausible, but it just won't work." He sat forward, his voice controlled and precise. "General, ever since they were children these people have been trained to accept that they were a closed group, and would never have contact with anyone else. On the unconscious level, on the level of their functional nervous systems, no one else in the world exists, for them the neuronic basis of reality is isolation. You'll never train them to invert their whole universe, any more than you can train a fish to fly. If you start to tamper with the fundamental patterns of their psyches you'll produce the sort of complete mental block you see when you try to teach a left-handed person to use his right."

Francis glanced at Dr. Kersh, who was nodding in agreement. Believe me General, contrary to what you and the Space Department naturally assume, the people in the dome do *not* want to come out. Given the choice they would prefer to stay there, just as the gold-fish prefers to stay in its bowl."

Short paused before replying, evidently re-assessing Francis. "You may be right, Doctor," he admitted. "But where does that get us? We've got 15 years, perhaps 25 at the outside."

"There's only one way to do it," Francis told him. "Let the project continue, exactly as before, but with one difference. Prevent them from marrying and having children. In 25 years only the present younger generation will still be alive, and a further five years from then they'll all be dead. A life span in the dome is little more than 45 years. At the age of 30 Abel will probably be an old man. When they start to die off no one will care about them any longer."

There was a full half minute's silence, and then Kersh said: "It's the best suggestion, General. Humane, and yet faithful both to the original project and the Department's instructions. The absence of children would be only a slight deviation from the conditioned pathway. The basic isolation of the group would be strengthened, rather than diminished, also their realization that they themselves will never see planet-fall. If we drop the pedagogical drills and play down the space flight they will soon become a small close community, little different from any other out-group on the road to extinction."

Chalmers cut in: "Another point, General. It would be far easier—and cheaper—to stage, and as the members died off we could progressively close down the ship until finally there might be only a single deck left, perhaps even a few cabins."

Short stood up and paced over to the window, looking out through the clear glass over the frosted panes at the great dome in the hangar.

"It sounds a dreadful prospect," he commented. "Completely insane. As you say, though, it may be the only way out."

Moving quietly among the trucks parked in the darkened hangar, Francis paused for a moment to look back at the lighted windows of the control deck. Two or three of the night staff sat watch over the line of TV screens, half asleep themselves as they observed the sleeping occupants of the dome.

He ducked out of the shadows and ran across to the dome, climbed the stairway to the entrance point thirty feet above. Opening the external lock, he crawled in and closed it behind him, then unfastened the internal entry hatch and pulled himself out of the sleeping cylinder into the silent cabin.

A single dim light glowed over the TV monitor screen as it revealed the three orderlies in the control deck, lounging back in a haze of cigarette smoke six feet from the camera.

Francis turned up the speaker volume, then tapped the mouthpiece sharply with his knuckle.

Tunic unbuttoned, sleep still shadowing his eyes, Colonel Chalmers leaned forward intently into the screen, the orderlies at his shoulder.

"Believe me, Roger, you're proving nothing. General Short and the Space Department won't withdraw their decision now that a special bill of enactment has been passed." When Francis still looked sceptical he added: "If anything, you're more likely to jeopardize them."

"I'll take a chance," Francis said. "Too many guarantees have been broken in the past. Here I'll be able to keep an eye on things." He tried to sound cool and unemotional; the cine-cameras would be recording the scene and it was important to establish the right impression. General Short would be only too keen to avoid a scandal. If he decided Francis was unlikely to sabotage the project he would probably leave him in the dome.

Chalmers pulled up a chair, his face earnest, "Roger, give yourself time to reconsider everything. You may be more of a discordant element than you realize. Remember, nothing would be easier than getting you out—a child could cut his way through the rusty hull with a blunt can-opener."

"Don't try it," Francis warned him quietly. "I'll be moving down to C-Deck, so if you come in after me they'll all know. Believe me, I won't try to interfere with the withdrawal programmes. And I won't arrange any teen-age marriages. But I think the people inside may need me now for more than eight hours a day."

"Francis!" Chalmers shouted. "Once you go down there you'll

never come out! Don't you realize you're entombing yourself in a situation that's totally unreal? You're deliberately withdrawing into a nightmare, sending yourself off on a non-stop journey to *nowhere*!'

Curtly, before he switched the set off for the last time, Francis replied: "Not nowhere, Colonel: Alpha Centauri."

Sitting down thankfully in the narrow bunk in his cabin, Francis rested briefly before setting off for the commissary. All day he had been busy coding the computer punch tapes for Abel, and his eyes ached with the strain of manually stamping each of the thousands of minuscule holes. For eight hours he had sat without a break in the small isolation cell, electrodes clamped to his chest, knees and elbows while Abel measured his cardiac and respiratory rhythms.

The tests bore no relation to the daily programmes Abel now worked out for his father, and Francis was finding it difficult to maintain his patience. Initially Abel had tested his ability to follow a prescribed set of instructions, producing an endless exponential function, then a digital representation of *pi* to a thousand places. Finally Abel had persuaded Francis to co-operate in a more difficult test—the task of producing a totally random sequence. Whenever he unconsciously repeated a simple progression, as he did if he was tired or bored, or a fragment of a larger possible progression, the computer scanning his progress sounded an alarm on the desk and he would have to start afresh. After a few hours the buzzer rasped out every ten seconds, snapping at him like a bad-tempered insect. Francis had finally hobbled over to the door that afternoon, entangling himself in the electrode leads, found to his annoyance that the door was locked (ostensibly to prevent any interruption by a fire patrol), then saw through the small porthole that the computer in the cubicle outside was running unattended.

But when Francis' pounding roused Abel from the far end of the next laboratory he had been almost irritable with the doctor for wanting to discontinue the experiment.

"Damn it, Abel, I've been punching away at these things for three weeks now." He winced as Abel disconnected him, brusquely tearing off the adhesive tape. "Trying to produce random sequences isn't all that easy—my sense of reality is beginning to fog." (Sometimes he wondered if Abel was secretly waiting for this.) "I think I'm entitled to a vote of thanks."

"But we arranged for the trial to last three days. Doctor," Abel pointed out. "It's only later that the valuable results begin to appear. It's the errors you make that are interesting. The whole experiment is pointless now."

"Well, it's probably pointless anyway. Some mathematicians used to maintain that a random sequence was impossible to define."

"But we can assume that it *is* possible," Abel insisted. "I was just giving you some practice before we started on the transfinite numbers."

Francis baulked here. "I'm sorry, Abel. Maybe I'm not so fit as I used to be. Anyway, I've got other duties to attend to."

"But they don't take long, Doctor. There's really nothing for you to do now."

He was right, as Francis was forced to admit. In the year he had spent in the dome Abel had remarkably streamlined the daily routines, provided himself and Francis with an excess of leisure time, particularly as the latter never went to conditioning (Francis was frightened of the sub-sonic voices—Chalmers and Short would be subtle in their attempts to extricate him, perhaps too subtle).

Life aboard the dome had been more of a drain on him than he anticipated. Chained to the routines of the ship, limited in his recreations and with few intellectual pastimes—there were no books aboard the ship—he found it increasingly difficult to sustain his former good humour, was beginning to sink into the deadening lethargy that had overcome most of the other crew members. Matthias Granger had retreated to his cabin, content to leave the programming to Abel, spent his time playing with a damaged clock, while the two Peters rarely strayed from Control. The three wives were almost completely inert, satisfied to knit and murmur to each other. The days passed indistinguishably. Sometimes Francis told himself wryly he nearly *did* believe that they were en route for Alpha Centauri. That would have been a joke for General Short!

At 6.30 when he went to the commissary for his evening meal, he found that he was a quarter of an hour late.

"Your meal time was changed this afternoon," Baker told him, lowering the hatchway. "I got nothing ready for you."

Francis began to remonstrate but the man was adamant. "I can't make a special dip into space-hold just because you didn't look at Routine Orders can I, Doctor?"

On the way out Francis met Abel, tried to persuade him to countermand the order. "You could have warned me, Abel. Damnation, I've been sitting inside your test rig all afternoon."

"But you went back to your cabin, Doctor," Abel pointed out smoothly. "You pass three SRO bulletins on your way from the laboratory. Always look at them at every opportunity, remember. Last-minute changes are liable at any time. I'm afraid you'll have to wait until 10.30 now."

Francis went back to his cabin, suspecting that the sudden change had been Abel's revenge on him for discontinuing the test. He would have to be more conciliatory with Abel, or the young man could make his life a hell, literally starve him to death. Escape from the dome was impossible now—there was a mandatory 20 year sentence on anyone making an unauthorized entry into the space simulator.

After resting for an hour or so, he left his cabin at 8 o'clock to carry out his duty checks of the pressure seals by the B-Deck Meteor Screen. He always went through the pretence of reading them, enjoying the sense of participation in the space flight which the exercise gave him, deliberately accepting the illusion.

The seals were mounted in the control point set at ten yard intervals along the perimeter corridor, a narrow circular passageway around the main corridor. Alone there, the servos clicking and snapping, he felt at peace within the space vehicle. "Earth itself is in orbit around the Sun," he mused as he checked the seals, "and the whole solar system is travelling at 40 miles a second towards the constellation Lyra. The degree of illusion that exists is a complex question."

Something cut through his reverie.

The pressure indicator was flickering slightly. The needle wavered between 0·001 and 0·0015 psi. The pressure inside the dome was fractionally above atmospheric, in order that dust might be expelled through untoward cracks (though the main object of the pressure seals was to get the crew safely into the vacuum-proof emergency cylinders in case the dome was damaged and required internal repairs).

For a moment Francis panicked, wondering whether Short had decided to come in after him—the reading, although meaningless, indicated that a breach had opened in the hull. Then the hand moved back to zero, and footsteps sounded along the radial corridor at right angles past the next bulkhead.

Quickly Francis stepped into its shadow. Before his death old Peters had spent a lot of time mysteriously pottering around the corridor, probably secreting a private food cache behind one of the rusting panels.

He leaned forward as the footsteps crossed the corridor.

Abel?

He watched the young man disappear down a stairway, then made his way into the radial corridor, searching the steel-grey sheeting for a retractable panel. Immediately adjacent to the end wall of the corridor, against the outer skin of the dome, was a small fire control booth.

A tuft of slate-white hairs lay on the floor of the booth.

Asbestos fibres!

Francis stepped into the booth, within a few seconds located a loosened panel that had rusted off its rivets. About ten inches by six, it slid back easily. Beyond it was the outer wall of the dome, a hand's breadth away. Here too was a loose plate, held in position by a crudely fashioned hook.

Francis hesitated, then lifted the hook and drew back the panel.

He was looking straight down into the hangar!

Below, a line of trucks was disgorging supplies on to the concrete floor under a couple of spotlights, a sergeant shouting orders at the labour squad. To the right was the control deck, Chalmers in his office on the evening shift.

The spy-hole was directly below the stairway, and the overhanging metal steps shielded it from the men in the hangar. The asbestos had been carefully frayed so that it concealed the retractable plate. The wire hook was as badly rusted as the rest of the hull, and Francis estimated that the window had been in use for over 30 or 40 years.

So almost certainly old Peters had regularly looked out

through the window, and knew perfectly well that the space ship was a myth. None the less he had stayed aboard, perhaps realizing that the truth would destroy the others, or preferring to be captain of an artificial ship rather than a self-exposed curiosity in the world outside.

Presumably he had passed on the secret. Not to his bleak taciturn son, but to the one other lively mind, one who would keep the secret and make the most of it. For his own reasons he too had decided to stay in the dome, realizing that he would soon be the effective captain, free to pursue his experiments in applied psychology. He might even have failed to grasp that Francis was not a true member of the crew. His confident mastery of the programming, his lapse of interest in Control, his casualness over the safety devices, all meant one thing—

Abel knew!

THE GARDEN OF TIME

TOWARDS evening, when the great shadow of the Palladian villa filled the terrace, Count Axel left his library and walked down the wide rococo steps among the time flowers. A tall, imperious figure in a black velvet jacket, a gold tie-pin glinting below his George V beard, cane held stiffly in a white-gloved hand, he surveyed the exquisite crystal flowers without emotion, listening to the sounds of his wife's harpsichord, as she played a Mozart rondo in the music room, echo and vibrate through the translucent petals.

The garden of the villa extended for some two hundred yards below the terrace, sloping down to a miniature lake spanned by a white bridge, a slender pavilion on the opposite bank. Axel rarely ventured as far as the lake; most of the time flowers grew in a small grove just below the terrace, sheltered by the high wall which encircled the estate. From the terrace he could see over the wall to the plain beyond, a continuous expanse of open ground that rolled in great swells to the horizon, where it rose slightly before finally dipping from sight. The plain surrounded the house on all sides, its drab emptiness emphasizing the seclusion and mellowed magnificence of the villa. Here, in the garden, the air seemed brighter, the sun warmer, while the plain was always dull and remote.

As was his custom before beginning his evening stroll, Count Axel looked out across the plain to the final rise, where the horizon was illuminated like a distant stage by the fading sun. As the Mozart chimed delicately around him, flowing from his wife's graceful hands, he saw that the advance column of an enormous army was moving slowly over the horizon. At first glance, the long ranks seemed to be progressing in orderly lines, but on closer inspection, it was apparent that, like the obscured detail of a Goya landscape, the army was composed of a vast throng of people, men and women, interspersed with a few soldiers in ragged uniforms, pressing forward in a disorganized tide. Some laboured under heavy loads suspended from crude yokes around their necks, others struggled with cumbersome wooden carts, their hands wrenching at the wheel spokes, a few trudged on alone, but all moved on at the same pace, bowed backs illuminated in the fleeting sun.

The advancing throng was almost too far away to be visible, but even as Axel watched, his expression aloof yet observant, it came perceptibly nearer, the vanguard of an immense rabble appearing from below the horizon. At last, as the daylight began to fade, the front edge of the throng reached the crest of the first swell below the horizon, and Axel turned from the terrace and walked down among the time flowers.

The flowers grew to a height of about six feet, their slender stems, like rods of glass, bearing a dozen leaves, the once transparent fronds frosted by the fossilized veins. At the peak of each stem was the time flower, the size of a goblet, the opaque outer petals enclosing the crystal heart. Their diamond brilliance contained a thousand faces, the crystal seeming to drain the air of its light and motion. As the flowers swayed slightly in the evening air, they glowed like flame-tipped spears.

Many of the stems no longer bore flowers, and Axel examined them all carefully, a note of hope now and then crossing his eyes as he searched for any further buds. Finally he selected a large flower on the stem nearest the wall, removed his gloves and with his strong fingers snapped it off.

As he carried the flower back on to the terrace, it began to sparkle and deliquesce, the light trapped within the core at last released. Gradually the crystal dissolved, only the outer petals remaining intact, and the air around Axel became bright and vivid, charged with slanting rays that flared away into the waning sunlight. Strange shifts momentarily transformed the evening, subtly altering its dimensions of time and space. The darkened portico of the house, its patina of age stripped away, loomed with a curious spectral whiteness as if suddenly remembered in a dream.

Raising his head, Axel peered over the wall again. Only the farthest rim of the horizon was lit by the sun, and the great throng, which before had stretched almost a quarter of the way across the plain, had now receded to the horizon, the entire concourse abruptly flung back in a reversal of time, and appeared to be stationary.

The flower in Axel's hand had shrunk to the size of a glass thimble, the petals contracting around the vanishing core. A faint sparkle flickered from the centre and extinguished itself, and Axel felt the flower melt like an ice-cold bead of dew in his hand.

Dusk closed across the house, sweeping its long shadows over the plain, the horizon merging into the sky. The harpsichord was silent, and the time flowers, no longer reflecting its music, stood motionlessly, like an embalmed forest.

For a few minutes Axel looked down at them, counting the flowers which remained, then greeted his wife as she crossed the terrace, her brocade evening dress rustling over the ornamental tiles.

"What a beautiful evening, Axel." She spoke feelingly, as if she were thanking her husband personally for the great ornate shadow across the lawn and the dark brilliant air. Her face was serene and intelligent, her hair, swept back behind her head into a jewelled clasp, touched with silver. She wore her dress low across her breast, revealing a long slender neck and high chin. Axel surveyed her with fond pride. He gave her his arm and together they walked down the steps into the garden.

"One of the longest evenings this summer," Axel confirmed,

adding: "I picked a perfect flower, my dear, a jewel. With luck it should last us for several days." A frown touched his brow, and he glanced involuntarily at the wall. "Each time now they seem to come nearer."

His wife smiled at him encouragingly and held his arm more tightly.

Both of them knew that the time garden was dying.

Three evenings later, as he had estimated (though sooner than he secretly hoped), Count Axel plucked another flower from the time garden.

When he first looked over the wall the approaching rabble filled the distant half of the plain, stretching across the horizon in an unbroken mass. He thought he could hear the low, fragmentary sounds of voices carried across the empty air, a sullen murmur punctuated by cries and shouts, but quickly told himself that he had imagined them. Luckily, his wife was at the harpsichord, and the rich contrapuntal patterns of a Bach fugue cascaded lightly across the terrace, masking any other noises.

Between the house and the horizon the plain was divided into four huge swells, the crest of each one clearly visible in the slanting light. Axel had promised himself that he would never count them, but the number was too small to remain unobserved, particularly when it so obviously marked the progress of the advancing army. By now the forward line had passed the first crest and was well on its way to the second; the main bulk of the throng pressed behind it, hiding the crest and the even vaster concourse spreading from the horizon. Looking to left and right of the central body, Axel could see the apparently limitless extent of the army. What had seemed at first to be the central mass was no more than a minor advance guard, one of many similar arms reaching across the plain. The true centre had not yet emerged, but from the rate of extension Axel estimated that when it finally reached the plain it would completely cover every foot of ground.

Axel searched for any large vehicles or machines, but all was amorphous and unco-ordinated as ever. There were no banners or flags, no mascots or pike-bearers. Heads bowed, the multitude pressed on, unaware of the sky.

Suddenly, just before Axel turned away, the forward edge of the throng appeared on top of the second crest, and swarmed down across the plain. What astounded Axel was the incredible distance it had covered while out of sight. The figures were now twice the size, each one clearly within sight.

Quickly, Axel stepped from the terrace, selected a time flower from the garden and tore it from the stem. As it released its compacted light, he returned to the terrace. When the flower had shrunk to a frozen pearl in his palm he looked out at the plain, with relief saw that the army had retreated to the horizon again.

Then he realized that the horizon was much nearer than previously, and that what he assumed to be the horizon was the first crest.

When he joined the Countess on their evening walk he told her nothing of this, but she could see behind his casual unconcern and did what she could to dispel his worry.

Walking down the steps, she pointed to the time garden. "What a wonderful display, Axel. There are so many flowers still."

Axel nodded, smiling to himself at his wife's attempt to reassure him. Her use of "still" had revealed her own unconscious anticipation of the end. In fact a mere dozen flowers remained of the many hundred that had grown in the garden, and several of these were little more than buds—only three or four were fully grown. As they walked down to the lake, the Countess's dress rustling across the cool turf, he tried to decide whether to pick the larger flowers first or leave them to the end. Strictly, it would be better to give the smaller flowers additional time to grow and mature, and this advantage would be lost if he retained the larger flowers to the end, as he wished to do, for the final repulse. However, he realized that it mattered little either way; the garden would soon die and the smaller flowers required far longer than he could give them to accumulate their compressed cores of time. During his entire lifetime he had failed to notice a single evidence of growth among the flowers. The larger blooms had always been mature, and none of the buds had shown the slightest development.

Crossing the lake, he and his wife looked down at their reflections in the still black water. Shielded by the pavilion on one side and the high garden wall on the other, the villa in the distance, Axel felt composed and secure, the plain with its

encroaching multitude a nightmare from which he had safely
awakened. He put one arm around his wife's smooth waist and
pressed her affectionately to his shoulder, realizing that he had
not embraced her for several years, though their lives together
had been timeless and he could remember as if yesterday when
he first brought her to live in the villa.

"Axel," his wife asked with sudden seriousness, "before the
garden dies . . . may I pick the last flower?"

Understanding her request, he nodded slowly.

One by one over the succeeding evenings, he picked the remaining
flowers, leaving a single small bud which grew just below the
terrace for his wife. He took the flowers at random, refusing to
count or ration them, plucking two or three of the smaller buds
at the same time when necessary. The approaching horde had now
reached the second and third crests, a vast concourse of labouring
humanity that blotted out the horizon. From the terrace Axel
could see clearly the shuffling, straining ranks moving down
into the hollow towards the final crest, and occasionally the sounds
of their voices carried across to him, interspersed with cries of
anger and the cracking of whips. The wooden carts lurched from
side to side on tilting wheels, their drivers struggling to control
them. As far as Axel could tell, not a single member of the throng
was aware of its overall direction. Rather, each one blindly
moved forward across the ground directly below the heels of the
person in front of him, and the only unity was that of the
cumulative compass. Pointlessly, Axel hoped that the true centre,
far below the horizon, might be moving in a different direction,
and that gradually the multitude would alter course, swing away
from the villa and recede from the plain like a turning tide.

On the last evening but one, as he plucked the time flower, the
forward edge of the rabble had reached the third crest, and was
swarming past it. While he waited for the Countess, Axel looked
at the two flowers left, both small buds which would carry them
back through only a few minutes of the next evening. The glass
stems of the dead flowers reared up stiffly into the air, but the
whole garden had lost its bloom.

Axel passed the next morning quietly in his library, sealing the
rarer of his manuscripts into the glass-topped cases between the

galleries. He walked slowly down the portrait corridor, polishing each of the pictures carefully, then tidied his desk and locked the door behind him. During the afternoon he busied himself in the drawing-rooms, unobtrusively assisting his wife as she cleaned their ornaments and straightened the vases and busts.

By evening, as the sun fell behind the house, they were both tired and dusty, and neither had spoken to the other all day. When his wife moved towards the music-room, Axel called her back.

"Tonight we'll pick the flowers together, my dear," he said to her evenly. "One for each of us."

He peered only briefly over the wall. They could hear, less than half a mile away, the great dull roar of the ragged army, the ring of iron and lash, pressing on towards the house.

Quickly, Axel plucked his flower, a bud no bigger than a sapphire. As it flickered softly, the tumult outside momentarily receded, then began to gather again.

Shutting his ears to the clamour, Axel looked around at the villa, counting the six columns in the portico, then gazed out across the lawn at the silver disc of the lake, its bowl reflecting the last evening light, and at the shadows moving between the tall trees, lengthening across the crisp turf. He lingered over the bridge where he and his wife had stood arm in arm for so many summers—

"*Axel!*"

The tumult outside roared into the air, a thousand voices bellowed only twenty or thirty yards away. A stone flew over the wall and landed among the time flowers, snapping several of the brittle stems. The Countess ran towards him as a further barrage rattled along the wall. Then a heavy tile whirled through the air over their heads and crashed into one of the conservatory windows.

"Axel!" He put his arms around her, straightening his silk cravat when her shoulder brushed it between his lapels.

"Quickly, my dear, the last flower!" He led her down the steps and through the garden. Taking the stem between her jewelled fingers, she snapped it cleanly, then cradled it within her palms.

For a moment the tumult lessened slightly and Axel collected himself. In the vivid light sparkling from the flower he saw his wife's white, frightened eyes. "Hold it as long as you can, my dear, until the last grain dies."

Together they stood on the terrace, the Countess clasping the brilliant dying jewel, the air closing in upon them as the voices outside mounted again. The mob was battering at the heavy iron gates, and the whole villa shook with the impact.

While the final glimmer of light sped away, the Countess raised her palms to the air, as if releasing an invisible bird, then in a final access of courage put her hands in her husband's, her smile as radiant as the vanished flower.

"Oh, Axel!" she cried.

Like a sword, the darkness swooped down across them.

Heaving and swearing, the outer edges of the mob reached the knee-high remains of the wall enclosing the ruined estate, hauled their carts over it and along the dry ruts of what once had been an ornate drive. The ruin, formerly a spacious villa, barely interrupted the ceaseless tide of humanity. The lake was empty, fallen trees rotting at its bottom, an old bridge rusting into it. Weeds flourished among the long grass in the lawn, over-running the ornamental pathways and carved stone screens.

Much of the terrace had crumbled, and the main section of the mob cut straight across the lawn, by-passing the gutted villa, but one or two of the more curious climbed up and searched among the shell. The doors had rotted from their hinges and the floors had fallen through. In the music-room an ancient harpsichord had been chopped into firewood, but a few keys still lay among the dust. All the books had been toppled from the shelves in the library, the canvases had been slashed, and gilt frames littered the floor.

As the main body of the mob reached the house, it began to cross the wall at all points along its length. Jostled together, the people stumbled into the dry lake, swarmed over the terrace and pressed through the house towards the open doors on the north side.

One area alone withstood the endless wave. Just below the terrace, between the wrecked balcony and the wall, was a dense, six-foot-high growth of heavy thorn-bushes. The barbed foliage formed an impenetrable mass, and the people passing stepped around it carefully, noticing the belladonna entwined among the branches. Most of them were too busy finding their footing among the upturned flagstones to look up into the centre of the thorn-bushes, where two stone statues stood side by side, gazing out over the grounds from their protected vantage point. The larger of the figures was the effigy of a bearded man in a high-collared jacket, a cane under one arm. Beside him was a woman in an elaborate full-skirted dress, her slim, serene face unmarked by the wind and rain. In her left hand she lightly clasped a single rose, the delicately formed petals so thin as to be almost transparent.

As the sun died away behind the house a single ray of light glanced through a shattered cornice and struck the rose, reflected off the whorl of petals on to the statues, lighting up the grey stone so that for a fleeting moment it was indistinguishable from the long-vanished flesh of the statues' originals.

THE CAGE OF SAND

AT sunset, when the vermilion glow reflected from the dunes along the horizon fitfully illuminated the white faces of the abandoned hotels, Bridgman stepped on to his balcony and looked out over the long stretches of cooling sand as the tides of purple shadow seeped across them. Slowly, extending their slender fingers through the shallow saddles and depressions, the shadows massed together like gigantic combs, a few phos-phorescing spurs of obsidian isolated for a moment between the tines, and then finally coalesced and flooded in a solid wave across the half-submerged hotels. Behind the silent façades, in the tilting sand-filled streets which had once glittered with cocktail bars and restaurants, it was already night. Haloes of moonlight beaded the lamp-standards with silver dew, and draped the shuttered windows and slipping cornices like a frost of frozen gas.

As Bridgman watched, his lean bronzed arms propped against the rusting rail, the last whorls of light sank away into the cerise funnel withdrawing below the horizon, and the first wind stirred across the dead Martian sand. Here and there miniature cyclones whirled about a sand-spur, drawing off swirling feathers of moon-washed spray, and a nimbus of white dust swept across the dunes and settled in the dips and hollows. Gradually the drifts accumulated, edging towards the former shoreline below the hotels. Already the first four floors had been inundated, and the sand now reached up to within two feet of Bridgman's balcony. After the next sandstorm he would be forced yet again to move to the floor above.

"Bridgman!"

The voice cleft the darkness like a spear. Fifty yards to his right, at the edge of the derelict sand-break he had once attempted to build below the hotel, a square stocky figure wearing a pair of frayed cotton shorts waved up at him. The moonlight etched the broad sinewy muscles of his chest, the powerful bowed legs sinking almost to their calves in the soft Martian sand. He was about forty-five years old, his thinning hair close-cropped so that he seemed almost bald. In his right hand he carried a large canvas hold-all.

Bridgman smiled to himself. Standing there patiently in the moonlight below the derelict hotel, Travis reminded him of some long-delayed tourist arriving at a ghost resort years after its extinction.

"Bridgman, are you coming?" When the latter still leaned on his balcony rail, Travis added: "The next conjunction is tomorrow."

Bridgman shook his head, a rictus of annoyance twisting his mouth. He hated the bi-monthly conjunctions, when all seven of the derelict satellite capsules still orbiting the Earth crossed the sky together. Invariably on these nights he remained in his room, playing over the old memo-tapes he had salvaged from the submerged chalets and motels further along the beach (the hysterical "This is Mamie Goldberg, 62955 Cocoa Boulevard, I really wanna protest against this crazy evacuation . . ." or resigned "Sam Snade here, the Pontiac convertible in the back garage belongs to anyone who can dig it out"). Travis and Louise Woodward always came to the hotel on the conjunction nights—it was the highest building in the resort, with an unrestricted view from horizon to horizon—and would follow the seven converging stars as they pursued their endless courses around the globe. Both would be oblivious of everything else, which the wardens knew only too well, and they reserved their most careful searches of the sand-sea for these bi-monthly occasions. Invariably Bridgman found himself forced to act as look-out for the other two.

"I was out last night," he called down to Travis. "Keep away from the north-east perimeter fence by the Cape. They'll be busy repairing the track."

Most nights Bridgman divided his time between excavating the buried motels for caches of supplies (the former inhabitants of the resort area had assumed the government would soon rescind its evacuation order) and disconnecting the sections of metal roadway laid across the desert for the wardens' jeeps. Each of the squares of wire mesh was about five yards wide and weighed over three hundred pounds. After he had snapped the lines of rivets, dragged the sections away and buried them among the dunes he would be exhausted, and spend most of the next day nursing his strained hands and shoulders. Some sections of the track were now permanently anchored with heavy steel stakes, and he knew that sooner or later they would be unable to delay the wardens by sabotaging the roadway.

Travis hesitated, and with a noncommittal shrug disappeared among the dunes, the heavy tool-bag swinging easily from one powerful arm. Despite the meagre diet which sustained him, his energy and determination seemed undiminished—in a single night Bridgman had watched him dismantle twenty sections of track and then loop together the adjacent limbs of a cross-road, sending an entire convoy of six vehicles off into the waste-lands to the south.

Bridgman turned from the balcony, then stopped when a faint tang of brine touched the cool air. Ten miles away, hidden by the lines of dunes, was the sea, the long green rollers of the middle Atlantic breaking against the red Martian strand. When he had first come to the beach five years earlier there had never been the faintest scent of brine across the intervening miles of sand. Slowly, however, the Atlantic was driving the shore back to its former margins. The tireless shoulder of the Gulf Stream drummed against the soft Martian dust and piled the dunes into grotesque rococo reefs which the wind carried away into the sand-sea. Gradually the ocean was returning, reclaiming its great smooth basin, sifting out the black quartz and Martian obsidian which would never be wind-borne and drawing these down into its deeps. More and more often the stain of brine would hang on the evening air, reminding Bridgman why he had first come to the beach and removing any inclination to leave.

Three years earlier he had attempted to measure the rate of approach, by driving a series of stakes into the sand at the water's edge, but the shifting contours of the dunes carried away the coloured poles. Later, using the promontory at Cape Canaveral, where the old launching gantries and landing ramps reared up into the sky like derelict pieces of giant sculpture, he had calculated by triangulation that the advance was little more than thirty yards per year. At this rate—without wanting to, he had automatically made the calculation—it would be well over five hundred years before the Atlantic reached its former littoral at Cocoa Beach. Though discouragingly slow, the movement was nonetheless in a forward direction, and Bridgman was happy to remain in his hotel ten miles away across the dunes, conceding towards its time of arrival the few years he had at his disposal.

Later, shortly after Louise Woodward's arrival, he had thought of dismantling one of the motel cabins and building himself a small chalet by the water's edge. But the shoreline had been too dismal and forbidding. The great red dunes rolled on for miles, cutting off half the sky, dissolving slowly under the impact of the slate-green water. There was no formal tide-line, but only a steep shelf littered with nodes of quartz and rusting fragments of Mars rockets brought back with the ballast. He spent a few days in a cave below a towering sand-reef, watching the long galleries of compacted red dust crumble and dissolve as the cold Atlantic stream sluiced through them, collapsing like the decorated colonnades of a baroque cathedral. In the summer the heat reverberated from the hot sand as from the slag of some molten sun, burning the rubber soles from his boots, and the light from the scattered flints of washed quartz flickered with diamond hardness. Bridgman had returned to the hotel grateful for his room overlooking the silent dunes.

Leaving the balcony, the sweet smell of brine still in his nostrils, he went over to the desk. A small cone of shielded light shone down over the tape-recorder and rack of spools. The rumble of the wardens' unsilenced engines always gave him at least five minutes' warning of their arrival, and it would have been safe to install another lamp in the room—there were no roadways between the hotel and the sea, and from a distance any light reflected on to the balcony was indistinguishable from the corona of glimmering phosphors which hung over the sand like myriads of fire-flies. However, Bridgman preferred to sit in the darkened suite, enclosed by the circle of books on the makeshift shelves, the shadow-filled air playing over his shoulders through the long night as he toyed with the memo-tapes, fragments of a vanished and unregretted past. By day he always drew the blinds, immolating himself in a world of perpetual twilight.

Bridgman had easily adapted himself to his self-isolation, soon evolved a system of daily routines that gave him the maximum of time to spend on his private reveries. Pinned to the walls around him were a series of huge white-prints and architectural drawings, depicting various elevations of a fantastic Martian city he had once designed, its glass spires and curtain walls rising like heliotropic jewels from the vermilion desert. In fact, the whole city was a vast piece of jewellery, each elevation brilliantly visualized but as symmetrical, and ultimately as lifeless, as a crown. Bridgman continually retouched the drawings, inserting more and more details, so that they almost seemed to be photographs of an original.

Most of the hotels in the town—one of a dozen similar resorts buried by the sand which had once formed an unbroken strip of motels, chalets and five-star hotels thirty miles to the south of Cape Canaveral—were well stocked with supplies of canned food abandoned when the area was evacuated and wired off. There were ample reservoirs and cisterns filled with water, apart from a thousand intact cocktail bars six feet below the surface of the sand. Travis had excavated a dozen of these in search of his favourite vintage bourbon. Walking out across the desert behind the town one would suddenly find a short flight of steps cut into the annealed sand and crawl below an occluded sign announcing "The Satellite Bar" or "The Orbit Room" into the inner sanctum, where the jutting deck of a chromium bar had been cleared as far as the diamond-paned mirror freighted with its rows of bottles and figurines. Bridgman would have been glad to see them left undisturbed.

The whole trash of amusement arcades and cheap bars on the outskirts of the beach resorts were a depressing commentary on the original space-flights, reducing them to the level of monster side-shows at a carnival.

Outside his room, steps sounded along the corridor, then slowly climbed the stairway, pausing for a few seconds at every landing. Bridgman lowered the memo-tape in his hand, listening to the familiar tired footsteps. This was Louise Woodward, making her invariable evening ascent to the roof ten storeys above. Bridgman glanced at the time-table pinned to the wall. Only two of the satellites would be visible, between 12.25 and 12.35 a.m., at an elevation of 62 degrees in the south-west, passing through Cetus and Eridanus, neither of them containing her husband. Although the siting was two hours away, she was already taking up her position, and would remain there until dawn.

Bridgman listened wanly to the feet recede slowly up the stairwell. All through the night the slim, pale-faced woman would sit out under the moon-lit sky, as the soft Martian sand her husband had given his life to reach sifted around her in the dark wind, stroking her faded hair like some mourning mariner's wife waiting for the sea to surrender her husband's body. Travis usually joined her later, and the two of them sat side by side against the elevator house, the frosted letters of the hotel's neon sign strewn around their feet like the fragments of a dismembered zodiac, then at dawn made their way down into the shadow-filled streets to their eyries in the nearby hotels.

Initially Bridgman often joined their nocturnal vigil, but after a few nights he began to feel something repellent, if not actually ghoulish, about their mindless contemplation of the stars. This was not so much because of the macabre spectacle of the dead astronauts orbiting the planet in their capsules, but because of the curious sense of unspoken communion between Travis and Louise Woodward, almost as if they were celebrating a private rite to which Bridgman could never be initiated. Whatever their original motives, Bridgman sometimes suspected that these had been overlaid by other, more personal ones.

Ostensibly, Louise Woodward was watching her husband's satellite in order to keep alive his memory, but Bridgman guessed that the memories she unconsciously wished to perpetuate were those of herself twenty years earlier, when her husband had been a celebrity and she herself courted by magazine columnists and TV reporters. For fifteen years after his death—Woodward had been killed testing a new lightweight launching platform—she had lived a nomadic existence, driving restlessly in her cheap car from motel to motel across the continent, following her husband's star as it disappeared into the eastern night, and had at last made her home at Cocoa Beach in sight of the rusting gantries across the bay.

Travis's real motives were probably more complex. To Bridgman, after they had known each other for a couple of years, he had confided that he felt himself bound by a debt of honour to maintain a watch over the dead astronauts for the example of courage and sacrifice they had set him as a child (although most of them had been piloting their wrecked capsules for fifty years before Travis's birth), and that now they were virtually forgotten he must singlehandedly keep alive the fading flame of their memory. Bridgman was convinced of his sincerity.

Yet later, going through a pile of old news magazines in the trunk of a car he excavated from a motel port, he came across a picture of Travis wearing an aluminium pressure suit and learned something more of his story. Apparently Travis had at one time himself been an astronaut—or rather, a would-be astronaut. A test pilot for one of the civilian agencies setting up orbital relay stations, his nerve had failed him a few seconds before the last "hold" of his count-down, a moment of pure unexpected funk that cost the company some five million dollars.

Obviously it was his inability to come to terms with this failure of character, unfortunately discovered lying flat on his back on a contour couch two hundred feet above the launching pad, which had brought Travis to Canaveral, the abandoned Mecca of the first heroes of astronautics.

Tactfully Bridgman had tried to explain that no one would blame him for this failure of nerve—less his responsibility than that of the selectors who had picked him for the flight, or at least the result of an unhappy concatenation of ambiguously-worded multiple-choice questions (crosses in the wrong boxes, some heavier to bear and harder to open than others! Bridgman had joked sardonically to himself). But Travis seemed to have reached his own decision about himself. Night after night, he watched the brilliant funerary convoy weave its gilded pathway towards the dawn sun, salving his own failure by identifying it with the greater, but blameless, failure of the seven astronauts. Travis still wore his hair in the regulation "mohican" cut of the space-man, still kept himself in perfect physical trim by the vigorous routines he had practised before his abortive flight. Sustained by the personal myth he had created, he was now more or less unreachable.

"Dear Harry, I've taken the car and deposit box. Sorry it should end like—"

Irritably, Bridgman switched off the memo-tape and its recapitulation of some thirty-year-old private triviality. For some reason he seemed unable to accept Travis and Louise Woodward for what they were. He disliked this failure of compassion, a nagging compulsion to expose other people's motives and strip away the insulating sheaths around their naked nerve strings, particularly as his own motives for being at Cape Canaveral were so suspect. Why was *he* there, what failure was *he* trying to expiate? And why choose Cocoa Beach as his penitential shore? For three years he had asked himself these questions so often that they had ceased to have any meaning, like a fossilized catechism or the blunted self-recrimination of a paranoiac.

He had resigned his job as the chief architect of a big space development company after the large government contract on which the firm depended, for the design of the first Martian city-settlement, was awarded to a rival consortium. Secretly, however, he realized that his resignation had marked his unconscious acceptance that despite his great imaginative gifts he was unequal to the specialized and more prosaic tasks of designing the settlement. On the drawing-board, as elsewhere, he would always remain earth-bound.

His dreams of building a new Gothic architecture of launching ports and control gantries, of being the Frank Lloyd Wright and Le Corbusier of the first city to be raised outside Earth, faded for ever, but leaving him unable to accept the alternative of turning out endless plans for low-cost hospitals in Ecuador and housing estates in Tokyo. For a year he had drifted aimlessly, but a few colour photographs of the vermilion sunsets at Cocoa Beach and a news story about the recluses living on in the submerged motels had provided a powerful compass.

He dropped the memo-tape into a drawer, making an effort to accept Louise Woodward and Travis on their own terms, a wife keeping watch over her dead husband and an old astronaut maintaining a solitary vigil over the memories of his lost comrades-in-arms.

The wind gusted against the balcony window, and a light spray of sand rained across the floor. At night dust-storms churned along the beach. Thermal pools isolated by the cooling desert would suddenly accrete like beads of quicksilver and erupt across the fluffy sand in miniature tornadoes.

Only fifty yards away, the dying cough of a heavy diesel cut through the shadows. Quickly Bridgman turned off the small desk light, grateful for his meanness over the battery packs plugged into the circuit, then stepped to the window.

At the leftward edge of the sand-break, half hidden in the long shadows cast by the hotel, was a large tracked vehicle with a low camouflaged hull. A narrow observation bridge had been built over the bumpers directly in front of the squat snout of the engine housing, and two of the beach wardens were craning up through the plexiglass windows at the balconies of the hotel, shifting their binoculars from room to room. Behind them, under the glass dome of the extended driving cabin, were three more wardens, controlling an outboard spotlight. In the centre of the bowl a thin mote of light pulsed with the rhythm of the engine, ready to throw its powerful beam into any of the open rooms.

Bridgman hid back behind the shutters as the binoculars focused upon the adjacent balcony, moved to his own, hesitated, and passed to the next. Exasperated by the sabotaging of the roadways, the wardens had evidently decided on a new type of vehicle. With their four broad tracks, the huge squat sand-cars would be free of the mesh roadways and able to rove at will through the dunes and sand-hills.

Bridgman watched the vehicle reverse slowly, its engine barely varying its deep base growl, then move off along the line of hotels, almost indistinguishable in profile among the shifting dunes and hillocks. A hundred yards away, at the first intersection, it turned towards the main boulevard, wisps of dust streaming from the metal cleats like thin spumes of steam. The men in the observation bridge were still watching the hotel. Bridgman was certain that they had seen a reflected glimmer of light, or perhaps some movement of Louise Woodward's on the roof. However reluctant to leave the car and be contaminated by the poisonous dust, the wardens would not hesitate if the capture of one of the beachcombers warranted it.

Racing up the staircase, Bridgman made his way to the roof, crouching below the windows that overlooked the boulevard. Like a huge crab, the sand-car had parked under the jutting overhang of the big department store opposite. Once fifty feet from the ground, the concrete lip was now separated from it by little more than six or seven feet, and the sand-car was hidden in the shadows below it, engine silent. A single movement in a window, or the unexpected return of Travis, and the wardens would spring from the hatchways, their long-handled nets and lassos pinioning them around the necks and ankles. Bridgman remembered one beachcomber he had seen flushed from his motel hide-out and carried off like a huge twitching spider at the centre of a black rubber web, the wardens with their averted faces and masked mouths like devils in an abstract ballet.

Reaching the roof, Bridgman stepped out into the opaque white moonlight. Louise Woodward was leaning on the balcony, looking out towards the distant, unseen sea. At the faint sound of the door creaking she turned and began to walk listlessly around the roof, her pale face floating like a nimbus. She wore a freshly ironed print dress she had found in a rusty spin drier in one of the launderettes, and her streaked blonde hair floated out lightly behind her on the wind.

"Louise!"

Involuntarily she started, tripping over a fragment of the neon sign, then moved backwards towards the balcony overlooking the boulevard.

"Mrs. Woodward!" Bridgman held her by the elbow, raised a hand to her mouth before she could cry out. "The wardens are down below. They're watching the hotel. We must find Travis before he returns."

Louise hesitated, apparently recognizing Bridgman only by an effort, and her eyes turned up to the black marble sky. Bridgman looked at his watch; it was almost 12.25. He searched the stars in the south-west.

Louise murmured: "They're nearly here now, I must see them. Where is Travis, he should be here?"

Bridgman pulled at her arm. "Perhaps he saw the sand-car. Mrs. Woodward, we should leave."

Suddenly she pointed up at the sky, then wrenched away from him and ran to the rail. "There they are!"

Fretting, Bridgman waited until she had filled her eyes with the two companion points of light speeding from the western horizon. These were Merril and Pokrovski—like every schoolboy he knew the sequences perfectly, a second system of constellations with a more complex but far more tangible periodicity and precession—the Castor and Pollux of the orbiting zodiac, whose appearance always heralded a full conjunction the following night.

Louise Woodward gazed up at them from the rail, the rising wind lifting her hair off her shoulders and entraining it horizontally behind her head. Around her feet the red Martian dust swirled and rustled, silting over the fragments of the old neon sign, a brilliant pink spume streaming from her long fingers as they moved along the balcony ledge. When the satellites finally disappeared among the stars along the horizon, she leaned forwards, her face raised to the milk-blue moon as if to delay their departure, then turned back to Bridgman, a bright smile on her face.

His earlier suspicions vanishing, Bridgman smiled back at her encouragingly. "Roger will be here tomorrow night, Louise. We must be careful the wardens don't catch us before we see him."

He felt a sudden admiration for her, at the stoical way she had sustained herself during her long vigil. Perhaps she thought of Woodward as still alive, and in some way was patiently waiting for him to return? He remembered her saying once: "Roger was only a boy when he took off, you know, I feel more like his mother now," as if frightened how Woodward would react to her dry skin and fading hair, fearing that he might even have forgotten her. No doubt the death she visualized for him was of a different order from the mortal kind.

Hand in hand, they tiptoed carefully down the flaking steps, jumped down from a terrace window into the soft sand below the wind-break. Bridgman sank to his knees in the fine silver moon-dust, then waded up to the firmer ground, pulling Louise after him. They climbed through a breach in the tilting palisades, then ran away from the line of dead hotels looming like skulls in the empty light.

"Paul, wait!" Her head still raised to the sky, Louise Woodward fell to her knees in a hollow between two dunes, with a laugh stumbled after Bridgman as he raced through the dips and saddles. The wind was now whipping the sand off the higher crests, flurries of dust spurting like excited wavelets. A hundred yards away, the town was a fading film set, projected by the camera obscura of the sinking moon. They were standing where the long Atlantic seas had once been ten fathoms deep, and Bridgman could scent again the tang of brine among the flickering white-caps of dust, phosphorescing like shoals of animalcula. He waited for any sign of Travis.

"Louise, we'll have to go back to the town. The sand-storms are blowing up, we'll never see Travis here."

They moved back through the dunes, then worked their way among the narrow alleyways between the hotels to the northern gateway to the town. Bridgman found a vantage point in a small apartment block, and they lay down looking out below a window lintel into the sloping street, the warm sand forming a pleasant cushion. At the intersections the dust blew across the roadway in white clouds, obscuring the warden's beach-car parked a hundred yards down the boulevard.

Half an hour later an engine surged, and Bridgman began to pile sand into the interval in front of them. "They're going. Thank God!"

Louise Woodward held his arm. "Look!"

Fifty feet away, his white vinyl suit half hidden in the dust clouds, one of the wardens was advancing slowly towards them, his lasso twirling lightly in his hand. A few feet behind was a second warden, craning up at the windows of the apartment block with his binoculars.

Bridgman and Louise crawled back below the ceiling, then dug their way under a transom into the kitchen at the rear. A window opened on to a sand-filled yard, and they darted away through the lifting dust that whirled between the buildings.

Suddenly, around a corner, they saw the line of wardens moving down a side-street, the sand-car edging along behind them. Before Bridgman could steady himself a spasm of pain seized his right calf, contorting the gastrocnemius muscle, and he fell to one knee. Louise Woodward pulled him back against the wall, then pointed at a squat, bow-legged figure trudging towards them along the curving road into town.

"Travis—"

The tool-bag swung from his right hand, and his feet rang faintly on the wire-mesh roadway. Head down, he seemed unaware of the wardens hidden by a bend in the road.

"Come on!" Disregarding the negligible margin of safety,

Bridgman clambered to his feet and impetuously ran out into the centre of the street. Louise tried to stop him, and they had covered only ten yards before the wardens saw them. There was a warning shout, and the spotlight flung its giant cone down the street. The sand-car surged forward, like a massive dust-covered bull, its tracks clawing at the sand.

"Travis!" As Bridgman reached the bend, Louise Woodward ten yards behind, Travis looked up from his reverie, then flung the tool-bag over one shoulder and raced ahead of them towards the clutter of motel roofs protruding from the other side of the street. Lagging behind the others, Bridgman again felt the cramp attack his leg, broke off into a painful shuffle. When Travis came back for him Bridgman tried to wave him away, but Travis pinioned his elbow and propelled him forward like an attendant straight-arming a patient.

The dust swirling around them, they disappeared through the fading streets and out into the desert, the shouts of the beach-wardens lost in the roar and clamour of the baying engine. Around them, like the strange metallic flora of some extra-terrestrial garden, the old neon signs jutted from the red Martian sand—"Satellite Motel", "Planet Bar", "Mercury Motel". Hiding behind them, they reached the scrub-covered dunes on the edge of the town, then picked up one of the trails that led away among the sand-reefs. There, in the deep grottoes of compacted sand which hung like inverted palaces, they waited until the storm subsided. Shortly before dawn the wardens abandoned their search, unable to bring the heavy sand-car on to the disintegrating reef.

Contemptuous of the wardens, Travis lit a small fire with his cigarette lighter, burning splinters of driftwood that had gathered in the gullies. Bridgman crouched beside it, warming his hands.

"This is the first time they've been prepared to leave the sand-car," he remarked to Travis. "It means they're under orders to catch us."

Travis shrugged. "Maybe. They're extending the fence along the beach. They probably intend to seal us in for ever."

"What?" Bridgman stood up with a sudden feeling of uneasiness. "Why should they? Are you sure? I mean, what would be the point?"

Travis looked up at him, a flicker of dry amusement on his bleached face. Wisps of smoke wreathed his head, curled up past the serpentine columns of the grotto to the winding interval of sky a hundred feet above. "Bridgman, forgive me saying so, but if you want to leave here, you should leave now. In a month's time you won't be able to."

Bridgman ignored this, and searched the cleft of dark sky overhead, which framed the constellation Scorpio, as if hoping to see a reflection of the distant sea. "They must be crazy. How much of this fence did you see?"

"About eight hundred yards. It won't take them long to complete. The sections are prefabricated, about forty feet high." He smiled ironically at Bridgman's discomfort. "Relax, Bridgman. If you do want to get out, you'll always be able to tunnel underneath it."

"I don't want to get out," Bridgman said coldly. "Damn them, Travis, they're turning the place into a zoo. You know it won't be the same with a fence all the way around it."

"A corner of Earth that is for ever Mars." Under the high forehead, Travis's eyes were sharp and watchful. "I see their point. There hasn't been a fatal casualty now"—he glanced at Louise Woodward, who was strolling about in the colonnades —"for nearly twenty years, and passenger rockets are supposed to be as safe as commuters' trains. They're quietly sealing off the past, Louise and I and you with it. I suppose it's pretty considerate of them not to burn the place down with flame-throwers. The virus would be a sufficient excuse. After all, we three are probably the only reservoirs left on the planet." He picked up a handful of red dust and examined the fine crystals with a sombre eye. "Well, Bridgman, what are you going to do?"

His thoughts discharging themselves through his mind like frantic signal flares, Bridgman walked away without answering.

Behind them, Louise Woodward wandered among the deep galleries of the grotto, crooning to herself in a low voice to the sighing rhythms of the whirling sand.

The next morning they returned to the town, wading through the deep drifts of sand that lay like a fresh fall of red snow between the hotels and stores, coruscating in the brilliant sunlight. Travis and Louise Woodward made their way towards their quarters in the motels further down the beach. Bridgman searched the still, crystal air for any signs of the wardens, but the sand-car had gone, its tracks obliterated by the storm.

In his room he found their calling-card.

A huge tide of dust had flowed through the french windows and submerged the desk and bed, three feet deep against the rear wall. Outside the sand-break had been inundated, and the contours of the desert had completely altered, a few spires of obsidian marking its former perspectives like buoys on a shifting sea. Bridgman spent the morning digging out his books and equipment, dismantled the electrical system and its batteries and carried everything to the room above. He would have moved to the penthouse on the top floor, but his lights would have been visible for miles.

Settling into his new quarters, he switched on the tape-recorder, heard a short, clipped message in the brisk voice which had shouted orders at the wardens the previous evening. "Bridgman, this is Major Webster, deputy commandant of Cocoa Beach Reservation. On the instructions of the Anti-Viral Sub-committee of the UN General Assembly we are now building a continuous fence around the beach area. On completion no further egress will be allowed, and anyone escaping will be immediately returned to the reservation. Give yourself up now, Bridgman, before—"

Bridgman stopped the tape, then reversed the spool and erased the message, staring angrily at the instrument. Unable to settle down to the task of rewiring the room's circuits, he paced about, fiddling with the architectural drawings propped against the wall. He felt restless and hyper-excited, perhaps because he had been trying to repress, not very successfully, precisely those doubts of which Webster had now reminded him.

He stepped on to the balcony and looked out over the desert, at the red dunes rolling to the windows directly below. For the fourth time he had moved up a floor, and the sequence of identical rooms he had occupied were like displaced images of himself seen through a prism. Their common focus, that elusive final definition of himself which he had sought for so long, still remained to be found. Timelessly the sand swept towards him, its shifting contours, approximating more closely than any other landscape he had found to complete psychic zero, enveloping his past failures and uncertainties, masking them in its enigmatic canopy.

Bridgman watched the red sand flicker and fluoresce in the steepening sunlight. He would never see Mars now, and redress the implicit failure of talent, but a workable replica of the planet was contained within the beach area.

Several million tons of the Martian top-soil had been ferried in as ballast some fifty years earlier, when it was feared that the continuous firing of planetary probes and space vehicles, and the transportation of bulk stores and equipment to Mars would fractionally lower the gravitational mass of the Earth and bring it into tighter orbit around the Sun. Although the distance involved would be little more than a few millimetres, and barely raise the temperature of the atmosphere, its cumulative effects over an extended period might have resulted in a loss into space of the tenuous layers of the outer atmosphere, and of the radiological veil which alone made the biosphere habitable.

Over a twenty-year period a fleet of large freighters had shuttled to and from Mars, dumping the ballast into the sea near the landing-grounds of Cape Canaveral. Simultaneously the Russians were filling in a small section of the Caspian Sea. The intention had been that the ballast should be swallowed by the Atlantic and Caspian waters, but all too soon it was found that the microbiological analysis of the sand had been inadequate.

At the Martian polar caps, where the original water vapour in the atmosphere had condensed, a residue of ancient organic matter formed the top-soil, a fine sandy loess containing the fossilized spores of the giant lichens and mosses which had been the last living organisms on the planet millions of years earlier. Embedded in these spores were the crystal lattices of the viruses which had once preyed on the plants, and traces of these were carried back to Earth with the Canaveral and Caspian ballast.

A few years afterwards a drastic increase in a wide range of plant diseases was noticed in the southern states of America and in the Kazakhstan and Turkmenistan republics of the Soviet Union. All over Florida there were outbreaks of blight and mosaic disease, orange plantations withered and died, stunted palms split by the roadside like dried banana skins, saw grass stiffened into paper spears in the summer heat. Within a few years the entire peninsula was transformed into a desert. The swampy jungles of the Everglades became bleached and dry, the rivers cracked husks strewn with the gleaming skeletons of crocodiles and birds, the forests petrified.

The former launching-ground at Canaveral was closed, and shortly afterwards the Cocoa Beach resorts were sealed off and evacuated, billions of dollars of real estate were abandoned to the virus. Fortunately never virulent to animal hosts, its influence was confined to within a small radius of the original loess which had borne it, unless ingested by the human organism, when it symbioted with the bacteria in the gut flora, benign and unknown to the host, but devastating to vegetation thousands of miles from Canaveral if returned to the soil.

Unable to rest despite his sleepless night, Bridgman played irritably with the tape-recorder. During their close escape from the wardens he had more than half hoped they would catch him. The mysterious leg cramp was obviously psychogenic. Although unable to accept consciously the logic of Webster's argument, he would willingly have conceded to the *fait accompli* of physical capture, gratefully submitted to a year's quarantine at the Parasitological Cleansing Unit at Tampa, and then returned to his career as an architect, chastened but accepting his failure.

As yet, however, the opportunity for surrender had failed to offer itself. Travis appeared to be aware of his ambivalent motives; Bridgman noticed that he and Louise Woodward had made no arrangements to meet him that evening for the conjunction.

In the early afternoon he went down into the streets, ploughed through the drifts of red sand, following the footprints of Travis and Louise as they wound in and out of the side-streets, finally saw them disappear into the coarser, flint-like dunes among the submerged motels to the south of the town. Giving up, he returned through the empty, shadowless streets, now and then shouted up into the hot air, listening to the echoes boom away among the dunes.

Later that afternoon he walked out towards the north-east, picking his way carefully through the dips and hollows, crouching in the pools of shadow whenever the distant sounds of the construction gangs along the perimeter were carried across to him

by the wind. Around him, in the great dust basins, the grains of
red sand glittered like diamonds. Barbs of rusting metal protruded
from the slopes, remnants of Mars satellites and launching stages
which had fallen on to the Martian deserts and then been carried
back again to Earth. One fragment which he passed, a complete
section of hull plate like a concave shield, still carried part of an
identification numeral, and stood upright in the dissolving sand
like a door into nowhere.

Just before dusk he reached a tall spur of obsidian that reared
up into the tinted cerise sky like the spire of a ruined church,
climbed up among its jutting cornices and looked out across the
intervening two or three miles of dunes to the perimeter.
Illuminated by the last light, the metal grilles shone with a
roseate glow like fairy portcullises on the edge of an enchanted sea.
At least half a mile of the fence had been completed, and as he
watched another of the giant prefabricated sections was canti-
levered into the air and staked to the ground. Already the eastern
horizon was cut off by the encroaching fence, the enclosed
Martian sand like the gravel scattered at the bottom of a cage.

Perched on the spur, Bridgman felt a warning tremor of pain
in his calf. He leapt down in a flurry of dust, without looking
back made off among the dunes and reefs.

Later, as the last baroque whorls of the sunset faded below
the horizon, he waited on the roof for Travis and Louise Woodward, peering impatiently into the empty moon-filled streets.

Shortly after midnight, at an elevation of 35 degrees in the south-
west, between Aquila and Ophiuchus, the conjunction began.
Bridgman continued to search the streets, and ignored the seven
points of speeding light as they raced towards him from the
horizon like an invasion from deep space. There was no indication
of their convergent orbital pathways, which would soon scatter
them thousands of miles apart, and the satellites moved as if they
were always together, in the tight configuration Bridgman had
known since childhood, like a lost zodiacal emblem, a constellation detached from the celestial sphere and for ever frantically
searching to return to its place.

"Travis! Confound you!" With a snarl, Bridgman swung away
from the balcony and moved along to the exposed section of rail
behind the elevator head. To be avoided like a pariah by Travis
and Louise Woodward forced him to accept that he was no longer

a true resident of the beach and now existed in a no-man's-land
between them and the wardens.

The seven satellites drew nearer, and Bridgman glanced up at
them cursorily. They were disposed in a distinctive but unusual
pattern resembling the Greek letter Χ, a limp cross, a straight
lateral member containing four capsules more or less in line
ahead—Connolly, Tkachev, Merril and Maiakovski—bisected
by three others forming with Tkachev an elongated Z—Pokrovski,
Woodward and Brodisnek. The pattern had been variously
identified as a hammer and sickle, an eagle, a swastika, and a
dove, as well as a variety of religious and runic emblems, but all
these were being defeated by the advancing tendency of the older
capsules to vaporize.

It was this slow disintegration of the aluminium shells that
made them visible—it had often been pointed out that the
observer on the ground was looking, not at the actual capsule,
but at a local field of vaporized aluminium and ionized hydrogen
peroxide gas from the ruptured attitude jets now distributed
within half a mile of each of the capsules. Woodward's, the most
recently in orbit, was a barely perceptible point of light. The
hulks of the capsules, with their perfectly preserved human
cargoes, were continually dissolving, and a wide fan of silver
spray opened out in a phantom wake behind Merril and
Pokrovski (1998 and 1999), like a double star transforming itself
into a nova in the centre of a constellation. As the mass of the
capsules diminished they sank into a closer orbit around the earth,
would soon touch the denser layers of the atmosphere and
plummet to the ground.

Bridgman watched the satellites as they moved towards him,
his irritation with Travis forgotten. As always, he felt himself
moved by the eerie but strangely serene spectacle of the ghostly
convoy endlessly circling the dark sea of the midnight sky, the
long-dead astronauts converging for the ten-thousandth time
upon their brief rendezvous and then setting off upon their lonely
flight-paths around the perimeter of the ionosphere, the tidal
edge of the beachway into space which had reclaimed them.

How Louise Woodward could bear to look up at her husband
he had never been able to understand. After her arrival he once
invited her to the hotel, remarking that there was an excellent
view of the beautiful sunsets, and she had snapped back bitterly:

"Beautiful? Can you imagine what it's like looking up at a sunset when your husband's spinning through it in his coffin?"

This reaction had been a common one when the first astronauts had died after failing to make contact with the launching platforms in fixed orbit. When these new stars rose in the west an attempt had been made to shoot them down—there was the unsettling prospect of the skies a thousand years hence, littered with orbiting refuse—but later they were left in this natural graveyard, forming their own monument.

Obscured by the clouds of dust carried up into the air by the sand-storm, the satellites shone with little more than the intensity of second-magnitude stars, winking as the reflected light was interrupted by the lanes of strato-cirrus. The wake of diffusing light behind Merril and Pokrovski which usually screened the other capsules seemed to have diminished in size, and he could see both Maiakovski and Brodisnek clearly for the first time in several months. Wondering whether Merril or Pokrovski would be the first to fall from orbit, he looked towards the centre of the cross as it passed overhead.

With a sharp intake of breath, he tilted his head back. In surprise he noticed that one of the familiar points of light was missing from the centre of the group. What he had assumed to be an occlusion of the conjoint vapour trails by dust clouds was simply due to the fact that one of the capsules—Merril's, he decided, the third of the line ahead—had fallen from its orbit.

Head raised, he sidestepped slowly across the roof, avoiding the pieces of rusting neon sign, following the convoy as it passed overhead and moved towards the eastern horizon. No longer overlaid by the wake of Merril's capsule. Woodward's shone with far greater clarity, and almost appeared to have taken the former's place, although he was not due to fall from orbit for at least a century.

In the distance somewhere an engine growled. A moment later, from a different quarter, a woman's voice cried out faintly. Bridgman moved to the rail, over the intervening roof-tops saw two figures silhouetted against the sky on the elevator head of an apartment block, then heard Louise Woodward call out again. She was pointing up at the sky with both hands, her long hair blown about her face, Travis trying to restrain her. Bridgman realized that she had misconstrued Merril's descent, assuming that the fallen astronaut was her husband. He climbed on to the edge of the balcony, watching the pathetic tableau on the distant roof.

Again, somewhere among the dunes, an engine moaned. Before Bridgman could turn around, a brilliant blade of light cleft the sky in the south-west. Like a speeding comet, an immense train of vaporizing particles stretching behind it to the horizon, it soared towards them, the downward curve of its pathway clearly visible. Detached from the rest of the capsules, which were now disappearing among the stars along the eastern horizon, it was little more than a few miles off the ground.

Bridgman watched it approach, apparently on a collision course with the hotel. The expanding corona of white light, like a gigantic signal flare, illuminated the roof-tops, etching the letters of the neon signs over the submerged motels on the outskirts of the town. He ran for the doorway, as he raced down the stairs saw the glow of the descending capsule fill the sombre streets like a hundred moons. When he reached his room, sheltered by the massive weight of the hotel, he watched the dunes in front of the hotel light up like a stage set. Three hundred yards away the low camouflaged hull of the wardens' beach-car was revealed poised on a crest, its feeble spotlight drowned by the glare.

With a deep metallic sigh, the burning catafalque of the dead astronaut soared overhead, a cascade of vaporizing metal pouring from its hull, filling the sky with incandescent light. Reflected below it, like an expressway illuminated by an aircraft's spot-lights, a long lane of light several hundred yards in width raced out into the desert towards the sea. As Bridgman shielded his eyes, it suddenly erupted in a tremendous explosion of detonating sand. A huge curtain of white dust lifted into the air and fell slowly to the ground. The sounds of the impact rolled against the hotel, mounting in a sustained crescendo that drummed against the windows. A series of smaller explosions flared up like opalescent fountains. All over the desert fires flickered briefly where fragments of the capsule had been scattered. Then the noise subsided, and an immense glistening pall of phosphorescing gas hung in the air like a silver veil, particles within it beading and winking.

Two hundred yards away across the sand was the running figure of Louise Woodward, Travis twenty paces behind her. Bridgman watched them dart in and out of the dunes, then abruptly felt the cold spotlight of the beach-car hit his face and flood the room behind him. The vehicle was moving straight towards him, two of the wardens, nets and lassos in hand, riding the outboard.

Quickly Bridgman straddled the balcony, jumped down into the sand and raced towards the crest of the first dune. He crouched and ran on through the darkness as the beam probed the air. Above, the glistening pall was slowly fading, the particles of vaporized metal sifting towards the dark Martian sand. In the distance the last echoes of the impact were still reverberating among the hotels of the beach colonies farther down the coast.

Five minutes later he caught up with Louise Woodward and Travis. The capsule's impact had flattened a number of the dunes, forming a shallow basin some quarter of a mile in diameter, and the surrounding slopes were scattered with the still glowing particles, sparkling like fading eyes. The beach-car growled somewhere four or five hundred yards behind him, and Bridgman broke off into an exhausted walk. He stopped beside Travis, who was kneeling on the ground, breath pumping into his lungs. Fifty yards away Louise Woodward was running up and down, distraughtly gazing at the fragments of smouldering metal. For a moment the spotlight of the approaching beach-car illuminated her, and she ran away among the dunes. Bridgman caught a glimpse of the inconsolable anguish in her face.

Travis was still on his knees. He had picked up a piece of the oxidized metal and was pressing it together in his hands.

"Travis, for God's sake tell her! This was Merril's capsule, there's no doubt about it! Woodward's still up there."

Travis looked up at him silently, his eyes searching Bridgman's face. A spasm of pain tore his mouth, and Bridgman realized that the barb of steel he clasped reverently in his hands was still glowing with heat.

"Travis!" He tried to pull the man's hands apart, the pungent stench of burning flesh gusting into his face, but Travis wrenched away from him. "Leave her alone, Bridgman! Go back with the wardens!"

Bridgman retreated from the approaching beach-car. Only thirty yards away, its spotlight filled the basin. Louise Woodward was still searching the dunes. Travis held his ground as the wardens jumped down from the car and advanced towards him with their nets, his bloodied hands raised at his sides, the steel barb flashing like a dagger. At the head of the wardens, the only one unmasked was a trim, neat-featured man with an intent, serious face. Bridgman guessed that this was Major Webster, and that the wardens had known of the impending impact and hoped to capture them, and Louise in particular, before it occurred.

Bridgman stumbled back towards the dunes at the edge of the basin. As he neared the crest he trapped his foot in a semicircular plate of metal, sat down and freed his heel. Unmistakably it was part of a control panel, the circular instrument housings still intact.

Overhead the pall of glistening vapour had moved off to the north-east, and the reflected light was directly over the rusting gantries of the former launching site at Cape Canaveral. For a few fleeting seconds the gantries seemed to be enveloped in a sheen of silver, transfigured by the vaporized body of the dead astronaut, diffusing over them in a farewell gesture, his final return to the site from which he had set off to his death a century earlier. Then the gantries sank again into their craggy shadows, and the pall moved off like an immense wraith towards the sea, barely distinguishable from the star glow.

Down below Travis was sitting on the ground surrounded by the wardens. He scuttled about on his hands like a frantic crab, scooping handfuls of the virus-laden sand at them. Holding tight to their masks, the wardens manœuvred around him, their nets and lassos at the ready. Another group moved slowly towards Bridgman.

Bridgman picked up a handful of the dark Martian sand beside the instrument panel, felt the soft glowing crystals warm his palm. In his mind he could still see the silver-sheathed gantries of the launching site across the bay, by a curious illusion almost identical with the Martian city he had designed years earlier. He watched the pall disappear over the sea, then looked around at the other remnants of Merril's capsule scattered over the slopes. High in the western night, between Pegasus and Cygnus, shone the distant disc of the planet Mars, which for both himself and the dead astronaut had served for so long as a symbol of unattained ambition. The wind stirred softly through the sand, cooling this replica of the planet which lay passively around him, and at last he understood why he had come to the beach and been unable to leave it.

Twenty yards away Travis was being dragged off like a wild dog, his thrashing body pinioned in the centre of a web of lassos. Louise Woodward had run away among the dunes towards the sea, following the vanished gas cloud.

In a sudden access of refound confidence, Bridgman drove his fist into the dark sand, buried his forearm like a foundation pillar. A flange of hot metal from Merril's capsule burned his wrist, bonding him to the spirit of the dead astronaut. Scattered around him on the Martian sand, in a sense Merril had reached Mars after all.

"Damn it!" he cried exultantly to himself as the wardens' lassos stung his neck and shoulders. "We made it!"

THE WATCH-TOWERS

THE next day, for some reason, there was a sudden increase of activity in the watch-towers. This began during the latter half of the morning, and by noon, when Renthall left the hotel on his way to see Mrs. Osmond, seemed to have reached its peak. People were standing at their windows and balconies along both sides of the street, whispering agitatedly to each other behind the curtains and pointing up into the sky.

Renthall usually tried to ignore the watch-towers, resenting even the smallest concession to the fact of their existence, but at the bottom of the street, where he was hidden in the shadow thrown by one of the houses, he stopped and craned his head up at the nearest tower.

A hundred feet away from him, it hung over the Public Library, its tip poised no more than twenty feet above the roof. The glass-enclosed cabin in the lowest tier appeared to be full of observers, opening and shutting the windows and shifting about what Renthall assumed were huge pieces of optical equipment. He looked around at the further towers, suspended from the sky at three hundred foot intervals in every direction, noticing an occasional flash of light as a window turned and caught the sun.

An elderly man wearing a shabby black suit and wing collar,

who usually loitered outside the library, came across the street to Renthall and backed into the shadows beside him.

"They're up to something all right." He cupped his hands over his eyes and peered up anxiously at the watch-towers. "I've never seen them like this as long as I can remember."

Renthall studied his face. However alarmed, he was obviously relieved by the signs of activity. "I shouldn't worry unduly," Renthall told him. "It's a change to see something going on at all."

Before the other could reply he turned on his heel and strode away along the pavement. It took him ten minutes to reach the street in which Mrs. Osmond lived, and he fixed his eyes firmly on the ground, ignoring the few passers-by. Although dominated by the watch-towers—four of them hung in a line exactly down its centre—the street was almost deserted. Half the houses were untenanted and falling into what would soon be an irreversible state of disrepair. Usually Renthall assessed each property carefully, trying to decide whether to leave his hotel and take one of them, but the movement in the watch-towers had caused him more anxiety than he was prepared to admit, and the terrace of houses passed unnoticed.

Mrs. Osmond's house stood half-way down the street, its gate swinging loosely on its rusty hinges. Renthall hesitated under the plane tree growing by the edge of the pavement, and then crossed the narrow garden and quickly let himself through the door.

Mrs. Osmond invariably spent the afternoon sitting out on the veranda in the sun, gazing at the weeds in the back garden, but today she had retreated to a corner of the sitting-room. She was sorting a suitcase full of old papers when Renthall came in.

Renthall made no attempt to embrace her and wandered over to the window. Mrs. Osmond had half drawn the curtains and he pulled them back. There was a watch-tower ninety feet away, almost directly ahead, hanging over the parallel terrace of empty houses. The lines of towers receded diagonally from left to right towards the horizon, partly obscured by the bright haze.

"Do you think you should have come today?" Mrs. Osmond asked, shifting her plump hips nervously in the chair.

"Why not?" Renthall said, scanning the towers, hands loosely in his pockets.

"But if they're going to keep a closer watch on us now they'll notice you coming here."

"I shouldn't believe all the rumours you hear," Renthall told her calmly.

"What do you think it means then?"

"I've absolutely no idea. Their movements may be as random and meaningless as our own." Renthall shrugged. "Perhaps they *are* going to keep a closer watch on us. What does it matter if all they do is stare?"

"Then you mustn't come here any more!" Mrs. Osmond protested.

"Why? I hardly believe they can see through walls."

"They're not that stupid," Mrs. Osmond said irritably. "They'll soon put two and two together, if they haven't already."

Renthall took his eyes off the tower and looked down at Mrs. Osmond patiently. "My dear, this house isn't tapped. For all they know we may be darning our prayer rugs or discussing the endocrine system of the tapeworm."

"Not you, Charles," Mrs. Osmond said with a short laugh. "Not if they know you." Evidently pleased by this sally, she relaxed and took a cigarette out of the box on the table.

"Perhaps they don't know me," Renthall said dryly. "In fact, I'm quite sure they don't. If they did I can't believe I should still be here."

He noticed himself stooping, a reliable sign that he was worrying, and went over to the sofa.

"Is the school going to start tomorrow?" Mrs. Osmond asked when he had disposed his long, thin legs around the table.

"It should do," Renthall said. "Hanson went down to the Town Hall this morning, but as usual they had little idea of what was going on."

He opened his jacket and pulled out of the inner pocket an old but neatly folded copy of a woman's magazine.

"Charles!" Mrs. Osmond exclaimed. "Where did you get this?"

She took it from Renthall and started leafing through the soiled pages.

"One of my sources," Renthall said. From the sofa he could still see the watch-tower over the houses opposite. "Georgina Simons. She has a library of them."

He rose, went over to the window and drew the curtains across.

"Charles, don't. I can't see."

"Read it later," Renthall told her. He lay back on the sofa again. "Are you coming to the recital this afternoon?"

"Hasn't it been cancelled?" Mrs. Osmond asked, putting the magazine down reluctantly.

"No, of course not."

"Charles, I don't think I want to go." Mrs. Osmond frowned. "What records is Hanson going to play?"

"Some Tchaikovsky. And Grieg." He tried to make it sound interesting. "You must come. We can't just sit about subsiding into this state of boredom and uselessness."

"I know," Mrs. Osmond said fractiously. "But I don't feel like it. Not today. All those records bore me. I've heard them so often."

"They bore me too. But at least it's something to do." He put an arm around Mrs. Osmond's shoulders and began to play with the darker unbleached hair behind her ears, tapping the large nickel ear-rings she wore and listening to them tinkle.

When he put his hand on to her knee Mrs. Osmond stood up and prowled aimlessly around the room, straightening her skirt.

"Julia, what is the matter with you?" Renthall asked irritably. "Have you got a headache?"

Mrs. Osmond was by the window, gazing up at the watch-towers. "Do you think they're going to come down?"

"Of course not!" Renthall snapped. "Where on earth did you get that idea?"

Suddenly he felt unbearably exasperated. The confined dimensions of the dusty sitting-room seemed to suffocate reason. He stood up and buttoned his jacket. "I'll see you this afternoon at the Institute, Julia. The recital starts at three."

Mrs. Osmond nodded vaguely, unfastened the french windows and ambled forwards across the veranda into full view of the watch-towers, the glassy expression on her face like a supplicant nun's.

As Renthall had expected, the school did not open the next day. When they tired of hanging around the hotel after breakfast he and Hanson went down to the Town Hall. The building was almost empty and the only official they were able to find was unhelpful.

"We have no instructions at present," he told them, "but as soon as the term starts you will be notified. Though from what I hear the postponement is to be indefinite."

"Is that the committee's decision?" Renthall asked. "Or just another of the town clerk's brilliant extemporizings?"

"The school committee is no longer meeting," the official said. "I'm afraid the town clerk isn't here today." Before Renthall could speak he added: "You will, of course, continue to draw your salaries. Perhaps you would care to call in at the treasurer's department on your way out?"

Renthall and Hanson left and looked about for a café. Finally they found one that was open and sat under the awning, staring vacantly at the watch-towers hanging over the roof-tops around them. Their activity had lessened considerably since the previous day. The nearest tower was only fifty feet away, immediately above a disused office building on the other side of the street. The windows in the observation tier remained shut, but every few minutes Renthall noticed a shadow moving behind the panes.

Eventually a waitress came out to them, and Renthall ordered coffee.

"I think I shall have to give a few lessons," Hanson remarked. "All this leisure is becoming too much of a good thing."

"It's an idea," Renthall agreed. "If you can find anyone interested. I'm sorry the recital yesterday was such a flop."

Hanson shrugged. "I'll see if I can get hold of some new records. By the way, I thought Julia looked very handsome yesterday."

Renthall acknowledged the compliment with a slight bow of his head. "I'd like to take her out more often."

"Do you think that's wise?"

"Why on earth not?"

"Well, just at present, you know." Hanson inclined a finger at the watch-towers.

"I don't see that it matters particularly," Renthall said. He disliked personal confidences and was about to change the subject when Hanson leaned forward across the table.

"Perhaps not, but I gather there was some mention of you at the last Council meeting. One or two members were rather critical of your little *ménage à deux*." He smiled thinly at Renthall, who was frowning into his coffee. "Sheer spite, no doubt, but your behaviour is a little idiosyncratic."

Controlling himself, Renthall pushed away the coffee cup. "Do you mind telling me what damned business it is of theirs?"

Hanson laughed. "None, really, except that they are the executive authority, and I suppose we should take our cue from them." Renthall snorted at this, and Hanson went on: "As a matter of interest, you may receive an official directive over the next few days."

"A *what*?" Renthall exploded. He sat back, shaking his head incredulously. "Are you serious?" When Hanson nodded he began to laugh harshly. "Those idiots! I don't know why we put up with them. Sometimes their stupidity positively staggers me."

"Steady on," Hanson demurred. "I do see their point. Bearing in mind the big commotion in the watch-towers yesterday the Council probably feel we shouldn't do anything that might antagonize them. You never know, they may even be acting on official instructions."

Renthall glanced contemptuously at Hanson. "Do you *really* believe that nonsense about the Council being in touch with the watch-towers? It may give a few simpletons a sense of security, but for heaven's sake don't try it on me. My patience is just about exhausted." He watched Hanson carefully, wondering which of the Council members had provided him with his information. The lack of subtlety depressed him painfully. "However, thanks for warning me. I suppose it means there'll be an overpowering air of embarrassment when Julia and I go to the cinema tomorrow."

Hanson shook his head. "No. Actually the performance has been cancelled. In view of yesterday's disturbances."

"But why—?" Renthall slumped back. "Haven't they got the intelligence to realize that it's just at this sort of time that we need every social get-together we can organize? People are hiding away in their back bedrooms like a lot of frightened ghosts. We've got to bring them out, give them something that will pull them together."

He gazed up thoughtfully at the watch-tower across the street. Shadows circulated behind the frosted panes of the observation windows. "Some sort of gala, say, or a garden fête. Who could organize it, though?"

Hanson pushed back his chair. "Careful, Charles. I don't know whether the Council would altogether approve."

"I'm sure they wouldn't." After Hanson had left he remained at the table and returned to his solitary contemplation of the watch-towers.

For half an hour Renthall sat at the table, playing absently with his empty coffee cup and watching the few people who passed along the street. No one else visited the café, and he was glad to be able to pursue his thoughts alone, in this miniature urban vacuum, with nothing to intervene between himself and the lines of watch-towers stretching into the haze beyond the roof-tops.

With the exception of Mrs. Osmond, Renthall had virtually no close friends in whom to confide. With his sharp intelligence and impatience with trivialities, Renthall was one of those men with whom others find it difficult to relax. A certain innate condescension, a reserved but unmistakable attitude of superiority held them away from him, though few people regarded him as anything but a shabby pedagogue. At the hotel he kept to himself. There was little social contact between the guests; in the lounge and dining-room they sat immersed in their old newspapers and magazines, occasionally murmuring quietly to each other. The only thing which could mobilize the simultaneous communion of the guests was some untoward activity in the watch-towers, and at such times Renthall always maintained an absolute silence.

Just before he stood up a square thick-set figure approached down the street. Renthall recognized the man and was about to turn his seat to avoid having to greet him, but something about his expression made him lean forward. Fleshy and dark-jowled, the man walked with an easy, rolling gait, his double-breasted check overcoat open to reveal a well-tended midriff. This was Victor Boardman, owner of the local flea-pit cinema, sometime bootlegger and procurer at large.

Renthall had never spoken to him, but he was aware that Boardman shared with him the distinction of bearing the stigma of the Council's disapproval. Hanson claimed that the Council had successfully stamped out Boardman's illicit activities, but the latter's permanent expression of smug contempt for the rest of the world seemed to belie this.

As he passed they exchanged glances, and Boardman's face

broke momentarily into a knowing smirk. It was obviously directed at Renthall, and implied a pre-judgement of some event about which Renthall as yet knew nothing, presumably his coming collision with the Council. Obviously Boardman expected him to capitulate to the Council without a murmur.

Annoyed, Renthall turned his back on Boardman, then watched him over his shoulder as he padded off down the street, his easy relaxed shoulders swaying from side to side.

The following day the activity in the watch-towers had subsided entirely. The blue haze from which they extended was brighter than it had been for several months, and the air in the streets seemed to sparkle with the light reflected off the observation windows. There was no sign of movement among them, and the sky had a rigid, uniform appearance that indicated an indefinite lull.

For some reason, however, Renthall found himself more nervous than he had been for some time. The school had not yet opened, but he felt strangely reluctant to visit Mrs. Osmond and remained indoors all morning, shunning the streets as if avoiding some invisible shadow of guilt.

The long lines of watch-towers stretching endlessly from one horizon to the other reminded him that he could soon expect to receive the Council's "directive"—Hanson would not have mentioned it by accident—and it was always during the lulls that the Council was most active in consolidating its position, issuing a stream of petty regulations and amendments.

Renthall would have liked to challenge the Council's authority on some formal matter unconnected with himself—the validity, for example, of one of the byelaws prohibiting public assemblies in the street—but the prospect of all the intrigue involved in canvassing the necessary support bored him utterly. Although none of them individually would challenge the Council, most people would have been glad to see it toppled, but there seemed to be no likely focus for their opposition. Apart from the fear that the Council was in touch with the watch-towers, no one would stand up for Renthall's right to carry on his affair with Mrs. Osmond.

Curiously enough, she seemed unaware of these cross-currents when he went to see her that afternoon. She had cleaned the house and was in high humour, the windows wide open to the brilliant air.

"Charles, what's the matter with you?" she chided him when he slumped inertly into a chair. "You look like a broody hen."

"I felt rather tired this morning. It's probably the hot weather." When she sat down on the arm of the chair he put one hand listlessly on her hip, trying to summon together his energies. "Recently I've been developing an *idée fixe* about the Council, I must be going through a crisis of confidence. I need some method of reasserting myself."

Mrs. Osmond stroked his hair soothingly with her cool fingers, her eyes watching him silkily. "What *you* need, Charles, is a little mother love. You're so isolated at that hotel, among all those old people. Why don't you rent one of the houses in this road? I'd be able to look after you then."

Renthall glanced up at her sardonically. "Perhaps I could move in here?" he asked, but she tossed her head back with a derisive snort and went over to the window.

She gazed up at the nearest watch-tower a hundred feet away, its windows closed and silent, the great shaft disappearing into the haze. "What do you suppose they're thinking about?"

Renthall snapped his fingers off-handedly. "They're probably not thinking about anything. Sometimes I wonder whether there's anyone there at all. The movements we see may be just optical illusions. Although the windows appear to open no one's ever actually *seen* any of them. For all we know this place may well be nothing more than an abandoned zoo."

Mrs. Osmond regarded him with rueful amusement. "Charles, you do pick some extraordinary metaphors. I often doubt if you're like the rest of us, I wouldn't dare say the sort of things you do in case—" She broke off, glancing up involuntarily at the watch-towers hanging from the sky.

Idly, Renthall asked: "In case what?"

"Well, in case—" Irritably, she said: "Don't be absurd, Charles, doesn't the thought of those towers hanging down over us frighten you at all?"

Renthall turned his head slowly and stared up at the watch-towers. Once he had tried to count them, but there seemed little point. "Yes, they frighten me," he said noncommittally. "In the same way that Hanson and the old people at the hotel and everyone else here does. But not in the sense that the boys at school are frightened of *me*."

Mrs. Osmond nodded, misinterpreting this last remark. "Children are very perceptive, Charles. They probably know you're not interested in them. Unfortunately they're not old enough to understand what the watch-towers mean."

She gave a slight shiver, and pulled her cardigan around her shoulders. "You know, on the days when they're busy behind their windows I can hardly move around, it's terrible. I feel so listless, all I want to do is sit and stare at the wall. Perhaps I'm more sensitive to their, er, radiations than most people."

Renthall smiled. "You must be. Don't let them depress you. Next time why don't you put on a paper hat and do a pirouette?"

"What? Oh, Charles, stop being cynical."

"I'm not. Seriously, Julia, do you think it would make any difference?"

Mrs. Osmond shook her head sadly. "You try, Charles, and then tell me. Where are you going?"

Renthall paused at the window. "Back to the hotel to rest. By the way, do you know Victor Boardman?"

"I used to, once. Why, what are you getting up to with him?"

"Does he own the garden next to the cinema car-park?"

"I think so." Mrs. Osmond laughed. "Are you going to take up gardening?"

"In a sense." With a wave, Renthall left.

He began with Dr. Clifton, whose room was directly below his own. Clifton's duties at his surgery occupied him for little more than an hour a day—there were virtually no deaths or illnesses— but he still retained sufficient initiative to cultivate a hobby. He had turned one end of his room into a small aviary, containing a dozen canaries, and spent much of his time trying to teach them tricks. His acerbic, matter-of-fact manner always tired Renthall, but he respected the doctor for not sliding into total lethargy like everyone else.

Clifton considered his suggestion carefully. "I agree with you, something of the sort is probably necessary. A good idea, Renthall. Properly conducted, it might well provide just the lift people need."

"The main question, Doctor, is one of organization. The only suitable place is the Town Hall."

Clifton nodded. "Yes, there's your problem. I'm afraid I've no influence with the Council, if that's what you're suggesting. I don't know what you can do. You'll have to get their permission of course, and in the past they haven't shown themselves to be very radical or original. They prefer to maintain the *status quo*."

Renthall nodded, then added casually: "They're only interested in maintaining their own power. At times I become rather tired of our Council."

Clifton glanced at him and then turned back to his cages. "You're preaching revolution, Renthall," he said quietly, a forefinger stroking the beak of one of the canaries. Pointedly, he refrained from seeing Renthall to the door.

Writing the doctor off, Renthall rested for a few minutes in his room, pacing up and down the strip of faded carpet, then went down to the basement to see the manager, Mulvaney.

"I'm only making some initial inquiries. As yet I haven't applied for permission, but Dr. Clifton thinks the idea is excellent, and there's no doubt we'll get it. Are you up to looking after the catering?"

Mulvaney's sallow face watched Renthall sceptically. "Of course I'm up to it, but how serious are you?" He leaned against his roll-top desk. "You think you'll get permission? You're wrong, Mr. Renthall, the Council wouldn't stand for the idea. They even closed the cinema, so they're not likely to allow a public party. Before you know what you'd have people dancing."

"I hardly think so, but does the idea appal you so much?"

Mulvaney shook his head, already bored with Renthall. "You get a permit, Mr. Renthall, and then we can talk seriously."

Tightening his voice, Renthall asked: "Is it necessary to get the Council's permission? Couldn't we go ahead without?"

Without looking up, Mulvaney sat down at his desk. "Keep trying, Mr. Renthall, it's a great idea."

During the next few days Renthall pursued his inquiries, in all approaching some half-dozen people. In general he met with the same negative response, but as he intended he soon noticed a subtle but nonetheless distinct quickening of interest around him. The usual fragmentary murmur of conversation would fade away abruptly as he passed the tables in the dining-room, and the service was fractionally more prompt. Hanson no longer took coffee with him in the mornings, and once Renthall saw him in guarded conversation with the town clerk's secretary, a young man called Barnes. This, he assumed, was Hanson's contact.

In the meantime the activity in the watch-towers remained at zero. The endless lines of towers hung down from the bright, hazy sky, the observation windows closed, and the people in the streets below sank slowly into their usual mindless torpor, wandering from hotel to library to café. Determined on his course of action, Renthall felt his confidence return.

Allowing an interval of a week to elapse, he finally called upon Victor Boardman.

The bootlegger received him in his office above the cinema, greeting him with a wry smile.

"Well, Mr. Renthall, I hear you're going into the entertainment business. Drunken gambols and all that. I'm surprised at you."

"A fête," Renthall corrected. The seat Boardman had offered him faced towards the window—deliberately, he guessed—and provided an uninterrupted view of the watch-tower over the roof of the adjacent furniture store. Only forty feet away, it blocked off half the sky. The metal plates which formed its rectangular sides were annealed together by some process Renthall was unable to identify, neither welded nor riveted, almost as if the entire tower had been cast *in situ*. He moved to another chair so that his back was to the window.

"The school is still closed, so I thought I'd try to make myself useful. That's what I'm paid for. I've come to you because you've had a good deal of experience."

"Yes, I've had a lot of experience, Mr. Renthall. Very varied. As one of the Council's employees, I take it you have its permission?"

Renthall evaded this. "The Council is naturally a conservative body, Mr. Boardman. Obviously at this stage I'm acting on my own initiative. I shall consult the Council at the appropriate moment later, when I can offer them a practicable proposition."

Boardman nodded sagely. "That's sensible, Mr. Renthall. Now what exactly do you want me to do? Organize the whole thing for you?"

"No, but naturally I'd be very grateful if you would. For the present I merely want to ask permission to hold the fête on a piece of your property."

"The cinema? I'm not going to take all those seats out, if that's what you're after."

"Not the cinema. Though we could use the bar and cloak-rooms," Renthall extemporized, hoping the scheme did not sound too grandiose. "Is the old beer-garden next to the car park your property?"

For a moment Boardman was silent. He watched Renthall shrewdly, picking his nails with his cigar-cutter, a faint suggestion of admiration in his eyes. "So you want to hold the fête in the open, Mr. Renthall? Is that it?"

Renthall nodded, smiling back at Boardman. "I'm glad to see you living up to your reputation for getting quickly to the point. Are you prepared to lend the garden? Of course, you'll have a big share of the profits. In fact, if it's any inducement, you can have all the profits."

Boardman put out his cigar. "Mr. Renthall, you're obviously a man of many parts. I underestimated you. I thought you merely had a grievance against the Council. I hope you know what you're doing."

"Mr. Boardman, will you lend the garden?" Renthall repeated.

There was an amused but thoughtful smile on Boardman's lips as he regarded the watch-tower framed by the window. "There are two watch-towers directly over the beer-garden, Mr. Rent-hall."

"I'm fully aware of that. It's obviously the chief attraction of the property. Now, can you give me an answer?"

The two men regarded each other silently, and then Boardman gave an almost imperceptible nod. Renthall realized that his scheme was being taken seriously by Boardman. He was obviously using Renthall for his own purposes, for once having flaunted the Council's authority he would be able to resume all his other, more profitable activities. Of course, the fête would never be held, but in answer to Boardman's questions he outlined a provisional programme. They fixed the date of the fête at a month ahead, and arranged to meet again at the beginning of the next week.

Two days later, as he expected, the first emissaries of the Council came to see him.

He was waiting at his usual table on the café terrace, the silent watch-towers suspended from the air around him, when he saw Hanson hurrying along the street.

"Do join me." Renthall drew a chair back. "What's the news?"

"Nothing—though you should know, Charles." He gave Renthall a dry smile, as if admonishing a favourite pupil, then gazed about the empty terrace for the waitress. "Service is appallingly bad here. Tell me, Charles, what's all this talk about you and Victor Boardman. I could hardly believe my ears."

Renthall leaned back in his chair. "I don't know, you tell me."

"We—er, I was wondering if Boardman was taking advantage of some perfectly innocent remark he might have overheard. This business of a garden party you're supposed to be organizing with him—it sounds absolutely fantastic."

"Why?"

"But Charles." Hanson leaned forward to examine Renthall carefully, trying to make sense of his unruffled pose. "Surely you aren't serious?"

"But why not? If I want to, why shouldn't I organize a garden party—fête, to be more accurate?"

"It doesn't make an iota of difference," Hanson said tartly. "Apart from any other reason"—here he glanced skyward—"the fact remains that you are an employee of the Council."

Hands in his trouser-pockets, Renthall tipped back his chair. "But that gives them no mandate to interfere in my private life. You seem to be forgetting, but the terms of my contract specifically exclude any such authority. I am not on the established grade, as my salary differential shows. If the Council disapprove, the only sanction they can apply is to give me the sack."

"They will, Charles, don't sound so smug."

Renthall let this pass. "Fair enough, if they can find anyone else to take on the job. Frankly I doubt it. They've managed to swallow their moral scruples in the past."

"Charles, this is different. As long as you're discreet no one gives a hoot about your private affairs, but this garden party is a public matter, and well within the Council's province."

Renthall yawned. "I'm rather bored with the subject of the Council. Technically, the fête will be a private affair, by invitation only. They've no statutory right to be consulted at all. If a breach of the peace takes place the Chief Constable can take action. Why all the fuss, anyway? I'm merely trying to provide a little harmless festivity."

Hanson shook his head. "Charles, you're deliberately evading the point. According to Boardman this fête will take place out of doors—directly under two of the watch-towers. Have you realized what the repercussions would be?"

"Yes." Renthall formed the word carefully in his mouth. "Nothing. Absolutely nothing."

"Charles!" Hanson lowered his head at this apparent blasphemy, glanced up at the watch-towers over the street as if expecting instant retribution to descend from them. "Look, my dear fellow, take my advice. Drop the whole idea. You don't stand a chance anyway of ever holding this mad jape, so why deliberately court trouble with the Council? Who knows what their real power would be if they were provoked?"

Renthall rose from his seat. He looked up at the watch-tower hanging from the air on the other side of the road, controlling himself when a slight pang of anxiety stirred his heart. "I'll send you an invitation," he called back, then walked away to his hotel.

The next afternoon the town clerk's secretary called upon him in his room. During the interval, no doubt intended as a salutary pause for reflection, Renthall had remained at the hotel, reading quietly in his armchair. He paid one brief visit to Mrs. Osmond, but she seemed nervous and irritable, evidently aware of the imminent clash. The strain of maintaining an appearance of unconcern had begun to tire Renthall, and he avoided the open streets whenever possible. Fortunately the school had still not opened.

Barnes, the dapper dark-haired secretary, came straight to the point. Refusing Renthall's offer of an armchair, he held a sheet of pink duplicated paper in his hand, apparently a minute of the last Council meeting.

"Mr. Renthall, the Council has been informed of your intention to hold a garden fête in some three weeks' time. I have been asked by the chairman of the Watch Committee to express the committee's grave misgivings, and to request you accordingly to terminate all arrangements and cancel the fête immediately, pending an inquiry."

"I'm sorry, Barnes, but I'm afraid our preparations are too far advanced. We're about to issue invitations."

Barnes hesitated, casting his eye around Renthall's faded room and few shabby books as if hoping to find some ulterior motive for Renthall's behaviour.

"Mr. Renthall, perhaps I could explain that this request is tantamount to a direct order from the Council."

"So I'm aware." Renthall sat down on his window-sill and gazed out at the watch-towers. "Hanson and I went over all this, as you probably know. The Council have no more right to order me to cancel this fête than they have to stop me walking down the street."

Barnes smiled his thin bureaucratic smirk. "Mr. Renthall, this is not a matter of the Council's statutory jurisdiction. This order is issued by virtue of the authority vested in it by its superiors. If you prefer, you can assume that the Council is merely passing on a direct instruction it has received." He inclined his head towards the watch-towers.

Renthall stood up. "Now we're at last getting down to business." He gathered himself together. "Perhaps you could tell the Council to convey to its superiors, as you call them, my polite but firm refusal. Do you get *my* point?"

Barnes retreated fractionally. He summed Renthall up carefully, then nodded. "I think so, Mr. Renthall. No doubt you understand what you're doing."

After he had gone Renthall drew the blinds over the window and lay down on his bed; for the next hour he made an effort to relax.

His final show-down with the Council was to take place the following day. Summoned to an emergency meeting of the Watch Committee, he accepted the invitation with alacrity, certain that with every member of the committee present the main council chamber would be used. This would give him a perfect opportunity to humiliate the Council by publicly calling their bluff.

Both Hanson and Mrs. Osmond assumed that he would capitulate without argument.

"Well, Charles, you brought it upon yourself," Hanson told him. "Still, I expect they'll be lenient with you. It's a matter of face now."

"More than that, I hope," Renthall replied. "They claim they were passing on a direct instruction from the watch-towers."

"Well, yes . . ." Hanson gestured vaguely. "Of course. Obviously the towers wouldn't intervene in such a trivial matter. They rely on the Council to keep a watching brief for them, as long as the Council's authority is respected they're prepared to remain aloof."

"It sounds an ideally simple arrangement. How do you think the communication between the Council and the watch-towers takes place?" Renthall pointed to the watch-tower across the street from the cabin. The shuttered observation tier hung emptily in the air like an out-of-season gondola. "By telephone? Or do they semaphore?"

But Hanson merely laughed and changed the subject.

Julia Osmond was equally vague, but equally convinced of the Council's infallibility.

"Of course they receive instructions from the towers, Charles. But don't worry, they obviously have a sense of proportion—they've been letting you come here all this time." She turned a monitory finger at Renthall, her broad-hipped bulk obscuring the towers from him. "That's your chief fault, Charles. You think you're more important than you are. Look at you now, sitting there all hunched up with your face like an old shoe. You think the Council and the watch-towers are going to give you some terrible punishment. But they won't, because you're not worth it."

Renthall picked uneagerly at his lunch at the hotel, conscious of the guests watching from the tables around him. Many had brought visitors with them, and he guessed that there would be a full attendance at the meeting that afternoon.

After lunch he retired to his room, made a desultory attempt to read until the meeting at half past two. Outside, the watch-towers hung in their long lines from the bright haze. There was no sign of movement in the observation windows, and Renthall studied them openly, hands in pockets, like a general surveying the dispositions of his enemy's forces. The haze was lower than usual, filling the interstices between the towers, so that in the distance, where the free space below their tips was hidden by the intervening roof-tops, the towers seemed to rise upwards into the air like rectangular chimneys over an industrial landscape, wreathed in white smoke.

The nearest tower was about seventy-five feet away, diagonally to his left, over the eastern end of the open garden shared by the other hotels in the crescent. Just as Renthall turned away, one of the windows in the observation deck appeared to open, the opaque glass pane throwing a spear of sharp sunlight directly towards him. Renthall flinched back, heart suddenly surging, then leaned forward again. The activity in the tower had subsided as instantly as it had arisen. The windows were sealed, no signs of movement behind them. Renthall listened to the sounds from the rooms above and below him. So conspicuous a motion of the window, the first sign of activity for many days, and a certain indication of more to come, should have brought a concerted rush to the balconies. But the hotel was silent, and below he could hear Dr. Clifton at his cages by the window, humming absently to himself.

Renthall scanned the windows on the other side of the garden but the lines of craning faces he expected were absent. He examined the watch-tower carefully, assuming that he had seen a window open in a hotel near by. Yet the explanation dissatisfied him. The ray of sunlight had cleft the air like a silver blade, with a curious luminous intensity that only the windows of the watch-towers seemed able to reflect, aimed unerringly at his head.

He broke off to glance at his watch, cursed when he saw that it was after a quarter past two. The Town Hall was a good half-mile away, and he would arrive dishevelled and perspiring.

There was a knock on his door. He opened it to find Mulvaney. "What is it? I'm busy now."

"Sorry, Mr. Renthall. A man called Barnes from the Council asked me to give you an urgent message. He said the meeting this afternoon has been postponed."

"Ha!" Leaving the door open, Renthall snapped his fingers contemptuously at the air. "So they've had second thoughts after all. Discretion is the better part of valour." Smiling broadly, he called Mulvaney back into his room. "Mr. Mulvaney! Just a moment!"

"Good news, Mr. Renthall?"

"Excellent. I've got them on the run." He added: "You wait and see, the next meeting of the Watch Committee will be held in private."

"You might be right, Mr. Renthall. Some people think they have over-reached themselves a bit."

"Really? That's rather interesting. Good." Renthall noted this mentally, then gestured Mulvaney over to the window. "Tell me, Mr. Mulvaney, just now while you were coming up the stairs, did you notice any activity out there?"

He gestured briefly towards the tower, not wanting to draw attention to himself by pointing at it. Mulvaney gazed out over the garden, shaking his head slowly. "Can't say I did, not more than usual. What sort of activity?"

"You know, a window opening . . ." When Mulvaney continued to shake his head, Renthall said: "Good. Let me know if that fellow Barnes calls again."

When Mulvaney had gone he strode up and down the room, whistling a Mozart rondo.

Over the next three days, however, the mood of elation gradually faded. To Renthall's annoyance no further date was fixed for the cancelled committee meeting. He had assumed that it would be held *in camera*, but the members must have realized that it would make little difference. Everyone would soon know that Renthall had successfully challenged their claim to be in communication with the watch-towers.

Renthall chafed at the possibility that the meeting had been postponed indefinitely. By avoiding a direct clash with Renthall the Council had cleverly side-stepped the danger before them.

Alternatively, Renthall speculated whether he had underestimated them. Perhaps they realized that the real target of his defiance was not the Council, but the watch-towers. The faint possibility—however hard he tried to dismiss it as childish fantasy the fear still persisted—that there *was* some mysterious collusion between the towers and the Council now began to grow in his mind. The fête had been cleverly conceived as an innocent gesture of defiance towards the towers, and it would be difficult to find something to take its place that would not be blatantly outrageous and stain him indelibly with the sin of hubris.

Besides, as he carefully reminded himself, he was not out to launch open rebellion. Originally he had reacted from a momentary feeling of pique, exasperated by the spectacle of the boredom and lethargy around him and the sullen fear with which everyone viewed the towers. There was no question of challenging their absolute authority—at least, not at this stage. He merely wanted to define the existential margins of their world—if they *were* caught in a trap, let them at least eat the cheese. Also, he calculated that it would take an affront of truly heroic scale to provoke any reaction from the watch-towers, and that a certain freedom by default was theirs, a small but valuable credit to their account built into the system.

In practical, existential terms this might well be considerable, so that the effective boundary between black and white, between good and evil, was drawn some distance from the theoretical boundary. This watershed was the penumbral zone where the majority of the quickening pleasures of life were to be found, and where Renthall was most at home. Mrs. Osmond's villa lay well within its territory, and Renthall would have liked to move himself over its margins. First, though, he would have to assess the extent of this "blue" shift, or moral parallax, but by cancelling the committee meeting the Council had effectively forestalled him.

As he waited for Barnes to call again a growing sense of frustration came over him. The watch-towers seemed to fill the sky, and he drew the blinds irritably. On the flat roof, two floors above, a continuous light hammering sounded all day, but he shunned the streets and no longer went to the café for his morning coffee.

Finally he climbed the stairs to the roof, through the doorway saw two carpenters working under Mulvaney's supervision. They were laying a rough board floor over the tarred cement. As he shielded his eyes from the bright glare a third man came up the stairs behind him, carrying two sections of wooden railing.

"Sorry about the noise, Mr. Renthall," Mulvaney apologized. "We should be finished by tomorrow."

"What's going on?" Renthall asked. "Surely you're not putting a sun garden here."

"That's the idea." Mulvaney pointed to the railings. "A few chairs and umbrellas, be pleasant for the old folk. Dr. Clifton suggested it." He peered down at Renthall, who was still hiding in the doorway. "You'll have to bring a chair up here yourself, you look as if you could use a little sunshine."

Renthall raised his eyes to the watch-tower almost directly over their heads. A pebble tossed underhand would easily have rebounded off the corrugated metal underside. The roof was completely exposed to the score of watch-towers hanging in the air around them, and he wondered whether Mulvaney was out of his mind—none of the old people would sit there for more than a second.

Mulvaney pointed to a roof-top on the other side of the garden, where similar activity was taking place. A bright yellow awning was being unfurled, and two seats were already occupied.

Renthall hesitated, lowering his voice. "But what about the watch-towers?"

"The what—?" Distracted by one of the carpenters, Mulvaney turned away for a moment, then rejoined him. "Yes, you'll be able to watch everything going on from up here, Mr. Renthall."

Puzzled, Renthall made his way back to his room. Had Mulvaney misheard his question, or was this a fatuous attempt to provoke the towers? Renthall grimly visualized his responsibility if a whole series of petty acts of defiance took place. Perhaps he had accidentally tapped all the repressed resentment that had been accumulating for years?

To Renthall's amazement, a succession of creaking ascents of the staircase the next morning announced the first party of residents to use the sun deck. Just before lunch Renthall went up to the roof, found a group of at least a dozen of the older guests sitting out below the watch-tower, placidly inhaling the cool air. None of them seemed in the least perturbed by the tower. At two or three points around the crescent sun-bathers had emerged, as if answering some deep latent call. People sat on makeshift porches or leaned from the sills, calling to each other.

Equally surprising was the failure of this upsurge of activity to be followed by any reaction from the watch-towers. Half-hidden behind his blinds, Renthall scrutinized the towers carefully, once caught what seemed to be a distant flicker of movement from an observation window half a mile away, but otherwise the towers remained silent, their long ranks receding to the horizon in all directions, motionless and enigmatic. The haze had thinned slightly, and the long shafts protruded further from the sky, their outlines darker and more vibrant.

Shortly before lunch Hanson interrupted his scrutiny. "Hello, Charles. Great news! The school opens tomorrow. Thank heaven for that, I was getting so bored I could hardly stand up straight."

7

Renthall nodded. "Good. What's galvanized them into life so suddenly?"

"Oh, I don't know. I suppose they had to reopen some time. Aren't you pleased?"

"Of course. Am I still on the staff?"

"Naturally. The Council doesn't bear childish grudges. They might have sacked you a week ago, but things are different now."

"What do you mean?"

Hanson scrutinized Renthall carefully. "I mean the school's opened. What is the matter, Charles?"

Renthall went over to the window, his eyes roving along the lines of sun-bathers on the roofs. He waited a few seconds in case there was some sign of activity from the watch-towers.

"When's the Watch Committee going to hear my case?"

Hanson shrugged. "They won't bother now. They know you're a tougher proposition than some of the people they've been pushing around. Forget the whole thing."

"But I don't want to forget it. I want the hearing to take place. Damn it, I deliberately invented the whole business of the fête to force them to show their hand. Now they're furiously back-pedalling."

"Well, what of it? Relax, they have their difficulties too." He gave a laugh. "You never know, they'd probably be only too glad of an invitation now."

"They won't get one. You know, I almost feel they've outwitted me. When the fête doesn't take place everyone will assume I've given in to them."

"But it will take place. Haven't you seen Boardman recently? He's going great guns, obviously it'll be a tremendous show. Be careful he doesn't cut you out."

Puzzled, Renthall turned from the window. "Do you mean Boardman's going ahead with it?"

"Of course. It looks like it anyway. He's got a big marquee over the car park, dozens of stalls, bunting everywhere."

Renthall drove a fist into his palm. "The man's insane!" He turned to Hanson. "We've got to be careful, something's going on. I'm convinced the Council are just biding their time, they're deliberately letting the reins go so we'll over-reach ourselves. Have you seen all these people on the roof-tops? Sun-bathing!"

"Good idea. Isn't that what you've wanted all along?"

"Not so blatantly as this." Renthall pointed to the nearest watch-tower. The windows were sealed, but the light reflected off them was far brighter than usual. "Sooner or later there'll be a short, sharp reaction. That's what the Council are waiting for."

"It's nothing to do with the Council. If people want to sit on the roof whose business is it but their own? Are you coming to lunch?"

"In a moment." Renthall stood quietly by the window, watching Hanson closely. A possibility he had not previously envisaged crossed his mind. He searched for some method of testing it. "Has the gong gone yet? My watch has stopped."

Hanson glanced at his wrist-watch. "It's twelve-thirty." He looked out through the window towards the clock tower in the distance over the Town Hall. One of Renthall's long-standing grievances against his room was that the tip of the nearby watch-tower hung directly over the clock-face, neatly obscuring it. Hanson nodded, re-setting his watch. "Twelve-thirty-one. I'll see you in a few minutes."

After Hanson had gone Renthall sat on the bed, his courage ebbing slowly, trying to rationalize this unforeseen development.

The next day he came across his second case.

Boardman surveyed the dingy room distastefully, puzzled by the spectacle of Renthall hunched up in his chair by the window.

"Mr. Renthall, there's absolutely no question of cancelling it now. The fair's as good as started already. Anyway, what would be the point?"

"Our arrangement was that it should be a fête," Renthall pointed out. "You've turned it into a fun-fair, with a lot of stalls and hurdy-gurdies."

Unruffled by Renthall's schoolmasterly manner, Boardman scoffed. "Well, what's the difference? Anyway, my real idea is to roof it over and turn it into a permanent amusement park. The Council won't interfere. They're playing it quiet now."

"Are they? I doubt it." Renthall looked down into the garden. People sat about in their shirt sleeves, the women in floral dresses, evidently oblivious of the watch-towers filling the sky a hundred feet above their heads. The haze had receded still further, and at least two hundred yards of shaft were now visible. There were no signs of activity from the towers, but Renthall was convinced that this would soon begin.

"Tell me," he asked Boardman in a clear voice. "Aren't you frightened of the watch-towers?"

Boardman seemed puzzled. "The what towers?" He made a spiral motion with his cigar. "You mean the big slide? Don't worry, I'm not having one of those, nobody's got the energy to climb all those steps."

He stuck his cigar in his mouth and ambled to the door. "Well, so long, Mr. Renthall. I'll send you an invite."

Later that afternoon Renthall went to see Dr. Clifton in his room below.

"Excuse me, Doctor," he apologized, "but would you mind seeing me on a professional matter?"

"Well, not here, Renthall, I'm supposed to be off-duty." He turned from his canary cages by the window with a testy frown, then relented when he saw Renthall's intent expression. "All right, what's the trouble?"

While Clifton washed his hands Renthall explained. "Tell me, Doctor, is there any mechanism known to you by which the simultaneous hypnosis of large groups of people could occur? We're all familiar with theatrical displays of the hypnotist's art, but I'm thinking of a situation in which the members of an entire small community—such as the residents of the hotels around this crescent—could be induced to accept a given proposition completely conflicting with reality."

Clifton stopped washing his hands. "I thought you wanted to see me professionally. I'm a doctor, not a witch doctor. What are you planning now, Renthall? Last week it was a fête, now you want to hypnotize an entire neighbourhood, you'd better be careful."

Renthall shook his head. "It's not I who want to carry out the hypnosis, Doctor. In fact I'm afraid the operation has already taken place. I don't know whether you've noticed anything strange about your patients?"

"Nothing more than usual," Clifton remarked dryly. He watched Renthall with increased interest. "Who's responsible for this mass hypnosis?" When Renthall paused and then pointed a forefinger at the ceiling Clifton nodded sagely. "I see. How sinister."

"Exactly. I'm glad you understand, Doctor." Renthall went over to the window, looking out at the sunshades below. He pointed to the watch-towers. "Just to clarify a small point, Doctor. You do see the watch-towers?"

Clifton hesitated fractionally, moving imperceptibly towards his valise on the desk. Then he nodded: "Of course."

"Good. I'm relieved to hear it." Renthall laughed. "For a while I was beginning to think that I was the only one in step. Do you realize that both Hanson and Boardman can no longer see the towers? And I'm fairly certain that none of the people down there can or they wouldn't be sitting in the open. I'm convinced that this is the Council's doing, but it seems unlikely that they would have enough power—" He broke off, aware that Clifton was watching him fixedly. "What's the matter? *Doctor!*"

Clifton quickly took his prescription pad from his valise. "Renthall, caution is the essence of all strategy. It's important that we beware of over-hastiness. I suggest that we both rest this afternoon. Now, these will give you some sleep—"

For the first time in several days he ventured out into the street. Head down, angry for being caught out by the doctor, he drove himself along the pavement towards Mrs. Osmond, determined to find at least one person who could still see the towers. The streets were more crowded than he could remember for a long time and he was forced to look upward as he swerved in and out of the ambling pedestrians. Overhead, like the assault craft from which some apocalyptic air-raid would be launched, the watch-towers hung down from the sky, framed between the twin spires of the church, blocking off a vista down the principal boulevard, yet unperceived by the afternoon strollers.

Renthall passed the café, surprised to see the terrace packed with coffee-drinkers, then saw Boardman's marquee in the cinema car park. Music was coming from a creaking wurlitzer, and the gay ribbons of the bunting fluttered in the air.

Twenty yards from Mrs. Osmond's he saw her come through her front door, a large straw hat on her head.

"Charles! What are you doing here? I haven't seen you for days, I wondered what was the matter."

Renthall took the key from her fingers and pushed it back into the lock. Closing the door behind them, he paused in the darkened hall, regaining his breath.

"Charles, what on earth is going on? Is someone after you? You look terrible, my dear. Your face—"

"Never mind my face." Renthall collected himself, and led the way into the living-room. "Come in here, quickly." He went over to the window and drew back the blinds, ascertained that the watch-tower over the row of houses opposite was still there. "Sit down and relax. I'm sorry to rush in like this but you'll understand in a minute." He waited until Mrs. Osmond settled herself reluctantly on the sofa, then rested his palms on the mantelpiece, organizing his thoughts.

"The last few days have been fantastic, you wouldn't believe it, and to cap everything I've just made myself look the biggest possible fool in front of Clifton. God, I could—"

"Charles—!"

"*Listen!* Don't start interrupting me before I've begun, I've got enough to contend with. Something absolutely insane is going on everywhere, by some freak I seem to be the only one who's still *compos mentis*. I know that sounds as if I'm completely mad, but in fact it's true. Why, I don't know; though I'm frightened it may be some sort of reprisal directed at me. However." He went over to the window. "Julia, what can you see out of that window?"

Mrs. Osmond dismantled her hat and squinted at the panes. She fidgeted uncomfortably. "Charles, what is going on?—I'll have to get my glasses." She subsided helplessly.

"Julia! You've never needed your glasses before to see these. Now tell me, what can you see?"

"Well, the row of houses, and the gardens . . ."

"Yes, what else?"

"The windows, of course, and there's a tree . . ."

"What about the sky?"

She nodded. "Yes, I can see that, there's a sort of haze, isn't there? Or is that my eyes?"

"No." Wearily, Renthall turned away from the window. For the first time a feeling of unassuageable fatigue had come over him. "Julia," he asked quietly. "Don't you remember the watch-towers?"

She shook her head slowly. "No, I don't. Where were they?"
A look of concern came over her face. She took his arm gently.
"Dear, what is going on?"

Renthall forced himself to stand upright. "I don't know." He
drummed his forehead with his free hand. "You can't remember
the towers at all, or the observation windows?" He pointed to the
watch-tower hanging down the centre of the window. "There—
used to be one over those houses. We were always looking at it.
Do you remember how we used to draw the curtains upstairs?"

"Charles! Be careful, people will hear. Where are you going?"

Numbly, Renthall pulled back the door. "Outside," he said
in a flat voice. "There's little point now in staying indoors."

He let himself through the front door, fifty yards from the house
heard her call after him, turned quickly into a side road and hurried towards the first intersection.

Above him he was conscious of the watch-towers hanging in the
bright air, but he kept his eyes level with the gates and hedges,
scanning the empty houses. Now and then he passed one that was
occupied, the family sitting out on the lawn, and once someone
called his name, reminding him that the school had started
without him. The air was fresh and crisp, the light glimmering
off the pavements with an unusual intensity.

Within ten minutes he realized that he had wandered into an
unfamiliar part of the town and completely lost himself, with
only the aerial lines of watch-towers to guide him, but he still
refused to look up at them.

He had entered a poorer quarter of the town, where the narrow
empty streets were separated by large waste dumps, and tilting
wooden fences sagged between ruined houses. Many of the
dwellings were only a single storey high, and the sky seemed even
wider and more open, the distant watch-towers along the horizon
like a continuous palisade.

He twisted his foot on a ledge of stone, and hobbled painfully
towards a strip of broken fencing that straddled a small rise in
the centre of the waste dump. He was perspiring heavily, and
loosened his tie, then searched the surrounding straggle of houses
for a way back into the streets through which he had come.

Overhead, something moved and caught his eye. Forcing
himself to ignore it, Renthall regained his breath, trying to master
the curious dizziness that touched his brain. An immense sudden

silence hung over the waste ground, so absolute that it was as if some inaudible piercing music was being played at full volume.

To his right, at the edge of the waste ground, he heard feet shuffle slowly across the rubble, and saw the elderly man in the shabby black suit and wing collar who usually loitered outside the Public Library. He hobbled along, hands in pockets, an almost Chaplinesque figure, his weak eyes now and then feebly scanning the sky as if he were searching for something he had lost or forgotten.

Renthall watched him cross the waste ground, but before he could shout the decrepit figure tottered away behind a ruined wall.

Again something moved above him, followed by a third sharp angular motion, and then a succession of rapid shuttles. The stony rubbish at his feet flickered with the reflected light, and abruptly the whole sky sparkled as if the air was opening and shutting.

Then, as suddenly, everything was motionless again.

Composing himself, Renthall waited for a last moment. Then he raised his face to the nearest watch-tower fifty feet above him, and gazed across at the hundreds of towers that hung from the clear sky like giant pillars. The haze had vanished and the shafts of the towers were defined with unprecedented clarity.

As far as he could see, all the observation windows were open. Silently, without moving, the watchers stared down at him.

CHRONOPOLIS

HIS trial had been fixed for the next day. Exactly when, of course, neither Newman nor anyone else knew. Probably it would be during the afternoon, when the principals concerned—judge, jury and prosecutor—managed to converge on the same court-room at the same time. With luck his defence attorney might also appear at the right moment, though the case was such an open and shut one that Newman hardly expected him to bother— besides, transport to and from the old penal complex was notoriously difficult, involved endless waiting in the grimy depot below the prison walls.

Newman had passed the time usefully. Luckily, his cell faced south and sunlight traversed it for most of the day. He divided its arc into ten equal segments, the effective daylight hours, marking the intervals with a wedge of mortar prised from the window ledge. Each segment he further subdivided into twelve smaller units.

Immediately he had a working timepiece, accurate to within virtually a minute (the final subdivision into fifths he made mentally). The sweep of white notches, curving down one wall, across the floor and metal bedstead, and up the other wall, would have been recognizable to anyone who stood with his back to the window, but no one ever did. Anyway, the guards were too stupid to understand, and the sundial had given Newman a tremendous advantage over them. Most of the time, when he wasn't recalibrating the dial, he would press against the grille, keeping an eye on the orderly room.

"Brocken!" he would shout out at 7.15, as the shadow line hit the first interval. "Morning inspection! On your feet, man!" The sergeant would come stumbling out of his bunk in a sweat, cursing the other warders as the reveille bell split the air.

Later, Newman sang out the other events on the daily roster: roll-call, cell fatigues, breakfast, exercise and so on round to the evening roll just before dusk. Brocken regularly won the block merit for the best-run cell deck and he relied on Newman to programme the day for him, anticipate the next item on the roster and warn him if anything went on for too long—in some of the other blocks fatigues were usually over in three minutes while breakfast or exercise could go on for hours, none of the warders knowing when to stop, the prisoners insisting that they had only just begun.

Brocken never inquired how Newman organized everything so exactly; once or twice a week, when it rained or was overcast, Newman would be strangely silent, and the resulting confusion reminded the sergeant forcefully of the merits of co-operation. Newman was kept in cell privileges and all the cigarettes he needed. It was a shame that a date for the trial had finally been named.

Newman, too, was sorry. Most of his research so far had been inconclusive. Primarily his problem was that, given a northward-facing cell for the bulk of his sentence, the task of estimating the time might become impossible. The inclination of the shadows in the exercise yards or across the towers and walls provided too blunt a reading. Calibration would have to be visual; an optical instrument would soon be discovered.

What he needed was an internal timepiece, an unconsciously operating psychic mechanism regulated, say, by his pulse or respiratory rhythms. He had tried to train his time sense, running an elaborate series of tests to estimate its minimum in-built error, and this had been disappointingly large. The chances of conditioning an accurate reflex seemed slim.

However, unless he could tell the exact time at any given moment, he knew he would go mad.

His obsession, which now faced him with a charge of murder, had revealed itself innocently enough.

As a child, like all children, he had noticed the occasional ancient clock tower, bearing the same white circle with its twelve intervals. In the seedier areas of the city the round characteristic dials often hung over cheap jewellery stores, rusting and derelict.

"Just signs," his mother explained. "They don't mean anything, like stars or rings."

Pointless embellishment, he had thought.

Once, in an old furniture shop, they had seen a clock with hands, upside down in a box full of fire-irons and miscellaneous rubbish.

"Eleven and twelve," he had pointed out. "What does it mean?"

His mother had hurried him away, reminding herself never to visit that street again. Time Police were still supposed to be around, watching for any outbreak. "Nothing," she told him sharply. "It's all finished." To herself she added experimentally: Five and twelve. Five *to* twelve. Yes.

Time unfolded at its usual sluggish, half-confused pace. They lived in a ramshackle house in one of the amorphous suburbs, a zone of endless afternoons. Sometimes he went to school, until he was ten spent most of his time with his mother queueing outside the closed food stores. In the evenings he would play with the neighbourhood gang around the abandoned railway station, punting a home-made flat car along the overgrown tracks, or break into one of the unoccupied houses and set up a temporary command post.

He was in no hurry to grow up; the adult world was unsynchronized and ambitionless. After his mother died he spent long days in the attic, going through her trunks and old clothes, playing with the bric-à-brac of hats and beads, trying to recover something of her personality.

In the bottom compartment of her jewellery case he came across a small flat gold-cased object, equipped with a wrist strap. The dial had no hands but the twelve-numbered face intrigued him and he fastened it to his wrist.

His father choked over his soup when he saw it that evening.

"Conrad, my God! Where in heaven did you get that?"

"In Mamma's bead box. Can't I keep it?"

"No. Conrad, give it to me! Sorry, son." Thoughtfully: "Let's see, you're fourteen. Look, Conrad, I'll explain it all in a couple of years."

With the impetus provided by this new taboo there was no need to wait for his father's revelations. Full knowledge came soon. The older boys knew the whole story, but strangely enough it was disappointingly dull.

"Is that all?" he kept saying. "I don't get it. Why worry so much about clocks? We have calendars, don't we?"

Suspecting more, he scoured the streets, carefully inspecting every derelict clock for a clue to the real secret. Most of the faces had been mutilated, hands and numerals torn off, the circle of minute intervals stripped away, leaving a shadow of fading rust. Distributed apparently at random all over the city, above stores, banks and public buildings, their real purpose was hard to discover. Sure enough, they measured the progress of time through twelve arbitrary intervals, but this seemed barely adequate grounds for outlawing them. After all, a whole variety of timers were in general use: in kitchens, factories, hospitals, wherever a fixed period of time was needed. His father had one by his bed at night. Sealed into the standard small black box, and driven by miniature batteries, it emitted a high penetrating whistle shortly before breakfast the next morning, woke him if he overslept. A clock was no more than a calibrated timer, in many ways less useful, as it provided you with a steady stream of irrelevant information. What if it was half past three, as the old reckoning put it, if you weren't planning to start or finish anything then?

Making his questions sound as naïve as possible, he conducted a long, carefull poll. Under fifty no one appeared to know anything at all about the historical background, and even the older people were beginning to forget. He also noticed that the less educated they were the more they were willing to talk, indicating that manual and lower-class workers had played no part in the revolution and consequently had no guilt-charged memories to repress. Old Mr. Crichton, the plumber who lived in the basement apartment, reminisced without any prompting, but nothing he said threw any light on the problem.

"Sure, there were thousands of clocks then, millions of them, everybody had one. Watches we called them, strapped to the wrist, you had to screw them up every day."

"But what did you *do* with them, Mr. Crichton?" Conrad pressed.

"Well, you just—looked at them, and you knew what time it was. One o'clock, or two, or half past seven—that was when I'd go off to work."

"But you go off to work now when you've had breakfast. And if you're late the timer rings."

Crichton shook his head. "I can't explain it to you, lad. You ask your father."

But Mr. Newman was hardly more helpful. The explanation promised for Conrad's sixteenth birthday never materialized. When his questions persisted Mr. Newman tired of side-stepping, shut him up with an abrupt: "Just stop thinking about it, do you understand? You'll get yourself and the rest of us into a lot of trouble."

Stacey, the young English teacher, had a wry sense of humour, liked to shock the boys by taking up unorthodox positions on marriage or economics. Conrad wrote an essay describing an imaginary society completely preoccupied with elaborate rituals revolving around a minute by minute observance of the passage of time.

Stacey refused to play, however, gave him a non-committal beta plus, after class quietly asked Conrad what had prompted the fantasy. At first Conrad tried to back away, then finally came out with the question that contained the central riddle.

"Why is it against the law to have a clock?"

Stacey tossed a piece of chalk from one hand to the other.

"Is it against the law?"

Conrad nodded. "There's an old notice in the police station offering a bounty of one hundred pounds for every clock or wrist-watch brought in. I saw it yesterday. The sergeant said it was still in force."

Stacey raised his eyebrows mockingly. "You'll make a million. Thinking of going into business?"

Conrad ignored this. "It's against the law to have a gun because you might shoot someone. But how can you hurt anybody with a clock?"

"Isn't it obvious? You can time him, know exactly how long it takes him to do something."

"Well?"

"Then you can make him do it faster."

At seventeen, on a sudden impulse, he built his first clock. Already his preoccupation with time was giving him a marked lead over his class-mates. One or two were more intelligent, others more conscientious, but Conrad's ability to organize his leisure and homework periods allowed him to make the most of his talents. When the others were lounging around the railway yard on their way home Conrad had already completed half his prep, allocating his time according to its various demands.

As soon as he finished he would go up to the attic playroom, now his workshop. Here, in the old wardrobes and trunks, he made his first experimental constructions: calibrated candles, crude sundials, sand-glasses, an elaborate clockwork contraption developing about half a horse power that drove its hands progressively faster and faster in an unintentional parody of Conrad's obsession.

His first serious clock was water-powered, a slowly leaking tank holding a wooden float that drove the hands as it sank downwards. Simple but accurate, it satisfied Conrad for several months while he carried out his ever-widening search for a real clock mechanism. He soon discovered that although there were innumerable table clocks, gold pocket watches and timepieces of every variety rusting in junk shops and in the back drawers of most homes, none of them contained their mechanisms. These, together with the hands, and sometimes the digits, had always been removed. His own attempts to build an escapement that would regulate the motion of the ordinary clockwork motor met with no success; everything he had heard about clock movements confirmed that they were precision instruments of exact design and construction. To satisfy his secret ambition—a portable timepiece, if possible an actual wrist-watch—he would have to find one, somewhere, in working order.

Finally, from an unexpected source, a watch came to him. One afternoon in a cinema an elderly man sitting next to Conrad had a sudden heart attack. Conrad and two members of the audience carried him out to the manager's office. Holding one of his arms, Conrad noticed in the dim aisle light a glint of metal inside the sleeve. Quickly he felt the wrist with his fingers, identified the unmistakable lens-shaped disc of a wrist-watch.

As he carried it home its tick seemed as loud as a death-knell. He clamped his hand around it, expecting everyone in the street to point accusingly at him, the Time Police to swoop down and seize him.

In the attic he took it out and examined it breathlessly, smothering it in a cushion whenever he heard his father shift about in the bedroom below. Later he realized that its noise was almost inaudible. The watch was of the same pattern as his mother's, though with a yellow and not a red face. The gold case was scratched and peeling, but the movement seemed to be in perfect condition. He pried off the rear plate, watched the frenzied flickering world of miniature cogs and wheels for hours, spellbound. Frightened of breaking the main spring, he kept the watch only half wound, packed away carefully in cotton wool.

In taking the watch from its owner he had not, in fact, been motivated by theft; his first impulse had been to hide the watch before the doctor discovered it feeling for the man's pulse. But once the watch was in his possession he abandoned any thought of tracing the owner and returning it.

That others were still wearing watches hardly surprised him. The water clock had demonstrated that a calibrated timepiece added another dimension to life, organized its energies, gave the countless activities of everyday existence a yardstick of significance. Conrad spent hours in the attic gazing at the small yellow dial, watching its minute hand revolve slowly, its hour hand press on imperceptibly, a compass charting his passage through the future. Without it he felt rudderless, adrift in a grey purposeless limbo of timeless events. His father began to seem idle and stupid, sitting around vacantly with no idea when anything was going to happen.

Soon he was wearing the watch all day. He stitched together a slim cotton sleeve, fitted with a narrow flap below which he could see the face. He timed everything—the length of classes, football games, meal breaks, the hours of daylight and darkness, sleep and waking. He amused himself endlessly by baffling his friends with demonstrations of this private sixth sense, anticipating the frequency of their heart beats, the hourly newscasts on the radio, boiling a series of identically consistent eggs without the aid of a timer.

Then he gave himself away.

Stacey, shrewder than any of the others, discovered that he was wearing a watch. Conrad had noticed that Stacey's English classes lasted exactly forty-five minutes, let himself slide into the habit of tidying his desk a minute before Stacy's timer pipped up. Once or twice he noticed Stacey looking at him curiously, but he could not resist the temptation to impress Stacey by always being the first one to make for the door.

One day he had stacked his books and clipped away his pen when Stacey pointedly asked him to read out a précis he had done. Conrad knew the timer would pip out in less than ten seconds, and decided to sit tight and wait for the usual stampede to save him the trouble.

Stacey stepped down from the dais, waiting patiently. One or two boys turned around and frowned at Conrad, who was counting away the closing seconds.

Then, amazed, he realized that the timer had failed to sound! Panicking, he first thought his watch had broken, just restrained himself in time from looking at it.

"In a hurry, Newman?" Stacey asked dryly. He sauntered down the aisle to Conrad, smiling sardonically. Baffled, and face reddening with embarrassment, Conrad fumbled open his exercise book, read out the précis. A few minutes later, without waiting for the timer, Stacey dismissed the class.

"Newman," he called out. "Here a moment."

He rummaged behind the rostrum as Conrad approached. "What happened then?" he asked. "Forget to wind up your watch this morning?"

Conrad said nothing. Stacey took out the timer, switched off the silencer and listened to the pip that buzzed out.

"Where did you get it from? Your parents? Don't worry, the Time Police were disbanded years ago."

Conrad examined Stacey's face carefully. "It was my mother's," he lied. "I found it among her things." Stacey held out his hand and Conrad nervously unstrapped the watch and handed it to him.

Stacey slipped it half out of its sleeve, glanced briefly at the yellow face. "Your mother, you say? Hmh."

"Are you going to report me?" Conrad asked.

"What, and waste some over-worked psychiatrist's time even further?"

"Isn't it breaking the law to wear a watch?"

"Well, you're not exactly the greatest living menace to public security." Stacey started for the door, gesturing Conrad with him. He handed the watch back. "Cancel whatever you're doing on Saturday afternoon. You and I are taking a trip."

"Where?" Conrad asked.

"Back into the past," Stacey said lightly. "To Chronopolis, the Time City."

Stacey had hired a car, a huge battered mastodon of chromium and fins. He waved jauntily to Conrad as he picked him up outside the public library.

"Climb into the turret," he called out. He pointed to the bulging briefcase Conrad slung on to the seat between them. "Have you had a look at those yet?"

Conrad nodded. As they moved off around the deserted square he opened the briefcase and pulled out a thick bundle of road maps. "I've just worked out that the city covers over 500 square miles. I'd never realized it was so big. Where is everybody?"

Stacey laughed. They crossed the main street, cut down into a long tree-lined avenue of semi-detached houses. Half of them were empty, windows wrecked and roofs sagging. Even the inhabited houses had a makeshift appearance, crude water towers on home-made scaffolding lashed to their chimneys, piles of logs dumped in over-grown front gardens.

"Thirty million people once lived in this city," Stacey remarked. "Now the population is little more than two, and still declining. Those of us left hang on in what were once the distal suburbs, so that the city today is effectively an enormous ring, five miles in width, encircling a vast dead centre forty or fifty miles in diameter."

They wove in and out of various back roads, past a small factory still running although work was supposed to end at noon, finally picked up a long, straight boulevard that carried them steadily westwards. Conrad traced their progress across successive maps. They were nearing the edge of the annulus Stacey had described. On the map it was overprinted in green so that the central interior appeared a flat, uncharted grey, a massive *terra incognita*.

They passed the last of the small shopping thoroughfares he remembered, a frontier post of mean terraced houses, dismal streets spanned by massive steel viaducts. Stacey pointed up at one as they drove below it. "Part of the elaborate railway system that once existed, an enormous network of stations and junctions that carried fifteen million people into a dozen great terminals every day."

For half an hour they drove on, Conrad hunched against the window, Stacey watching him in the driving mirror. Gradually, the landscape began to change. The houses were taller, with coloured roofs, the sidewalks were railed off and fitted with pedestrian lights and turnstiles. They had entered the inner suburbs, completely deserted streets with multi-level supermarkets, towering cinemas and department stores.

Chin in one hand, Conrad stared out silently. Lacking any means of transport he had never ventured into the uninhabited interior of the city, like the other children always headed in the opposite direction for the open country. Here the streets had died twenty or thirty years earlier; plate-glass shopfronts had slipped and smashed into the roadway, old neon signs, window frames and overhead wires hung down from every cornice, trailing a ragged webwork of disintegrating metal across the pavements. Stacey drove slowly, avoiding the occasional bus or truck abandoned in the middle of the road, its tyres peeling off their rims.

Conrad craned up at the empty windows, into the narrow alleys and side-streets, but nowhere felt any sensation of fear or anticipation. These streets were merely derelict, as unhaunted as a half-empty dustbin.

One suburban centre gave way to another, to long intervening stretches of congested ribbon developments. Mile by mile, the architecture altered its character; buildings were larger, ten- or fifteen-storey blocks, clad in facing materials of green and blue tiles, glass or copper sheathing. They were moving forward in time rather than, as Conrad had expected, back into the past of a fossil city.

Stacey worked the car through a nexus of side-streets towards a six-lane expressway that rose on tall concrete buttresses above the roof-tops. They found a side road that circled up to it, levelled out and then picked up speed sharply, spinning along one of the clear centre lanes.

Conrad craned forward. In the distance, two or three miles away, the tall rectilinear outlines of enormous apartment blocks reared up thirty or forty storeys high, hundreds of them lined shoulder to shoulder in apparently endless ranks, like giant dominoes.

"We're entering the central dormitories here," Stacey told him. On either side buildings overtopped the motorway, the congestion mounting so that some of them had been built right up against the concrete palisades.

In a few minutes they passed between the first of the apartment batteries, the thousands of identical living units with their slanting balconies shearing up into the sky, the glass in-falls of the aluminium curtain walling speckling in the sunlight. The smaller houses and shops of the outer suburbs had vanished. There was no room on the ground level. In the narrow intervals between the blocks there were small concrete gardens, shopping complexes, ramps banking down into huge underground car parks.

And on all sides there were the clocks. Conrad noticed them immediately, at every street corner, over every archway, three-quarters of the way up the sides of buildings, covering every conceivable angle of approach. Most of them were too high off the ground to be reached by anything less than a fireman's ladder and still retained their hands. All registered the same time: 12.01.

Conrad looked at his wrist-watch, noted that it was just 2.45 p.m.

"They were driven by a master clock," Stacey told him. "When that stopped they all seized at the same moment. One minute after midnight, thirty-seven years ago."

The afternoon had darkened, as the high cliffs cut off the sunlight, the sky a succession of narrow vertical intervals opening and closing around them. Down on the canyon floor it was dismal and oppressive, a wilderness of concrete and frosted glass. The expressway divided and pressed on westwards. After a few more miles the apartment blocks gave way to the first office buildings in the central zone. These were even taller, sixty or seventy storeys high, linked by spiralling ramps and causeways. The expressway was fifty feet off the ground yet the first floors of the office blocks were level with it, mounted on massive stilts that straddled the glass-enclosed entrance bays of lifts and escalators. The streets were wide but featureless. The sidewalks of parallel roadways merged below the buildings, forming a continuous concrete apron. Here and there were the remains of cigarette kiosks, rusting stairways up to restaurants and arcades built on platforms thirty feet in the air.

Conrad, however, was looking only at the clocks. Never had he visualized so many, in places so dense that they obscured each other. Their faces were multi-coloured: red, blue, yellow, green. Most of them carried four or five hands. Although the master hands had stopped at a minute past twelve, the subsidiary hands had halted at varying positions, apparently dictated by their colour.

"What were the extra hands for?" he asked Stacey. "And the different colours?"

"Time zones. Depending on your professional category and the consumer-shifts allowed. Hold on, though, we're almost there."

They left the expressway and swung off down a ramp that fed them into the north-east corner of a wide open plaza, eight hundred yards long and half as wide, down the centre of which had once been laid a continuous strip of lawn, now rank and over-grown. The plaza was empty, a sudden block of free space bounded by tall glass-faced cliffs that seemed to carry the sky.

Stacey parked, and he and Conrad climbed out and stretched themselves. Together they strolled across the wide pavement towards the strip of waist-high vegetation. Looking down the vistas receding from the plaza Conrad grasped fully for the first time the vast perspectives of the city, the massive geometric jungle of buildings.

Stacey put one foot up on the balustrade running around the lawn bed, pointed to the far end of the plaza, where Conrad saw a low-lying huddle of buildings of unusual architectural style, nineteenth-century perpendicular, stained by the atmosphere and badly holed by a number of explosions. Again, however, his attention was held by the clock face built into a tall concrete tower just behind the older buildings. This was the largest clock dial he had ever seen, at least a hundred feet across, huge black hands halted at a minute past twelve. The dial was white, the first they had seen, but on wide semicircular shoulders built out off the tower below the main face were a dozen smaller faces, no more than twenty feet in diameter, running the full spectrum of colours. Each had five hands, the inferior three halted at random.

"Fifty years ago," Stacey explained, gesturing at the ruins below the tower, "that collection of ancient buildings was one of the world's greatest legislative assemblies." He gazed at it quietly for a few moments, then turned to Conrad. "Enjoy the ride?"

Conrad nodded fervently. "It's impressive, all right. The people who lived here must have been giants. What's really remarkable is that it looks as if they left only yesterday. Why don't we go back?"

"Well, apart from the fact that there aren't enough of us now, even if there were we couldn't control it. In its hey-day this city was a fantastically complex social organism. The communications problems are difficult to imagine merely by looking at these blank façades. It's the tragedy of this city that there appeared to be only one way to solve them."

"Did they solve them?"

"Oh, yes, certainly. But they left themselves out of the equation. Think of the problems, though. Transporting fifteen million office workers to and from the centre every day, routeing in an endless stream of cars, buses, trains, helicopters, linking every office, almost every desk, with a videophone, every apartment with television, radio, power, water, feeding and entertaining this enormous number of people, guarding them with ancillary services, police, fire squads, medical units—it all hinged on one factor."

Stacey threw a fist out at the great tower clock. "Time! Only

by synchronizing every activity, every footstep forward or back-
ward, every meal, bus-halt and telephone call, could the organism
support itself. Like the cells in your body, which proliferate into
mortal cancers if allowed to grow in freedom, every individual
here had to subserve the overriding needs of the city or fatal
bottlenecks threw it into total chaos. You and I can turn on the
tap any hour of the day or night, because we have our own
private water cisterns, but what would happen here if everybody
washed the breakfast dishes within the same ten minutes?"

They began to walk slowly down the plaza towards the clock
tower. "Fifty years ago, when the population was only ten million,
they could just provide for a potential peak capacity, but even
then a strike in one essential service paralysed most of the others;
it took workers two or three hours to reach their offices, as long
again to queue for lunch and get home. As the population climbed
the first serious attempts were made to stagger hours; workers
in certain areas started the day an hour earlier or later than those
in others. Their railway passes and car number plates were
coloured accordingly, and if they tried to travel outside the
permitted periods they were turned back. Soon the practice
spread; you could only switch on your washing-machine at a
given hour, post a letter or take a bath at a specific period."

"Sounds feasible," Conrad commented, his interest mounting.
"But how did they enforce all this?"

"By a system of coloured passes, coloured money, an elaborate
set of schedules published every day like the TV or radio programmes. And, of course, by all the thousands of clocks you can
see around you here. The subsidiary hands marked out the
number of minutes remaining in any activity period for people
in the clock's colour category."

Stacey stopped, pointed to a blue-faced clock mounted on one
of the buildings overlooking the plaza. "Let's say, for example,
that a lower-grade executive leaving his office at the allotted
time, 12 o'clock, wants to have lunch, change a library book, buy
some aspirin, and telephone his wife. Like all executives, his
identity zone is blue. He takes out his schedule for the week, or
looks down the blue-time columns in the newspaper, and notes
that his lunch period for that day is 12.15 to 12.30. He has fifteen
minutes to kill. Right, he then checks the library. Time code
for today is given as 3, that's the third hand on the clock. He looks

at the nearest blue clock, the third hand says 37 minutes past—
he has 23 minutes, ample time, to reach the library. He starts
down the street, but finds at the first intersection that the
pedestrian lights are only shining red and green and he can't get
across. The area's been temporarily zoned off for lower-grade
women office workers—red, and manuals—greens."

"What would happen if he ignored the lights?" Conrad asked.

"Nothing immediately, but all blue clocks in the zoned area
would have returned to zero, and no shops or the library would
serve him, unless he happened to have red or green currency
and a forged set of library tickets. Anyway, the penalties were too
high to make the risk worthwhile, and the whole system was
evolved for his convenience, no one else's. So, unable to reach
the library, he decides on the chemist. The time code for the
chemist is 5, the fifth, smallest hand. It reads 54 minutes past:
he has six minutes to find a chemist and make his purchase. This
done, he still has five minutes before lunch, decides to phone his
wife. Checking the phone code he sees that no period has been
provided for private calls that day—or the next. He'll just have
to wait until he sees her that evening."

"What if he did phone?"

"He wouldn't be able to get his money in the coin box, and
even then, his wife, assuming she is a secretary, would be in a
red time zone and no longer in her office for that day—hence the
prohibition on phone calls. It all meshed perfectly. Your time
programme told you when you could switch on your TV set
and when to switch off. All electric appliances were fused, and
if you strayed outside the programmed periods you'd have a hefty
fine and repair bill to meet. The viewer's economic status
obviously determined the choice of programme, and vice versa,
so there was no question of coercion. Each day's programme listed
your permitted activities: you could go to the hairdresser's,
cinema, bank, cocktail bar, at stated times, and if you went then
you were sure of being served quickly and efficiently."

They had almost reached the far end of the plaza. Facing them
on its tower was the enormous clock face, dominating its constellation of twelve motionless attendants.

"There were a dozen socio-economic categories: blue for
executives, gold for professional classes, yellow for military and
government officials—incidentally, it's odd your parents ever got

hold of that wrist-watch, none of your family ever worked for the government—green for manual workers and so on. But, naturally, subtle subdivisions were possible. The lower-grade executive I mentioned left his office at 12, but a senior executive, with exactly the same time codes, would leave at 11.45, have an extra fifteen minutes, would find the streets clear before the lunch-hour rush of clerical workers."

Stacey pointed up at the tower. "This was the Big Clock, the master from which all others were regulated. Central Time Control, a sort of Ministry of Time, gradually took over the old parliamentary buildings as their legislative functions diminished. The programmers were, effectively, the city's absolute rulers."

As Stacey continued Conrad gazed up at the battery of time-pieces, poised helplessly at 12.01. Somehow time itself seemed to have been suspended, around him the great office buildings hung in a neutral interval between yesterday and tomorrow. If one could only start the master clock the entire city would probably slide into gear and come to life, in an instant be repeopled with its dynamic jostling millions.

They began to walk back towards the car. Conrad looked over his shoulder at the clock face, its gigantic arms upright on the silent hour.

"Why did it stop?" he asked.

Stacey looked at him curiously. "Haven't I made it fairly plain?"

"What do you mean?" Conrad pulled his eyes off the scores of clocks lining the plaza, frowned at Stacey.

"Can you imagine what life was like for all but a few of the thirty million people here?"

Conrad shrugged. Blue and yellow clocks, he noticed, out-numbered all others; obviously the major governmental agencies had operated from the plaza area. "Highly organized but better than the sort of life we lead," he replied finally, more interested in the sights around him. "I'd rather have the telephone for one hour a day than not at all. Scarcities are always rationed, aren't they?"

"But this was a way of life in which everything was scarce. Don't you think there's a point beyond which human dignity is surrendered?"

Conrad snorted. "There seems to be plenty of dignity here.

Look at these buildings, they'll stand for a thousand years. Try comparing them with my father. Anyway, think of the beauty of the system, engineered as precisely as a watch."

"That's all it was," Stacey commanded dourly. "The old metaphor of the cog in the wheel was never more true than here. The full sum of your existence was printed for you in the newspaper columns, mailed to you once a month from the Ministry of Time."

Conrad was looking off in some other direction and Stacey pressed on in a slightly louder voice. "Eventually, of course, revolt came. It's interesting that in any industrial society there is usually one social revolution each century, and that successive revolutions receive their impetus from progressively higher social levels. In the eighteenth century it was the urban proletariat, in the nineteenth the artisan classes, in this revolt the white collar office worker, living in his tiny so-called modern flat, supporting through credit pyramids an economic system that denied him all freedom of will or personality, chained him to a thousand clocks . . ." He broke off. "What's the matter?"

Conrad was staring down one of the side streets. He hesitated, then asked in a casual voice: "How were these clocks driven? Electrically?"

"Most of them. A few mechanically. Why?"

"I just wondered . . . how they kept them all going." He dawdled at Stacey's heels, checking the time from his wrist-watch and glancing to his left. There were twenty or thirty clocks hanging from the buildings along the side street, indistinguishable from those he had seen all afternoon.

Except for the fact that one of them was working!

It was mounted in the centre of a black glass portico over an entrance-way fifty yards down the right-hand side, about eighteen inches in diameter, with a faded blue face. Unlike the others its hands registered 3.15, the correct time. Conrad had nearly mentioned this apparent coincidence to Stacey when he had suddenly seen the minute hand move on an interval. Without doubt someone had restarted the clock; even if it had been running off an inexhaustible battery, after thirty-seven years it could never have displayed such accuracy.

He hung behind Stacey, who was saying: "Every revolution has its symbol of oppression . . ."

The clock was almost out of view. Conrad was about to bend
down and tie his shoelace when he saw the minute hand jerk
downwards, tilt slightly from the horizontal.

He followed Stacey towards the car, no longer bothering to
listen to him. Ten yards from it he turned and broke away, ran
swiftly across the roadway towards the nearest building.

"Newman!" he heard Stacey shout. "Come back!" He
reached the pavement, ran between the great concrete pillars
carrying the building. He paused for a moment behind an elevator
shaft, saw Stacey climbing hurriedly into the car. The engine
coughed and roared out, and Conrad sprinted on below the
building into a rear alley that led back to the side-street. Behind
him he heard the car accelerating, a door slam as it picked up
speed.

When he entered the side-street the car came swinging off the
plaza thirty yards behind him. Stacey swerved off the roadway,
bumped up on to the pavement and gunned the car towards
Conrad, throwing on the brakes in savage lurches, blasting the
horn in an attempt to frighten him. Conrad side-stepped out of its
way, almost falling over the bonnet, hurled himself up a narrow
stairway leading to the first floor and raced up the steps to a short
landing that ended in tall glass doors. Through them he could
see a wide balcony that ringed the building. A fire-escape criss-
crossed upwards to the roof, giving way on the fifth floor to a
cafeteria that spanned the street to the office building opposite.

Below he heard Stacey's feet running across the pavement. The
glass doors were locked. He pulled a fire-extinguisher from its
bracket, tossed the heavy cylinder against the centre of the plate.
The glass slipped and crashed to the tiled floor in a sudden
cascade, splashing down the steps. Conrad stepped through on to
the balcony, began to climb the stairway. He had reached the
third floor when he saw Stacey below, craning upwards. Hand
over hand, Conrad pulled himself up the next two flights, swung
over a bolted metal turnstile into the open court of the cafeteria.
Tables and chairs lay about on their sides, mixed up with the
splintered remains of desks thrown down from the upper floors.

The doors into the covered restaurant were open, a large pool
of water lying across the floor. Conrad splashed through it, went
over to a window and peered down past an old plastic plant into
the street. Stacey seemed to have given up. Conrad crossed the

rear of the restaurant, straddled the counter and climbed through a window on to the open terrace running across the street. Beyond the rail he could see into the plaza, the double line of tyre marks curving into the street below.

He had almost crossed to the opposite balcony when a shot roared out into the air. There was a sharp tinkle of falling glass and the sound of the explosion boomed away among the empty canyons.

For a few seconds he panicked. He flinched back from the exposed rail, his ear drums numbed, looking up at the great rectangular masses towering above him on either side, the endless tiers of windows like the faceted eyes of gigantic insects. So Stacey had been armed, almost certainly was a member of the Time Police!

On his hands and knees Conrad scurried along the terrace, slid through the turnstiles and headed for a half-open window on the balcony.

Climbing through, he quickly lost himself in the building.

He finally took up a position in a corner office on the sixth floor, the cafeteria just below him to the right, the stairway up which he had escaped directly opposite.

All afternoon Stacey drove up and down the adjacent streets, sometimes free-wheeling silently with the engine off, at others blazing through at speed. Twice he fired into the air, stopping the car afterwards to call out, his words lost among the echoes rolling from one street to the next. Often he drove along the pavements, swerved about below the buildings as if he expected to flush Conrad from behind one of the banks of escalators.

Finally he appeared to drive off for good, and Conrad turned his attention to the clock in the portico. It had moved on to 6.45, almost exactly the time given by his own watch. Conrad reset this to what he assumed was the correct time, then sat back and waited for whoever had wound it to appear. Around him the thirty or forty other clocks he could see remained stationary at 12.01.

For five minutes he left his vigil, scooped some water off the pool in the cafeteria, suppressed his hunger and shortly after midnight fell asleep in a corner behind the desk.

He woke the next morning to bright sunlight flooding into the office. Standing up, he dusted his clothes, turned around to find a small grey-haired man in a patched tweed suit surveying him with sharp eyes. Slung in the crook of his arm was a large black-barrelled weapon, its hammers menacingly cocked.

The man put down a steel ruler he had evidently tapped against a cabinet, waited for Conrad to collect himself.

"What are you doing here?" he asked in a testy voice. Conrad noticed his pockets were bulging with angular objects that weighed down the sides of his jacket.

"I . . . er . . ." Conrad searched for something to say. Something about the old man convinced him that this was the clock-winder. Suddenly he decided he had nothing to lose by being frank, and blurted out: "I saw the clock working. Down there on the left. I want to help wind them all up again."

The old man watched him shrewdly. He had an alert bird-like face, twin folds under his chin like a cockerel's.

"How do you propose to do that?" he asked.

Stuck by this one, Conrad said lamely: "I'd find a key somewhere."

The old man frowned. "One key? That wouldn't do much good." He seemed to be relaxing slowly, shook his pockets with a dull chink.

For a few moments neither of them said anything. Then Conrad had an inspiration, bared his wrist. "I have a watch," he said. "It's 7.45."

"Let me see." The old man stepped forward, briskly took Conrad's wrist, examined the yellow dial. "Movado Super-matic," he said to himself. "CTC issue." He stepped back, lowering the shot-gun, seemed to be summing Conrad up. "Good," he remarked at last. "Let's see. You probably need some breakfast."

They made their way out of the building, began to walk quickly down the street.

"People sometimes come here," the old man said. "Sightseers and police. I watched your escape yesterday, you were lucky not to be killed." They swerved left and right across the empty streets, the old man darting between the stairways and buttresses. As he walked he held his hands stiffly to his sides, preventing his pockets from swinging. Glancing into them, Conrad saw that they were full of keys, large and rusty, of every design and combination.

"I presume that was your father's watch," the old man remarked.

"Grandfather's," Conrad corrected. He remembered Stacey's lecture, and added: "He was killed in the plaza."

The old man frowned sympathetically, for a moment held Conrad's arm.

They stopped below a building, indistinguishable from the others nearby, at one time a bank. The old man looked carefully around him, eyeing the high cliff walls on all sides, then led the way up a stationary escalator.

His quarters were on the second floor, beyond a maze of steel grilles and strongdoors, a stove and a hammock slung in the centre of a large workshop. Lying about on thirty or forty desks in what had once been a typing pool, was an enormous collection of clocks, all being simultaneously repaired. Tall cabinets surrounded them, loaded with thousands of spare parts in neatly labelled correspondence trays—escapements, ratchets, cogwheels, barely recognizable through the rust.

The old man led Conrad over to a wall chart, pointed to the total listed against a column of dates. "Look at this. There are now 278 running continuously. Believe me, I'm glad you've come. It takes me half my time to keep them wound."

He made breakfast for Conrad, told him something about himself. His name was Marshall. Once he had worked in Central Time Control as a programmer, had survived the revolt and the Time Police, ten years later returned to the city. At the beginning of each month he cycled out to one of the perimeter towns to cash his pension and collect supplies. The rest of the time he spent winding the steadily increasing number of functioning clocks and searching for others he could dismantle and repair.

"All these years in the rain hasn't done them any good," he explained, "and there's nothing I can do with the electrical ones."

Conrad wandered off among the desks, gingerly feeling the dismembered timepieces that lay around like the nerve cells of some vast unimaginable robot. He felt exhilarated and yet at the same time curiously calm, like a man who has staked his whole life on the turn of a wheel and is waiting for it to spin.

"How can you make sure that they all tell the same time?" he asked Marshall, wondering why the question seemed so important.

Marshall gestured irritably. "I can't, but what does it matter? There is no such thing as a perfectly accurate clock. The nearest you can get is one that has stopped. Although you never know when, it *is* absolutely accurate twice a day."

Conrad went over to the window, pointed to the great clock visible in an interval between the rooftops. "If only we could start that, and run all the others off it."

"Impossible. The entire mechanism was dynamited. Only the chimer is intact. Anyway, the wiring of the electrically driven clocks perished years ago. It would take an army of engineers to recondition them."

Conrad nodded, looked at the scoreboard again. He noticed that Marshall appeared to have lost his way through the years— the completion dates he listed were seven and a half years out. Idly, Conrad reflected on the significance of this irony, but decided not to mention it to Marshall.

For three months Conrad lived with the old man, following him on foot as he cycled about on his rounds, carrying the ladder and the satchel full of keys with which Marshall wound up the clocks, helping him to dismantle recoverable ones and carry them back to the workshop. All day, and often through half the night, they worked together, repairing the movements, restarting the clocks and returning them to their original positions.

All the while, however, Conrad's mind was fixed upon the great clock in its tower dominating the plaza. Once a day he managed to sneak off and make his way into the ruined Time buildings. As Marshall had said, neither the clock nor its twelve satellites would ever run again. The movement house looked like the engine-room of a sunken ship, a rusting tangle of rotors and drive wheels exploded into contorted shapes. Every week he would climb the long stairway up to the topmost platform two hundred feet above, look out through the bell tower at the flat roofs of the office blocks stretching away to the horizon. The hammers rested against their trips in long ranks just below him. Once he kicked one of the treble trips playfully, sent a dull chime out across the plaza.

The sound drove strange echoes into his mind.

Slowly he began to repair the chimer mechanism, rewiring the hammers and the pulley systems, trailing fresh wire up the great height of the tower, dismantling the winches in the movement room below and renovating their clutches.

He and Marshall never discussed their self-appointed tasks. Like animals obeying an instinct they worked tirelessly, barely aware of their own motives. When Conrad told him one day that he intended to leave and continue the work in another sector of the city, Marshall agreed immediately, gave Conrad as many tools as he could spare and bade him good-bye.

Six months later, almost to the day, the sounds of the great clock chimed out across the rooftops of the city, marking the hours, the half-hours and the quarter-hours, steadily tolling the progress of the day. Thirty miles away, in the towns forming the perimeter of the city, people stopped in the streets and in doorways, listening to the dim haunted echoes reflected through the long aisles of apartment blocks on the far horizon, involuntarily counting the slow final sequences that told the hour. Older people whispered to each other: "Four o'clock, or was it five? They have started the clock again. It seems strange after these years."

And all through the day they would pause as the quarter and half hours reached across the miles to them, a voice from their childhoods reminding them of the ordered world of the past. They began to reset their timers by the chimes, at night before they slept they would listen to the long count of midnight, wake to hear them again in the thin clear air of the morning.

Some went down to the police station and asked if they could have their watches and clocks back again.

After sentence, twenty years for the murder of Stacey, five for fourteen offences under the Time Laws, to run concurrently, Newman was led away to the holding cells in the basement of the court. He had expected the sentence and made no comment when invited by the judge. After waiting trial for a year the afternoon in the courtroom was nothing more than a momentary intermission.

He made no attempt to defend himself against the charge of killing Stacey, partly to shield Marshall, who would be able to continue their work unmolested, and partly because he felt indirectly responsible for the policeman's death. Stacey's body, skull fractured by a twenty- or thirty-storey fall, had been discovered in the back seat of his car in a basement garage not far from the plaza. Presumably Marshall had discovered him prowling around and dealt with him single-handed. Newman recalled that one day Marshall had disappeared altogether and had been curiously irritable for the rest of the week.

The last time he had seen the old man had been during the three days before the police arrived. Each morning as the chimes boomed out across the plaza Newman had seen his tiny figure striding briskly down the plaza towards him, waving up energetically at the tower, bareheaded and unafraid.

Now Newman was faced with the problem of how to devise a clock that would chart his way through the coming twenty years. His fears increased when he was taken the next day to the cell block which housed the long-term prisoners—passing his cell on the way to meet the superintendent he noticed that his window looked out on to a small shaft. He pumped his brains desperately as he stood to attention during the superintendent's homilies, wondering how he could retain his sanity. Short of counting the seconds, each one of the 86,400 in every day, he saw no possible means of assessing the time.

Locked into his cell, he sat limply on the narrow bed, too tired to unpack his small bundle of possessions. A moment's inspection confirmed the uselessness of the shaft. A powerful light mounted half-way up masked the sunlight that slipped through a steel grille fifty feet above.

He stretched himself out on the bed and examined the ceiling. A lamp was recessed into its centre, but a second, surprisingly, appeared to have been fitted to the cell. This was on the wall, a few feet above his head. He could see the curving bowl of the protective case, some ten inches in diameter.

He was wondering whether this could be a reading light when he realized that there was no switch.

Swinging round, he sat up and examined it, then leapt to his feet in astonishment.

It was a clock! He pressed his hands against the bowl, reading the circle of numerals, noting the inclination of the hands. 4.53, near enough the present time. Not simply a clock, but one in running order! Was this some sort of macabre joke, or a misguided attempt at rehabilitation?

His pounding on the door brought a warder.

"What's all the noise about? The clock? What's the matter with it?" He unlocked the door and barged in, pushing Newman back.

"Nothing. But why is it here? They're against the law."

"Oh, is that what's worrying you." The warder shrugged. "Well, you see, the rules are a little different in here. You lads have got a lot of time ahead of you, it'd be cruel not to let you know where you stood. You know how to work it, do you? Good." He slammed the door, bolted it fast, smiled at Newman through the cage. "It's a long day here, son, as you'll be finding out, that'll help you get through it."

Gleefully, Newman lay on the bed, his head on a rolled blanket at its foot, staring up at the clock. It appeared to be in perfect order, electrically driven, moving in rigid half-minute jerks. For an hour after the warder left he watched it without a break, then began to tidy up his cell, glancing over his shoulder every few minutes to reassure himself that it was still there, still running efficiently. The irony of the situation, the total inversion of justice, delighted him, even though it would cost him twenty years of his life.

He was still chuckling over the absurdity of it all two weeks later when for the first time he noticed the clock's insanely irritating tick . . .